Berkley Prime Crime titles by Carolyn Hart

LETTER FROM HOME
WHAT THE CAT SAW

Death on Demand Mysteries

DEATH COMES SILENTLY
DEAD, WHITE, AND BLUE

Bailey Ruth Ghost Mysteries

GHOST GONE WILD

PRAISE FOR

What the Cat Saw

continued . . .

PRAISE FOR

Death Comes Silently

"Sparkling . . . A bucolic setting, colorful characters, and frequent knowledgeable recommendations of mystery authors and books old and new help make this another winning entry in a cozy series that shows no sign of age."
—*Publishers Weekly*

"Fans of this popular cozy series will not be disappointed with Hart's latest entry. It is always a pleasure to read about the current obsession of Annie's well-meaning mother-in-law, Laurel Darling Roethke, and the competition between Henny and resident mystery writer, Emma Clyde, over the bookstore's monthly mystery contest. Recommended for all cozy mystery fans, especially those who like to read Joan Hess, Leslie Meier, and Jill Churchill." —*Library Journal*

"[Hart] serves up a beautifully constructed puzzle mystery."
—*The Connecticut Post*

"The latest Death on Demand cozy is a superb entry that keeps the series fresh . . . Carolyn Hart has written another strong whodunit." —*Genre Go Round Reviews*

"There are lots of reasons Carolyn Hart's books are all national bestsellers. They are just great." —*Cozy Library*

"*Death Comes Silently* does not disappoint. I was immediately engaged . . . As usual, Hart's storyline flows."
—MyShelf.com

"Any book by Hart is guaranteed to include a top-notch mystery delivering an enjoyable reading experience. Hart is a master storyteller and her popular Death on Demand series continues to include strong plotlines and characterizations."
—*RT Book Reviews*

What the Cat Saw

CAROLYN HART

BERKLEY PRIME CRIME, NEW YORK

THE BERKLEY PUBLISHING GROUP
Published by the Penguin Group
Penguin Group (USA)
375 Hudson Street, New York, New York 10014, USA

USA | Canada | UK | Ireland | Australia | New Zealand | India | South Africa | China

Penguin Books Ltd., Registered Offices: 80 Strand, London WC2R 0RL, England
For more information about the Penguin Group, visit penguin.com.

WHAT THE CAT SAW

A Berkley Prime Crime Book / published by arrangement with the author

Berkley Prime Crime Books are published by The Berkley Publishing Group.
BERKLEY® PRIME CRIME and the PRIME CRIME logo are trademarks of
Penguin Group (USA).

For information, address: The Berkley Publishing Group,
a division of Penguin Group (USA),
375 Hudson Street, New York, New York 10014.

ISBN: 978-0-425-25228-4

PUBLISHING HISTORY
Berkley Prime Crime hardcover edition / October 2012
Berkley Prime Crime mass-market edition / October 2013

PRINTED IN THE UNITED STATES OF AMERICA

10 9 8 7 6 5 4 3 2 1

Cover photo: *Tabby looking through window* by Getty Junophoto.
Cover design by George Long.

ALWAYS LEARNING   PEARSON

To Trent and Adrienne with love, always.

— 1 —

On the upside, the airport was small. On the downside, a blustery wind took Nela Farley's breath away as she stepped out of the terminal, pulling her small wheeled bag. She shivered in her light coat. She'd expected cold temperatures, but she'd not expected a wind that buffeted her like a hurried shopper in a crowded mall. She'd also known she wouldn't be met. Still, arriving in a strange place without anyone to greet her was a reminder that she was alone.

Alone . . .

She walked faster, hurried across the double drive to a parking garage. Chloe's call this morning had been even more fragmented than usual. ". . . on the fourth level, slot A forty-two. Leland's car is an old VW, I mean really old. Pink stripes. You can't miss it."

In the parking garage elevator, Nela opened her purse and found the keys that had arrived by overnight FedEx from her sister. They dangled from what seemed to be a rabbit's foot. Nela held it gingerly. In the dusky garage, she followed numbers, chilled by the wind whistling and moaning through the concrete interior.

She spotted Leland's VW with no difficulty. Why pink stripes? The decals in the rear window would have been distinctive enough. In turn, they featured a mustachioed cowboy in an orange cowboy hat and orange chaps with *OSU* down one leg, a huge openmouthed bass fish, a long-eared dog with the caption, *My Best Friend Is a Coonhound*, and a gleaming Harley with the caption, *Redneck at the Ready*.

Nela unlocked the driver's door. Soon she would be off on an Oklahoma adventure, all because Chloe had roared off one sunny California day on the back of her new boyfriend's Harley, destination the red dirt state. Plus, Nela had lost her job on a small SoCal daily and was free to answer Chloe's call that she come to Craddock, Oklahoma.

Nela was both irritated with her sister—one more call for a rescue, this time to protect her job—and grateful to have somewhere to go, something to fill leaden days. As for Chloe's job, she would have been pleased if she'd had an inkling of what to expect, but in her usual fashion, Chloe had spoken of her job only peripherally.

Nela expected she'd manage. It definitely would be different to be in Oklahoma. Everything was going to be new, including subbing at Chloe's job, whatever it was. Knowing Chloe, the job could be raising guppies or painting plastic plates or transcribing medical records. Only Chloe could hold a job for several months and, despite hour-long sisterly confabs on their cells, always be vague about where she worked or what she did. Nela had a hazy idea she worked in an office of some kind. On the phone, Chloe was more interested in talking about what she and Leland had done or were going to do. *The wind blows all the time, but it's kind of fun . . . Hamburger Heaven really is . . . There's a farm with llamas . . . went to see the Heavener*

Runestone . . . However, she'd promised to leave a packet full of "stuff" on the front passenger seat.

Nela popped her suitcase in the backseat. She breathed a sigh of relief as she slid behind the wheel. Indeed, there was a folder and on it she saw her sister's familiar scrawl: *Everything You Need to Know.* Nestled next to the folder was a golden box—oh, she shouldn't have spent that much money—of Godiva. A sticky note read: *Road treats.* Confetti dangled from the rearview mirror. Taped to the wheel was a card. She pulled the card free, opened the envelope. The card showed an old-fashioned derrick spewing oil. She opened it. Chloe had written: *I gush for you. Nela, you're a life saver. Thanks and hugs and kisses—Love—Chloe*

Nela's brief irritation subsided. She smiled. She wished her little—though so much taller—sister was here and she could give her a hug, look into those cornflower blue eyes, and be sure everything was right in Chloe's world. So long as she could, Nela knew she would gladly come when her sister called.

She picked up the folder, opened it to find a garage parking ticket, a letter, and a map with directions to I-35.

. . . turn south. It's an hour and a half drive to Craddock. They say Hiram Craddock, a rail gang supervisor for the Santa Fe railroad, took a horseback ride one Sunday in 1887 and saw a cloud of butterflies stopped by the river. When the tracks were laid, he quit his job to stay and build the first shack in what later became Craddock. This fall when the monarchs came through, I loved thinking about him seeing them and saying, This is beautiful, I'll stay here. He married a Chickasaw woman. That was real common for white men who wanted to be able to stay in the Chickasaw Nation. He opened a trading post. Anyway, I don't know if I

*explained about staying at Miss Grant's apartment after
she died. I did it as a favor and I know you won't mind.
It's because of Jugs. You'll love him. In case your plane's
delayed, there's plenty of food and water, but the last I
checked, your flights were on time. Anyway, it's sad
about Miss Grant but I didn't mind helping out. Nobody
knows you're coming in today and I didn't take time to
explain but I left a note and said Jugs was taken care
of. But they do expect you Monday morning and there
are directions in the folder. The key with the pink ribbon is to Miss Grant's place. Oh, I left my car coat in
the backseat. I won't need a coat in Tahiti! There's a
pizza in the fridge. Anchovies, of course, for you. (Shud-
der.) When you get to Craddock . . .*

Nela scanned the rest of the disjointed message, obviously written in haste. But Chloe could have a day or a week
or a month at her disposal and her communications would
still careen from thought to fact to remembrance to irrele-
vance. Nela retrieved Chloe's map and the ribbon-tagged
key. She placed the map on the passenger seat and dropped
the key into her purse.

Nela drove out of the garage into a brilliant day. She
squinted against a sun that was surely stronger than in LA.
Whatever happened, she intended to have fun, leaving behind
the grayness now that was LA, and the sadness.

Bill wouldn't want her to be sad.

Occasional winter-bare trees dotted softly rolling dun-
colored countryside. Nela passed several horse farms.
Cattle huddled with their backs to the north wind. The usual
tacky billboards dotted the roadside. Nela felt more and
more relaxed. The little VW chugged sturdily south despite
its age. The traffic was fairly heavy and it was nearer two

hours when she turned onto the exit to Craddock. After checking the map, she drove east into town, passing red-brick shops, several banks, and a library, and glancing at Chloe's directions, turned off again to the south on Cimarron. Ranch-style houses predominated. After a few blocks, the homes grew more substantial, the lots larger, the houses now two and three stories, including faux colonials, Mediterranean villas, and French mansards.

Nela noted house numbers. She was getting close. She came around a curve. Her eyes widened at a majestic home high on a ridge, a Georgian mansion built of limestone with no houses visible on either side, the grounds stretching to woods. Nela slowed. Surely not . . . Chloe had clearly written of a garage apartment.

Nela stopped at stone pillars that marked the entrance and scrabbled through Chloe's notes.

. . . so funny . . . I use the tradesman's entrance. Keep going past the main drive around a curve to a blacktop road into the woods. It dead ends behind the house. That's where the old garage is and Miss Grant's apartment. It's kind of prehistoric. You'll see the newer garages, much bigger, but they kept the old one. It isn't like Miss Grant rented it. People like Blythe Webster don't have renters. Miss Grant started living there when she first came to work for Harris Webster. He was Blythe's father and he made a fortune in oil. That's the money that funds everything. She went from being his personal assistant to helping run the whole deal. Now that she's gone, I imagine they'll close up the apartment, maybe use it for storage. Anyway, it's a lot more comfortable than Leland's trailer so it's great that someone needs to be with Jugs. Be sure and park in the garage. Miss Webster had a fit about the VW, didn't want it visible from the terrace. No opener or anything, just pull

up the door. It's kind of like being the crazy aunt in the attic, nobody's supposed to know the VW's there. It offends Miss Webster's "sensibilities." I'll bet she didn't tell Miss Grant where to park! Anyway the Bug fits in next to Miss Grant's Mercedes. Big contrast. The apartment's way cool. Like I said, nicer than a trailer, but I'd take a trailer with Leland anytime. So everything always works out for the best. I mean, except for Miss Grant.

Even with the disclaimer, the message reflected Chloe's unquenchable cheer.

Nela pressed the accelerator. Names bounced in her mind like errant Ping-Pong balls . . . Grant, Webster, Jugs . . . as she chugged onto the winding road. If delivery trucks actually came this way, their roofs would scrape low-hanging tree limbs. In the second decade of the twenty-first century, Nela felt sure that FedEx, UPS, and any other delivery service would swing through the stone pillars into the main drive. Tradesmen entrances had gone the way of horse-drawn buggies, milk bottles, and typewriters.

As the lane curved out of the woods, she gazed at the back of the magnificent house. A rose garden that would be spectacular in summer spread beneath steps leading up to a paved terrace. Lights blazed from huge windows, emphasizing the gathering winter darkness that leached light and color from the dormant garden. Lights also gleamed from lantern-topped stone pillars near the massive garages Chloe had described as new. Almost lost in the gloom was an old wooden two-door garage with a second-floor apartment. The windows were dark.

Nela coasted to a stop. She put the car in park but left the motor running while she pulled up the garage door. The Bug fit with room to spare next to the Mercedes coupe. She glanced at the elegant car as she retrieved her suitcase. Very sporty. It would be interesting to see Miss Grant's apartment. It would be odd to stay in the apartment of a woman whom she'd never met. But ten days would speed past.

And then?

Nela shook away any thought of the future. For now, she was hungry and looking forward to pizza with anchovies and taking sanctuary in a dead woman's home. *Miss Grant, wherever you are, thank you.*

She didn't take time to put on Chloe's coat, which surely would hang to her knees. She stepped out of the garage and lowered the overhead door. Pulling her suitcase, carrying Chloe's coat over one arm, she hurried to the wooden stairs, the sharp wind ruffling her hair, penetrating her thin cotton blouse and slacks.

On the landing, she fumbled in her purse until she found the ribbon-tagged key, unlocked the door. Stepping inside, she flicked a switch. She was pleasantly surprised. Despite January gloom beyond the windows, the room was crisp and bright, lemon-painted walls with an undertone of orange, vivid Rothko matted prints, blond Danish modern furniture, the sofa and chairs upholstered with peonies splashed against a pale purple background. A waist-high blond wood bookcase extended several feet into the room to the right of the door.

Her gaze stopped at car keys lying there next to a Coach bag. Had the purse belonged to Miss Grant? Certainly Chloe had never owned a Coach bag and, if she had, she wouldn't have left it carelessly in an empty apartment. Nela shrugged away the presence of the purse. The contents of the apartment were none of her business.

As for Miss Grant, she wasn't the person Nela had imagined. When Chloe wrote, *Too bad about Miss Grant*, Nela knew she'd been guilty of stereotyping. Miss Grant was dead so she was old. Until she'd read Chloe's note, Nela had pictured a plump elderly woman, perhaps with white curls and a sweet smile. This apartment had not belonged to an old woman.

So much for preconceived ideas. Nela closed the door behind her. She set the suitcase down and turned to explore the rest of the apartment. She took two steps, then, breath gone, pulse pounding, stared across the room. She reached out to grip the back of a chair, willing herself to stay upright. She began to tremble, defenses gone, memory flooding, not hot, but cold and dark and drear.

The cat's huge round eyes seemed to grow larger and larger.

Lost in the intensity of the cat's gaze, she was no longer in a strange apartment half a continent from home. Instead, numb and aching, she was at Bill's house with Bill's mother, face etched in pain, eyes red-rimmed, and his sobbing sisters and all of his huge and happy family, which had gathered in sorrow. Bill's brother Mike spoke in a dull monotone: *He was on patrol . . . stepped on an IED . . .*

Unbearable images had burned inside. She had turned away, dropped into a chair in the corner of the room. Bill's cat was lying on the piano bench, looking at her. Splotches of white marked Big Man's round black face.

Big Man stared with mesmerizing green eyes. *". . . He's gone . . . dead . . . yesterday . . . legs blown away . . . blood splashing . . ."*

Through the next frozen week, Big Man's thoughts recurred like the drumbeat of a dirge. But, of course, they were her thoughts, too hideous to face and so they came to her reflected from the cat Bill loved.

The next week an emaciated feral cat confronted her in the alley behind the apartment house. Gaunt, ribs showing, the cat whirled toward her, threat in every tense line. She looked into pale yellow eyes. *". . . starving . . . That's my rat . . . Get out of my way . . ."*

Rat? She'd jerked around and seen a flash of gray fur

near the Dumpster. Back in her apartment, she'd tried to
quell her quick breaths. Her mind had been jumbled, that's
all. She'd seen a desperate cat and known there was garbage
and of course there might be rats. She had not read the cat's
thoughts.

Of course she hadn't.

Like calendar dates circled in red, she remembered other
episodes. At the beauty shop, a cuddly white cat turned sea
blue eyes toward her. "... *The woman in the third chair's
afraid* ... *The redhead is mean* ... *The skinny woman's
smile is a lie* ..." At a beach taco stand, a rangy black tom
with a white-tipped tail and a cool, pale gaze. "... *rank
beef* ... *People want the baggies from the blue cooler* ...
afraid of police ..." On a neighbor's front porch swing, an
imperious Persian with a malevolent face. "... *I'm the
queen* ... *I saw the suitcase* ... *If she boards me, she'll be
sorry* ..."

Now, a few feet away from her, a lean brown tabby with
distinctive black stripes and oversize ears stood in a circle
of light from an overhead spot—of course the cat chose that
spot seeking warmth from the bulb—and gazed at Nela
with mournful eyes. "... *Dead* ... *Dead and gone* ... *She
loved me* ... *board rolled on the second step* ..."

Nela fought a prickle of hysteria. She was tired. Maybe
she was crazy. Boards didn't roll ... Unless he meant a
skateboard. Skateboards were rolling boards. Was that how
a cat would describe a skateboard? Was she losing her mind?
Cats and a board that rolled and skateboards. How weird to
think of a skateboard on a step. She hadn't thought of skateboards in years. Bill had done the best ollies in the neighborhood. His legs were stocky and strong. The IED ... Oh
God. Maybe it was because the cat had such distinctive
black stripes. Bill's skateboard had been shiny orange with
black stripes. She had to corral her mind, make her thoughts
orderly. No one saw what was in a cat's mind. She was

making it up. From a board that rolled to skateboards. Maybe she needed to see a doctor. No. This would pass.

The cat gave a sharp chirp, walked across the parquet flooring.

She backed away, came up hard with her back against the front door.

The cat looked up. *". . . Hungry . . . Feed me . . . We're both sad . . ."*

With the beauty of movement peculiar to cats, he moved swiftly past her toward the kitchen.

We're both sad . . .

Nela looked after him. Slowly her frantic breathing eased. The cat—he had to be Jugs with ears like those—was not a threat. She was fighting to keep away memories that hurt. It made sense that she'd ascribe sadness to a cat with a dead mistress. Cats needed attention. Maybe he'd let her pet him. As for imagining his thoughts, her mind was playing a trick. Maybe she wasn't quite crazy. She struggled to remember the professor's droning voice in Psych 1. What had he said? Then she remembered. Displacement. That's what she was doing. Displacement. She clung to the word.

It took every fiber of her will but she quieted her quick breaths, moved with deliberation toward the kitchen. Food would help and the welcome distraction of finding her way about in a strange place.

Next to the refrigerator, she spotted a sheet of paper taped to a cabinet door. Chloe had printed, neatly for her:

Feed Jugs a.m. and p.m., one-half can and one full scoop dry food. Fresh water. He's a sweetie. He adored Marian. Of course I called her Miss Grant at the office. You remember Marlene Dietrich in a black pillbox in No Highway in the Sky? *That was Marian Grant, a cool blonde, always efficient, knew everybody and everything and scared everyone to death.*

Jugs stood on his back paws, scratched at the cabinet door.

Now she was able to look at the cat without a sense of dread. They were fellow creatures, both of them hungry, both of them grieving. "All right, Jugs." As Nela gently opened the door, Jugs dropped to the floor and moved toward his bowl. She emptied a half can into a blue ceramic bowl with *Jugs* painted in white on one side. Nela placed the bowl on newspaper already spread on the floor. She added a scoop of chicken-flavored dry pellets to a yellow bowl with his name in blue. She poured fresh water in a white bowl.

Nela found, as promised, pizza in the fridge. In only a moment, thanks to the microwave, she settled at the kitchen table with two slices of hot crisp anchovy pizza, a small Caesar salad, and a glass of iced tea.

Jugs thumped onto the other end of the table. He made no move to come toward the food. Instead, he settled on his stomach, front paws flat on the table.

Nela studied him gravely as she ate. "You are obviously a privileged character. But you have very good manners. Did Miss Grant allow you to sit on the table when she ate?"

The cat blinked. *". . . She was worried . . . She didn't know what to do . . ."*

Determinedly, Nela looked away. That was the human condition. Worry about the rain. Worry about cancer. Worry about war. Worry about money. Worry about . . . The list could go on and on, big worries and little, everyone had them. Whatever worries had plagued Marian Grant, she was now beyond their reach. Nela felt puzzled. Chloe spoke of Miss Grant as if she'd seen her recently at the office but she'd made no mention of illness. If Marian Grant hadn't been old or sick, how had she died? Why had she been worried?

Nela finished the second slice. She'd do the dishes and look through the rest of Chloe's notes. Surely, tucked in somewhere, she'd left directions to her job and explained what she did.

Nela carried Chloe's folder into the living room. She looked around the room at colorful Rothko prints. Nela's gaze stopped at a bright red cat bed near the desk. Jugs was curved into a ball, one paw across his face, taking an after-dinner snooze. She was, of course, wide awake. It was almost ten here and darkness pressed against the windows, but her body was still on California time. Oh well, she was in no hurry. No one expected her to do anything until Monday morning.

No one would call who really mattered to her. Not since Bill died . . .

Nela hurried to the chintz sofa, sank onto one end, opened the folder, looked at a haphazard pile of loose sheets. She began to read the handwritten notes, glad to push away remembrance.

> . . . *different world. You know, the rich. They really are different. If I had Blythe Webster's money, I'd go around the world. But I guess she's been there, done that. She's pretty nice. She just started spending a lot of time at the foundation last fall. Blythe's around forty, kind of stiff and prim. Think Olivia de Havilland . . .*

Nela's stiff shoulders relaxed. It was almost as comforting as pulling up one of her grandmother's afghans. She and Chloe had grown up on old movies, the free ones on Turner Classic Movies.

> . . . *in* The Heiress, *dark hair, one of those cameo-smooth faces, neat features, but something about her makes you remember her. It's probably all that money. You think? She's looked washed-out since Miss Grant died. I don't know if she can handle things by herself. Miss Grant's the one that made the place go.*

Nela felt a spurt of exasperation. What place, Chloe? Nela scanned more tidbits about people.

. . . Abby's soooo serious. I mean, you'd think Indian baskets were like religious relics. Sure, the mess was a shame but a basket's a basket. If she'd use a little makeup, she has gorgeous eyes, but with those sandy brows you kind of don't notice them. Of course, Miss Grant took everything seriously, too. Maybe that's why she ran four miles every morning. You'd think handing out money would be easy as pie. I could hand out money and not act like I had boulders on my shoulders. Anyway, everything's been kind of nuts since the fire alarm and the sprinklers. I was afraid Louise was going to have a stroke. Usually she's pretty nice. The director's kind of like James Stewart in The Shop Around the Corner. *When he walks by women, it's boobs up, butts tucked. They don't even realize they're doing it!!!*

Nela smiled at the triple exclamation points though she'd chide Chloe for her language. Or maybe not. Chloe was Chloe.

. . . He's tall and angular and has this bony appealing face. I'm pretty sure I glimpsed lust even in the eyes of the T. People call Miss Webster the T because she's the trustee. Not to her face, of course. I wonder if the job description for director of the Haklo Foundation stipulated: Only handsome dudes need apply.

Nela seized on the clue: Haklo Foundation. A few sentences later, she hit pay dirt.

. . . It's a five-minute drive. Kind of quaint after LA. Hills and trees and cows and stuff. The foundation's a

*yellow stucco building with a red-tile roof. When you
leave the apartment, turn right on Cimarron and keep
going. You can't miss it. Leland's dad—his mom's dead—
had me over to dinner when we got to Craddock. His dad
had some connection to the foundation. He tried to get
me a job there but they didn't need anybody. Louise told
him if anything opened up, they'd be glad to have me.
When Louise's assistant quit, I got the job. Louise is the
top dog secretary. I was lucky there was an opening.
She probably wouldn't have left except for the car fire.
She shouldn't have left her car unlocked. I didn't know
there was any place in the world where people didn't lock
their cars. Of course, she wasn't in the car when it happened and I think the foundation got her a new car. At
least that's what Rosalind told me and she always knows
everything and she loves to talk. She's a sweetheart. Anyway, I'll bet it was just somebody raising hell, though
Rosalind thinks the point was to screw things up for the
T. She's kind of under fire from some of the old hands
because she's the one that brought in the new director
and has made a bunch of changes. But I mean, that's a
pretty roundabout way. Anyway, I got the job and Leland
drops me off and picks me up. How about that! Chauf-
feur service and . . . Oh well, you get the picture.*

Nela's lips curved. In a perfect world, she'd like to see
Chloe walking down the aisle with a regular guy, not hop-
ping on the back of a vagabond's Harley. On a positive note,
Leland had brought her to his hometown and introduced
her to his father. As usual, Nela wasn't clear what Leland
did—if anything—but Chloe always sounded happy when
she called. Besides—one of Chloe's favorite words—her
sister's boyfriends might have their quirks, from a vegetar-
ian chef to a treasure hunter, but so far they'd all turned out
to be nice men. Otherwise, Nela would have been worried

about a faraway jaunt to Tahiti with a guy Chloe had known only since last summer.

Nela closed the folder. Tomorrow she'd scout around, spot the foundation, do some grocery shopping.

A creak startled her.

She looked up in time to see a cat door flap fall as lean hindquarters and a tall black tail disappeared into darkness through the front door. So Jugs was an indoor-outdoor fellow. He'd had his nap and was ready to roam.

An in and out cat. That meant he went down the garage apartment stairs. That's how he would see if a board rolled on the second step . . . Nonsense. Boards didn't roll and that's all there was to it.

Except for skateboards.

"That's enough, Nela." She spoke aloud. That was enough, more than enough, of her odd and silly imaginings about the thoughts of cats. She forced herself to focus on what she felt was an improvement. She and Jugs were sharing space. That was definitely a step in the right direction. Thankfully, he'd remained aloof. Maybe the next time she looked at him, she'd be able to discipline her mind. Maybe his presence would help prove she had nothing to fear from cats. Maybe she'd finally be able to face what was in her mind, come to grips with grief.

Bill . . .

She pushed up from the couch, willing away memory. She walked swiftly to the bookcases that lined one wall, looked at titles to try to force other thoughts into her mind. It hurt too much to think of Bill and their plans that ended in blood and death. The phone rang.

Startled, Nela turned. After a moment's hesitation, she walked swiftly to the cream-colored phone on the desk near the bookshelves. "Hello." Her answer was tentative.

"Nela, you're there! How's everything? Did you find the pizza? Isn't Jugs a honeybunch?"

Nela had felt so alone when she arrived. Hearing Chloe's husky voice was like a welcoming hug. "He's great. I'm great. How about you and Leland?"

"Oooooh." It was halfway between a squeal and a coo. "You can't believe how gorgeous everything is. We had to catch a red-eye to get to LA in time for our flight but we made it. We just checked in and we're leaving to ride an outrigger. Doesn't that sound like fun? He's already downstairs so I better scoot. Thanks, Nela. You're the best."

Nela shook her head as she replaced the receiver in the cradle. Talking to Chloe was like trying to catch a shooting star. None of her questions were answered: What was the job? Exactly where was it? What happened to Miss Grant? Perhaps she should follow Chloe's example and let the good times roll. In Chloe's world, everything seemed to work out. Nela smiled. *Have fun, sweetie. Be happy. Love him because . . .*

Again there were images to block, pain to forestall. She swung again to the bookshelves. She'd find a weighty tome, read until she felt sleepy. Midway through the first shelf, she pulled out a large picture book and carried it to the sofa. The cover photograph featured a marble statue of a tall, lean man. Even in cold stone, the hard-ridged face compelled attention. Deep-set eyes, a beaked nose, and jutting chin proclaimed power, strength, and ruthless determination. Behind the statue rose wide steps leading to a pale yellow stucco building. The title was in red Gothic letters: *The Haklo Foundation, the Story of Harris Webster and the Fortune He Shared.*

She thumbed through the beautifully crafted book. No expense had been spared in its production. She turned back to the introduction. Harris Webster was the descendant of an early Craddock family. Caleb Webster arrived in the Chickasaw Nation in 1885. After his marriage to Mary Castle, a member of the Chickasaw Nation, he began to prosper.

He wrangled horses for her father, later opened an early dry goods store, apparently on very thin credit. He prospered, added a livery stable, and established a bank. His son, Lewis, increased the family's wealth with a cattle ranch. The Websters were one of Craddock's leading families, but the great wealth came from Caleb's grandson, Harris, a hugely successful wildcatter in the 1950s and '60s. He sold Webster Exploration to Exxon for one hundred million dollars in 1988. Harris Webster married Ellen White in 1970. Their first child died at birth. A daughter, Blythe, was born in 1973, and a second daughter, Grace, in 1985. Ellen died in 1987 from cancer.

Webster set up a trust, establishing the foundation in 1989 with an endowment of fifty million dollars. He served as the sole trustee until his death in 2007. His designated successor as sole trustee was his oldest daughter, Blythe.

The following facing pages featured portraits in oval frames. Caleb Webster's blunt, square-jawed face looked young and appealing, the black-and-white photo likely taken when he was in his late twenties. His hair was parted in the middle, his collar high and stiff. Mary Castle's dark hair was drawn back in a bun, emphasizing the severity of her features: the deep-set eyes, high-bridged nose and high cheekbones, thin lips pursed. She had looked gravely into the camera with a questioning gaze. The rest of the portraits were in color. Lewis Webster was dark-haired and narrow-faced with a strong chin. A merry smile curved the lips of his round-faced, blond wife, Lillian.

Harris Webster's color portrait, taken possibly when he was in his forties, exuded vigor and strength. Unlike the other photographs, he was pictured outdoors against a leafy background, a breeze ruffling thick black curls. Bronze skin suggested hours spent under the sun. His brown eyes stared confidently into the camera. His smile was that of a man who met any challenge with complete expectation of victory.

His pale blond wife Ellen appeared fragile. Her expression was pensive, a woman turned inward.

The portraits of the Webster daughters hung side by side, affording an interesting contrast. Blythe Webster looked intelligent, imperious, and reserved. Ebony hair framed an oval face with a pleasant, though aloof, expression. The straight, unwavering stare of her dark brown eyes hinted at unknown depths. Her much younger sister Grace was blue-eyed with a fair complexion. Strawberry blond hair cascaded in thick curls. Her smile was amused, possibly wry, but there was something in the cast of her face which suggested a will that would not bend.

Nela bunched a pillow behind her and began to read.

— 2 —

Fasten seat belt sign . . . nattering shrill voices behind her . . . rain like tears . . . cat's eyes . . . alone, alone, alone . . .

Nela moved restlessly, swimming up from the depths of sleep. She'd tossed and turned for hours before drifting into fitful slumber. Her eyes opened. She stared at unfamiliar shadows, felt the strangeness of the bed. She blinked at the luminous dial of the bedside clock. Almost half past one. One in the morning. In a dead woman's apartment.

She'd chosen a guest room. There was no way she would use Miss Grant's bedroom where a red silk robe lay across the arm of the empire sofa. Had Miss Grant dropped the robe there with no thought that there would not be time ever again to straighten the room?

Nela had firmly shut the door to the guest bedroom in case Jugs was accustomed to sharing a bed, though surely when he came back inside he would seek out Miss Grant's room.

A splintering crash sounded from the living room.

Nela jerked upright, heart pounding. Had the cat knocked something over? But cats were agile, moving silently through time and space.

A heavy thud.

Nela swung her legs over the bedside. A line of light shone beneath the closed bedroom door. She had turned off the living room light before she came into the bedroom. Someone had turned on that light. Someone was in the apartment.

Fully awake now, adrenaline charged her mind and body. In one swift movement, she was on her feet and moving across the floor. An uncle who was an LA cop had drilled into his young nieces: React. Move. Don't freeze. Fight. Scream. Yell. Run.

Nela's mind closed in on the first necessity. Lock the door. Set up a barrier. Don't make it easy.

More crashes.

Nela reached the door. Her hands touched cold wood. The door panel was smooth. Guest rooms did not come equipped with deadbolts. She slipped her hand down, found the knob, pushed the button lock.

Now for her cell . . . Her purse was on the dresser. She turned, moved through the velvety darkness, hands outstretched. She tried to judge where she'd left her suitcase. She veered a little, but one knee caught the case. Losing her balance, she tumbled forward. Scrambling up, she thudded into the chest, but her purse was there. She yanked out the cell phone, opened it. As the cell phone glowed, she punched 911.

Not a breath of sound came from beyond the closed door but she sensed menace. She felt threatened not only by the alien presence in the living room, but the darkness that surrounded her. She hurried to the wall and turned on the overhead light, welcoming the brightness.

A brisk voice. "Craddock nine-one-one. What is your emergency?"

"Someone's broken in." Her voice was shaky but forceful. "Send the police."

"Ma'am, please speak louder. Where are you?"

"Oh God, I don't know the address. I'm in a garage apartment behind a big mansion on Cimarron." She scrambled to remember. "The Webster house on Cimarron. Blythe Webster. Behind the house there's a garage apartment. Call the Craddock police. I need—"

The doorknob rattled.

Nela backed away. "I'm in a bedroom. Someone's trying to get inside. Send help." *Fight. Scream. Yell.* She lowered the cell, shouted, "The police are coming. They're on their way."

"Ma'am, try to be calm. We need the address."

"The garage apartment behind the Webster house on Cimarron." Again, she held the phone away, yelled, "The police are coming."

In the background behind the responder's calm tone, she heard a male voice. "Ten-sixty-seven. Ten-seventy. Possible four-fifty-nine."

"I have that, ma'am. Residence listed to Marian Grant." Her voice fainter, the responder spoke quickly, "Garage apartment One Willow Lane behind residence at Nine-thirteen Cimarron."

In the distance, a man's voice repeated her words. "Officers en route."

The woman's calm voice was loud and clear. "Help is on the way, ma'am. Can you describe the intruder?"

Beyond the door, there was a thud of running feet.

The responder continued to speak. "Officers will arrive in less than three minutes. Tell the intruder help is on the way."

Nela's shouts hurt her throat. "The police are coming. They're coming."

She heard the slam of a door. She was breathless as she spoke to the responder. "I think he's leaving. Hurry. Please hurry."

The responder continued to speak calmly.

Nela held the phone but she scarcely listened. Finally, a siren wailed. Nela approached the bedroom door, leaned against the panel, drawing in deep gulps of air. More sirens shrieked.

A pounding on the front door. "Police. Open up. Police."

In the bedroom, Nela took time to grab a heavy silver-backed hand mirror from the dresser, then turned the knob. She plunged into the living room, makeshift weapon raised high, ready to dart and squirm.

She moved fast, focused on the door. She turned the lock, yanked open the front door.

Two policemen entered, guns in hand.

Nela backed up until she was hard against the wall. "He got away. I heard the door slam."

The older officer, eyes flicking around the room, spoke into a transmitter clipped to his collar. "Cars two and three. Search grounds for prowler." He nodded at his younger companion. "Cover me." He glanced at Nela, his eyes cool. "Stay where you are, ma'am." With that warning, he moved warily across the room, alert, intent, ready for trouble.

Nela shivered, was suddenly aware of her cotton pj's. The night air was cold. As she turned to watch the officers, her eyes widened at the swath of destruction in the once cool and elegant room.

The officers moved fast. Doors banged against walls. They were in the kitchen. One of them muttered, "Nobody here. Window secure."

They moved back into the living room, oblivious to her. At the closed door to Miss Grant's bedroom, the lead officer shouted, "Police," flung back the door, stood to one side as he flipped on the light. There was silence in the bedroom. Cautiously, he edged inside, his backup advancing with him.

Outside, car doors slammed and men shouted. Cold night air swirled through the open front door.

Finally, the officers returned, guns put away. The tall man stopped in front of her, his face impassive, his hooded eyes moving around the room. "You hurt, ma'am?" His voice was gruff but kind. The younger officer closed the front door, but the room was already achingly cold.

"I'm fine." Maybe not fine. Maybe still a little breathless, pulse racing, but standing in the trashed room, she felt safe, safe and grateful for the quick response of the Craddock police.

"Check the living room windows, Pierce."

The stocky officer began a circuit of the windows.

The officer in charge cleared his throat. "Ma'am, can you describe the intruder?" He looked into her face, his eyes probing.

Nela clasped her hands together. "I never saw him. I heard him. I was in the guest bedroom." She realized she was shaking with cold. "Please, let me get my jacket. It's right by the door." She moved fast and yanked Chloe's long car coat from a coat tree near the front door. She shrugged into it, knew she looked absurd in the big floppy coat, bare legs and feet sticking out below the hem.

When she turned back, the officer held a small electronic notepad in one hand. "Name?"

"Nela Farley. Actually, it's Cornelia, but I'm called Nela." With every moment that passed, she felt more assured.

"Cornelia Farley." He spelled the name as he swiped the keys. His questions came fast. She answered, wishing she could be more help, knowing that all she had to report was noise.

Shouts and calls sounded outside. Officer Pierce made a slow circuit of the room, making notes.

The inquiring officer's nose wrinkled above a thin black mustache. "So you got here tonight. Anybody know you were here?"

"My sister."

He nodded. "I got it. You're in town to take her job. Anyone else know you're here?"

"They're expecting me at her office Monday."

"Do they know"—he was patient—"that you're staying here?" He jerked a thumb at the room.

"No." Chloe hadn't mentioned that Nela would be in Miss Grant's apartment.

The officer's gaze was intent. "You know anyone at the office?"

"Not a soul. I don't know anyone in Craddock."

"So, nobody came here because you're here." He surveyed the litter. The computer was lying on the floor. Drawers were pulled out and upended. Glass from a smashed mirror sparkled on the floor. The cracked mirror hung crookedly on a wall. "More than likely, somebody saw the death notice in the *Clarion* and thought the apartment was empty." He sounded satisfied. "Did the intruder make this mess?"

Nela nodded. "The noise woke me up."

"I'll bet it did. Wake anybody up." His tone was dry. "Looks like the perp got mad. Tossed that little statue and totaled the mirror. Maybe he didn't find cash. Or whatever he was looking for."

Nela, too, looked at the broken mirror. Lying on the floor was a crystal statuette of a horse that had been on the desk.

A woman's imperious voice rose above the hubbub outside. Footsteps rattled on the steps. "Of course I can go upstairs." The voice was rather high and thin and utterly confident. "The place belongs to me."

The front door opened.

Nela and her inquisitor—she noted his name tag: Officer T. B. Hansen—looked toward the open doorway.

A slender woman strode inside. Blue silk pajama legs were visible beneath a three-quarter-length mink coat. She wore running shoes.

She was followed by a middle-aged, redheaded patrol woman who gave Officer Hansen a worried look.

He made a slight hand gesture and the officer looked relieved.

The newcomer held her fur coat folded over against her for warmth. Her black hair appeared disheveled from sleep, but her stare at the officer was wide awake and demanding. "What's going on here?"

Officer Hansen stood straighter. "Reports of a prowler, Miss Webster."

The woman's eyes widened in surprise. "Here?" She glanced around the room. "Who made this mess?"

The officer's tone was noncommittal. "The young lady said an intruder is responsible."

The woman stared at Nela with narrowed eyes. "Who are you?" Her tone was just this side of accusing.

Nela took a quick breath. "Nela Farley, Chloe's sister."

The woman raised one sleek dark eyebrow in inquiry. "You don't look like her."

"No." Nela glimpsed herself in the remnants of mirror. Not only did she not resemble her tall, willowy sister, she looked like a bedraggled waif, dark eyes huge in a pale face, slender bare legs poking from beneath the overlarge coat. "I'm five-four and dark haired. She's five-nine and blond."

Miss Webster asked sharply, "Did Chloe give you Marian's keys?"

Nela nodded. "She asked me to stay here and take care of Jugs. I flew in this afternoon and drove down. I arrived about six. I'm driving Chloe's boyfriend's VW. Chloe told me to park the VW in the garage."

"Oh." Miss Webster's tone was considering now, not hostile. "That car. God knows that monstrosity should be kept in a garage. Or driven into a lake." She sped a quick smile toward Nela. "Thanks for putting the VW in the garage. I didn't know you were staying here. I hadn't thought about it." Her tone was careless. Clearly, the habitation of employees was not her concern. "Louise told me the cat was taken care of. I didn't ask how." Also clearly, the care of a dead employee's animal was not her responsibility. These kinds of things were handled by others. "I suppose this is a convenient place to stay while you're visiting, and having you here puts off deciding what to do with the cat. We have to find him a home. Marian was crazy about that animal." She shook her head, looked abruptly sad. "I can't believe she's gone. And to have someone break in her home makes me furious. Did you see the burglar? I heard the sirens. By the time I reached a window, police were milling around with flashlights and yelling. I thought I was in the middle of a war zone."

Once again Nela told her story, climbing from the deep pit of sleep, bangs and crashes in the living room, hurrying to lock the bedroom door, calling for help, the turning of the knob, the arrival of the police.

Blythe Webster's eyes glinted with anger. "Someone must have read about Marian's death in the newspaper and come like a vulture to pick over her things. Look at this mess. I'm glad you were here. Who knows what might have happened to the rest of her things if you hadn't been here? It would be awful to think of a robber stealing from Marian. So everything's worked out for the best."

The echo of Chloe's favorite phrase was strangely disturbing to Nela. Was it all for the best that she'd known moments of dark fear?

Blythe must have sensed Nela's reaction. She turned over a hand in appeal. "Forgive me. It's dreadful that you have come to help us and run into something like this. Thank you for being here and calling for help. I don't know what we should do now." She looked at Officer Hansen in appeal. "What do you suggest?" Her gesture included the shattered mirror and the emptied drawers.

"Nothing for the moment. We'll send a tech tomorrow to see about prints. But I doubt we'll find anything helpful. Would you"—he directed his question to Blythe Webster—"know if anything is missing?"

"I have no idea about Marian's belongings. I guess they were looking for money." Her gaze settled on the Coach purse atop a bookcase near the front door. "That's Marian's purse. Why didn't a thief grab the purse?" She looked at Nela. "I guess he must have intended to take it but got scared when he heard you. He must have been shocked out of his pants when he realized someone was in the bedroom. Well, no harm done apparently, except for a bad introduction to Craddock for you." Her glance at Nela was sympathetic. "I'm sorry you've had such a rough welcome. We'll make it up to you. By the way, I'm Blythe Webster. I own all of this." She waved a casual hand. "Marian worked for me. I run the foundation. I'll be seeing you there." She turned toward the patrolman. "Send me a report." She moved to the door, looked back at the police officer, a faint frown on her face. "How did the thief get in?"

Hansen said carefully, "We haven't found evidence of a break-in." His hooded gaze settled on Nela. "When we arrived, the front door was locked. Ms. Farley opened the door for us."

Blythe Webster looked puzzled. "If nobody broke in and the door was locked, how did someone get in?"

Nela felt her face tighten. "I don't know." She didn't like the searching looks turned toward her. "Maybe someone had a key."

Blythe Webster's brown eyes narrowed. "I suppose some-where up at the house we may have a key in case of an emergency. I'll ask my housekeeper. But I can't imagine that Marian passed out keys to her apartment. That would be very unlike her."

The officer turned to Nela. "Are you sure you locked the front door?"

"Positive."

He didn't appear impressed. He'd probably been told many things by many witnesses that turned out to be mistaken or false. "There was a real nice story in the *Clarion* about Miss Grant and a funeral notice. The intruder counted on the place being empty. Maybe he found the door unlocked."

Nela started to speak.

He forestalled her. "Or maybe he didn't. Maybe he jiggled a credit card, got lucky. It's an old door. Once inside, he locked the door to keep anyone from surprising him. When he heard you calling for help, he ran out and slammed the front door behind him." He glanced toward the door, gave a satisfied nod. "It's an old lock, one where the lock doesn't pop up when the inside handle is turned. Then it took only a minute to get down the stairs and disappear in the dark." He looked from Nela to Miss Webster. "Did either of you hear a car?"

Nela shook her head. Inside the apartment, she had been acutely aware of sounds from outside, waiting for the police to arrive. She hadn't heard anything until the sirens rose and fell.

Blythe Webster was dismissive. "I was asleep. The sirens woke me. But most cars don't make much noise these days."

Officer Pierce yanked a thumb toward the front door. "They haven't found any trace outside. It looks like he got clean away."

"Whoever came is long gone now." Blythe sounded relieved. She turned to Nela. "As soon as the police finish, you can lock up and feel quite safe. Can't she, Officer?"

Officer Hansen's face was studiously unexpressive. "You may be right, Miss Webster."

Officer Pierce, who had arrived with Hansen, spoke quickly. "Right. Once you scare 'em away, they won't come back."

The redheaded patrol woman, who had followed Blythe Webster inside, nodded in agreement.

"I locked the door." Nela was insistent.

Blythe Webster nodded. "You thought you did." Her tone was understanding. "Anyway, these things happen. I'm glad you're fine. I expect you're very tired. As for me, I'm ready for a nightcap . . . Oh, here's Jugs."

Nela distinctly remembered engaging the front-door lock. She would have objected again, continued to insist, but at the mention of the cat, she swung to look toward the doorway.

The big-eared brown tabby strolled past them, his gaze flicking around the room.

Nela looked into the cat's huge pupils, still dilated for night vision. *". . . Cars . . . strangers . . . like the day She died . . . lying on the concrete . . ."* The cat moved away, heading straight for the open door to Marian Grant's bedroom.

Blythe Webster's face abruptly tightened, cheekbones jutting. "Do you suppose he's hunting for Marian? I hate that." There was a quiver in her voice. "Anyway, now that everything's under control, I'll say good night." In a flurry, she was gone.

Nela scarcely heard the clatter as Blythe Webster hurried down the wooden steps. . . . *lying on the concrete* . . . There was a square of concrete to one side of the apartment stairs, possibly at one time intended for outdoor parking.

Officer Hansen adjusted his earpiece, spoke into the lapel transmitter. "Officer Hansen. Garage apartment behind

Webster home. Possible intruder. No trace of perp. Search of living room apparent. Unknown if any valuables are missing. Alarm raised at one thirty-five a.m. by guest Cornelia Farley. She didn't see anyone but heard sounds in living room. Search of grounds yielded no suspects or witnesses." He stopped, listened. "Yes, sir. I'll do that, sir. Ten-four." He was brisk as he turned toward Nela.

She stood stiffly, watching as Jugs disappeared into Marian's bedroom.

"Ma'am—"

Nela felt a surge of irritation. Why did he call her ma'am? She wasn't an old lady. "I'm Nela."

His eyes flickered. "Ms. Farley"—his tone was bland—"a technician will arrive at nine a.m. tomorrow to fingerprint the desk and the front door and the materials on the floor. Sometimes we get lucky and pick up some prints. Usually, we don't. If you have any further trouble, call nine-one-one." He stared to turn away.

Nela spoke sharply. "I locked the door. Someone had a key."

His pale brown eyes studied her. "The chances are the intruder knew Miss Grant was dead and thought the apartment was empty. Now it's obvious the place is occupied. I don't think you'll have any more trouble." He gestured toward the desk. "It looks like somebody was interested in the desk and not looking to bother you." He cleared his throat. "To be on the safe side, get a straight chair out of the kitchen, tilt it, and wedge the top rail under the knob. Anybody who pushes will force the back legs tight against the floor. Nobody will get in. Tomorrow you can pick up a chain lock at Walmart."

"That's good advice, ma'am." The redheaded police-woman was earnest. "I was in the first car the morning Miss Grant died. The housekeeper told me she ran up the steps to call from here because it was quicker. She didn't have a key. She used a playing card she always carries in her pocket. The seven of hearts. For luck." The officer raised her eyebrows, obviously amused at the superstition. "Anyway, she got inside. Like Officer Hansen said, it doesn't take much to jiggle these old locks. Not that it made any difference for Miss Grant that we got here quick."

"What happened to her?" Nela glimpsed Jugs in her peripheral vision.

The redheaded patrol woman was brisk. "She fell over the stair rail last Monday morning, straight down to the concrete. I was in the first car to arrive." The redheaded officer—Officer L. T. Baker—gestured toward the opening into darkness. "The housekeeper found her beside the stairs. It looked like Miss Grant tripped and went over the railing and pretty much landed on her head. Broken neck. Apparently she jogged early every morning. When we saw her, it was obvious she'd taken a header over the railing. Massive head wound. She must have laid there for a couple of hours."

Nela's eyes shifted to Jugs.

The cat's sea green eyes gazed at Nela. *". . . They took Her away . . ."*

Paramedics came and found death and carried away a broken and bruised body. Nela didn't need to look at the woman's cat to know this.

"A header?" *. . . board rolled on the second step . . .* Nela felt a twist of foreboding. "Did you find what tripped her?"

Officer Baker shrugged. "Who knows? The stairs are steep. Accidents happen. She was wearing new running shoes. Maybe a toe of a shoe caught on a step."

No mention of a skateboard. "Did you find anything on the ground that could have caused her to fall?"

The policewoman waved a hand in dismissal. "These grounds are tidy. Not even a scrap of paper in a twenty-foot radius from the stairs."

"She probably started down the stairs too fast." Officer

Hansen shook his head. "She was a hard charger. She always helped at the Kiwanis pancake suppers, made more pancakes than anybody. There were a bunch of stories in the paper. She was a big deal out at the foundation. Anybody looking for an easy way to make a buck would have known her place was empty." His look was earnest. "Craddock's a real nice place, Ms. Farley, but we got our no-goods like any other town. It seems pretty clear what we had here tonight was intent to rob. Now that the perp knows you're here, you should be fine." He gave a brief nod to officers Pierce and Baker and they moved through the doorway. He paused on the threshold long enough to gesture toward the kitchen. "Wedge that chair if you're nervous. I guarantee you'll be okay."

−3−

Jugs wrinkled his nose, cautiously sniffed the Walmart sack on the bookcase near the front door.

Nela inserted a nine-volt battery into a doorstop alarm. When shoved beneath the bottom of the door, the wedge prevented anyone from opening the door, with or without a key, plus any pressure activated an alarm. She didn't feel she could install a deadbolt in an apartment that, as Miss Webster had made clear, belonged to her.

Nela felt as though she'd been in the garage apartment for an eon with only the short foray to Walmart as a respite. She glanced around the living room, wished she found the decor as appealing as when she first arrived.

In her peripheral vision, she was aware of the shattered mirror. Slowly she turned her head to look at it fully. The crystal horse still lay among shards of glass. There was something wanton in that destruction. If she had the money, she'd move to a motel. But she didn't have enough cash to rent a room for a week. Besides, the cat needed to be cared for.

The blond desk held only a few traces of powder. The police technician, a talkative officer with bright brown eyes and a ready smile, had arrived punctually at nine a.m., fingerprinted the front doorknob inside and out, the desk, the scattered drawers, the tipped-over chair, the statuette. He cleaned up after himself. He'd kept up a nonstop chatter. He'd quickly identified Miss Grant's prints from a hairbrush in the master bath. "Lots of hers on the desk and some unidentified prints, but the drawer handles are smudged. Good old gloves. It takes a dumb perp to leave fingerprints. Usually we only find them at unpremed scenes." He'd departed still chatting. ". . . Not too many prowler calls . . . usually a bar fight on Saturday nights . . ."

Now she was left with the mess and her new defense against invasion.

Jugs batted at the sack. The plastic slid from the table and the muscular cat flowed to the floor. He used a twist of his paw to fling the bag in the air.

She ripped off the doorstop plastic cover and threw it across the room, a better toy than a plastic sack.

Jugs crossed the floor in a flash, flicked the plastic, chased, jumped, rolled on his back to toss his play prey into the air, then gripped the plastic with both paws.

"Pity a mouse. Staying in shape until spring?"

Ignoring her, Jugs twisted to his feet and crouched, the tip of his tail flicking. After a final fling and pounce and flurry, Jugs strolled away, game done, honors his.

She stared after him as he moved toward the front door. Every time she saw him, she remembered that searing moment yesterday when their eyes had first met. She blurted out her thought while berating herself for what was rapidly becoming an obsession. "There wasn't a skateboard," she

called after him. Her voice sounded loud in the quiet room.
"They would have found a skateboard."

Her only answer was the clap of the flap as Jugs disappeared through the cat door.

Now she was talking out loud to a cat. Possibly he wondered what the weird-sounding syllables—skateboard—meant. More than likely his thoughts were now focused on a bird, a rustle in a bush, the scent of another cat.

Anyway, what difference did it make?

The difference between sanity and neuroses.

No matter what made her think of a skateboard, there was no connection between the vagrant thought, a pet cat, and the accidental death of a woman who moved fast.

Nela felt cheered. Monday she would go to the foundation, try to please Chloe's boss, and enjoy the not-exactly holiday but definite departure from her normal life. The normal life that an IED had transformed from quiet happiness to dull gray days that merged into each other without borders, without hope.

Nela looked down at the doorstop. There was no need to put the piece in place now. She shoved the doorstop into the corner between the door and the wall. So much for that. At least tonight she would feel safe.

She still felt unsettled by the knowledge that Marian Grant had fallen to her death. The police seemed competent. If there had been a skateboard in the vicinity of the body, the police would have found it. There hadn't been a skateboard—a board that rolled—on a step. Certainly not. But the image persisted.

She turned, walked restlessly across the room, stopped and stared at the desk and the litter on the floor and the upended drawers. Why rifle a desk? Did people keep money in desks? Maybe.

However . . . She turned back toward the front door. Only

two items lay atop the waist-high blond bookcase to the right as a visitor entered. A set of keys. A black leather Coach bag. Last night Blythe Webster said the purse belonged to Marian Grant.

When the intruder had turned on the living room's overhead light, he couldn't have missed seeing the expensive purse, especially if the purpose of entry was to steal. Wouldn't a petty thief grab the purse first? Maybe he had. Maybe he'd rifled the purse first, then searched the desk. They hadn't looked inside the purse last night. Wasn't that an oversight?

Nela stopped by the bookcase. She reached out for the purse, then drew her hand back. She hurried to the kitchen, fumbled beneath the sink, found a pair of orange rubber gloves, and yanked them on. She didn't stop to sort out her thoughts, but fingerprints loomed in her mind. She had no business looking in the purse, but she would feel reassured if there was no money, if a billfold and credit cards were gone.

Nela carried the purse to the kitchen table. She undid the catch. The interior of the purse was as austere and tidy as the apartment. She lifted out a quilted wallet in a bright red and orange pattern. It took only a moment to find a driver's license. She gazed at an unsmiling face, blond hair, piercing blue eyes: Marian Denise Grant. Birth date: November 16, 1965. Address: One Willow Lane. As Blythe had said, the purse belonged to Marian Grant, had likely rested atop the bookcase since she'd arrived home the night before she died.

Nela pulled apart the bill chamber. Two fifties, four twenties, a ten, three fives, seven ones. Four credit cards, one of them an American Express Platinum. She and Chloe always lived from paycheck to paycheck but, after she'd lost her writing job, she'd waited tables at an upscale restaurant in Beverly Hills and she remembered snatches of conversation over lunch at a producer's table, the advantages of this particular card, automatic hotel upgrades, delayed four p.m. checkout times, free access to all airline hospitality suites, and more.

An intruder could not have missed seeing the purse, but instead of rifling through the billfold, taking easy money, the intruder had walked on to the desk.

Nela placed the quilted billfold on the table. One by one, she lifted out the remaining contents: lip gloss, a silver compact, comb, small perfume atomizer, pill case, pencil flashlight, BlackBerry, Montblanc pen with the initials *MDG*.

Resting on the bottom of the purse was a neatly folded pair of women's red leather gloves. She almost returned the other contents, but, always thorough, she picked up the gloves. Her hand froze in the air. Lying in a heap at the bottom of the bag, hidden from view until now by the folded gloves, was a braided gold necklace inlaid with what looked like diamonds. Nela had a quick certainty that the stones were diamonds. They had a clarity and glitter that faux stones would lack.

Nela held up the necklace, felt its weight, admired the intricacies of the gold settings. A thief would have hit pay dirt if he'd grabbed the purse as he ran. She returned the objects to the interior compartments and carried the purse to the bookcase. She replaced the bag precisely where it had earlier rested.

And so?

There were lots of maybes. Maybe the thief planned to take the purse but her 911 call induced panic. Maybe the thief knew of something valuable in the desk. Maybe Marian Grant collected old stamps or coins. Maybe Marian Grant had a bundle of love letters the writer could not afford for anyone to see. Her mouth twisted. Maybe there was a formula for Kryptonite or a treasure map or nothing at all. Lots of maybes and none of them satisfactory.

The cat flap slapped.

Nela turned to face Jugs. He sauntered past her, beauty in motion, sinuous, graceful, silent.

"It's your fault that I'm worried." Her tone was accusing.

The cat flicked a glance over his shoulder. "... *My territory* ... *I showed him* ..." He disappeared into the kitchen.

Nela wondered if he had vanquished a neighboring tom or if she was simply thinking what he might have done when outside. What difference did it make whether the thought was hers or Jugs?

A big difference.

Either the cat remembered a board that rolled on a step or she had dredged up a long-ago memory of a teenage Bill on a skateboard in happy, sunny days.

What if the cat was right? What if Marian Grant hadn't seen a skateboard on the step when she hurried out to jog early that January morning? The police surmised she'd caught a toe on a steep step, that she'd been going too fast. There had been no skateboard near the stairs when her body was discovered. But there could be reasons. Maybe some kid lived in that big house. Maybe the housekeeper saw the skateboard and either unthinkingly or perhaps quite deliberately removed it. Maybe the cat was thinking about some other skateboard on some other steps. Maybe the cat wasn't thinking a damn thing.

Moreover, a skateboard on the steps might explain why Marian Grant fell, but again so what? She fell because she caught her toe or slipped on a skateboard or simply took a misstep. Her death had been adjudged an accident. To think otherwise was absurd.

Then why did someone creep into the dead woman's apartment last night and search the desk?

This was the easiest answer of all. As Officer Henson said, every town had its no-goods and last night one of them had taken a chance on finding something valuable in a dead woman's apartment.

Still . . . Why the desk and not the purse?

The apartment was utterly quiet. She felt a light pressure on her leg. She looked down. Jugs twined around her leg, whisking the side of his face against her, staking claim to her. She reached down, paused to remove one rubber glove, and stroked his silky back.

His upright tail curved slightly forward. *". . . You're all right . . . I like you . . ."*

Nela felt a catch in her throat. "I like you, too."

The sound of her voice emphasized the silence surrounding them. There was no one to see them. With a decisive nod, she walked toward the door, retrieved the doorstop, pushed it beneath the door. Moving around the living room, she closed the blinds in the windows. She pulled back on the rubber glove and crossed to the desk.

She wasn't sure why she was wearing the gloves now. Maybe she had the instincts of a crook. After all, wasn't it reasonable for her to clean up the mess around the desk, make the room presentable again?

Although Nela was sure she was unobserved, she worked fast as she stacked papers. The cleanup turned out to be reasonably easy. In keeping with Chloe's judgment of Marian Grant as efficient, each folder had a neat tab and it soon became apparent that the drawers had been emptied but the papers had fallen not far from the appropriate folder and showed no signs of having been checked over.

Nela was looking for something to explain what drew an intruder past an expensive purse to this sleek desk. She started with the drawer emptied nearest the desk, turned it right side up. She restored Miss Grant's personal papers to the proper folder—insurance policies, a car title, medical records, bank and credit card statements, travel receipts, copies of tax submissions. Near the next drawer, she found clips of news stories about individuals, research programs, fellowships, and educational institutions. Each person or group featured had received a grant from the Haklo Foundation. She was getting good at her project and quickly placed clips in the correct folders. The second drawer slid into its place.

Doggedly, Nela continued until the floor was clear, the drawers replaced with the proper contents.

When she'd finished, she stared at the desk with a puzzled frown. She had a conviction that the searcher had emptied the drawers not to mess up the papers or even to check them, but to be sure there wasn't something hidden among the folders.

She looked across the room at the Coach bag. Instead of finding reassurance, she felt more uneasy. Had the searcher been hunting for that obviously expensive necklace? If so, why not look in the purse? Why the desk? But who knew what a thief thought or why?

Nela stripped off the rubber gloves, returned them to the kitchen. She found a broom closet, picked up a broom and dustpan. Soon the last of the broken mirror had been swept up and dumped into the trash container. Lips pressed firmly together, she carefully eased the frame with the remnants of the mirror from the hook on the wall. When she'd placed the frame inside Miss Grant's bedroom, she returned to the living room. She opened the blinds, welcoming bright shafts of winter sunlight.

Yet the apartment held no cheer. She had rarely felt so alone, so cut off from human contact. She wouldn't be around anyone until she went to Chloe's job Monday. The job . . . There probably wouldn't be anyone at the foundation on a Saturday but she could take a drive, find the way, make Monday morning easier. She grabbed her purse and Chloe's coat.

She was almost to the door when she paused. The Coach purse now seemed huge to her because she knew that it contained a large sum of cash and an obviously expensive necklace. She yanked wool gloves from Chloe's pockets. She put them on and picked up the Coach bag.

In the kitchen, she knelt by the cabinet that held Jugs's canned food. In only a moment, the purse rested snugly behind cans stacked four high. Maybe a thief would head unerringly for the cat food cabinet. But she felt better. Monday at work, she'd find out how to contact Marian Grant's sister and suggest that the purse, bank books, and other obvious valuables be removed from the apartment. She didn't have to admit she knew the purse's contents to suggest that it be put away for safekeeping.

She was considerably cheered as she stepped out on the high porch. The wind had died down. The day was cold, possibly in the thirties, but brilliant sunshine and a pale winter blue sky were exhilarating.

As she started down the steep steps, a streak of dark blue on the second baluster caught her gaze. She stopped and stared. An oblique line marred the white paint about sixteen inches above the step. The scrape on the wood indicated that something had struck the baluster, leaving an uneven mark on the paint.

Nela pictured early-morning darkness and a woman in a hurry, moving fast, not thinking about a familiar stairway. Likely her right foot would have come down on the first step, her left on the second. A skateboard could have flipped up to strike the baluster while flinging her sideways to tumble over the railing.

The police had searched the area and found nothing, certainly not a skateboard.

The streak looked new and fresh. Nela was abruptly irritated with herself. Since when was she an expert on a marred surface on a white post? Since never. The scrape might have been there for months.

She started down the steps. Carefully.

H aklo Foundation glittered in faux gold letters in an arch over stone pillars. Nela turned in. Leafless trees bordered well-kept grounds. Winter-bare branches seemed even more bleak in contrast to a green lawn of fescue. The velvety grass emphasized the Mediterranean glow of the two-story golden stucco building atop a ridge.

At the foundation entrance, an impressive portico covered shallow stone steps. The imposing statue of Harris Webster gazed into infinity at the base of the steps. The red tile roof made Nela feel homesick. There were so many Spanish colonial buildings in old LA. Even the ornate stonework on oversize windows seemed familiar, but there should have been palm trees, not leafless sycamores.

A discreet sign with an arrow pointed to the right: PARKING.

Obediently Nela turned right. She passed a line of evergreens. The short spur ended at a cross street. A sign to the right announced: GUEST PARKING. The guest parking lot was out of sight behind the evergreens. A sign to the left: STAFF ONLY.

She turned left. A wing extended the length of the drive. At the end of the building, she turned left again. A matching wing extended from the other side with a courtyard in between. Arched windows overlooked a courtyard garden with a tiled fountain, waterless in January. A cocktail reception could easily spill out into the courtyard in good weather. She glanced about but saw no parking areas. Once past the building, another discreet sign led to the staff parking lot, also screened by evergreens. Beyond the evergreens, a half dozen outbuildings likely provided either storage or housed maintenance. On the far side of sycamores that stood sentinel alongside the building, she glimpsed several rustic cabins.

She was a little surprised to see a car in the lot, a beige Camry. Nela turned into the parking area and chose the slot next to the Camry. It would take only a minute to spot the entrance she should use Monday.

When she stepped out of the VW and closed the door, the sound seemed loud, the country silence oppressive. She wasn't accustomed to stillness. There was always noise in LA. She followed a covered walkway to the end of the near wing. The walk ended in a T. To her left was a doorway helpfully marked: STAFF ONLY. To the right, the sidewalk led past the sycamores to the cabins.

There were two keys on Chloe's key ring. One fit the VW. Nela assumed the other afforded entrance to the building. The key to Marian Grant's apartment had been separate, identifiable by a pink ribbon.

However, the foundation locks might be rigged so that any entrance outside of work hours triggered an alarm. As Nela hesitated, the heavy oak door opened.

A middle-aged woman with frizzy brown hair peered out. Pale brown eyes, magnified by wire-rim glasses perched on a bony nose, looked at her accusingly. "This is private property. The foundation is closed to the public until Monday. I heard a car and if you continue to trespass I will call the police."

Nela had no wish to deal further with law enforcement personnel. She spoke quickly, embarrassed and uncomfortable. "I'm Chloe Farley's sister, Nela. Chloe gave me directions and I came by to be sure I knew the way on Monday."

"Oh." The brown eyes blinked rapidly. "I should have recognized you. Chloe has a picture on her bookcase. But so many things have happened and I'm here by myself. Oh dear. I hope you will forgive me. Please come in. I'm Louise

Spear, the executive secretary. I'll show you around." She
held the door wide. "That will make everything easier Monday. Do you have a key?"

As she stepped inside, Nela held up the key ring. "Is the
bronze one the key to the staff entrance?"

Louise peered. "That's it. Did you intend to try it to be
sure?"

Nela smiled. "No. I thought I could knock Monday morning if necessary. I was afraid to use the key after hours in
case it triggered an alarm."

Louise shook her head. "Only broken windows sound an
alarm. We can go in and out with a key at any time. The
key works for all the outer doors." She closed the door.

Nela looked up a wide marbled hallway with office doors
on one side and windowed alcoves overlooking the courtyard on the other. The marble flooring was a swirl of golden
tones. Between the alcoves, paintings of Western scenes
hung on the walls.

Louise reached out, touched a panel of lights. Recessed
lighting glowed to illuminate the paintings. She was proud.
"Isn't it beautiful? The paintings in this hall are from various places in Oklahoma. Our state has an amazingly varied
terrain, everything from hills to prairies to mesas. There
are beautiful paintings all through the foundation. I'm glad
I can show you everything today when we don't have to
hurry. Mondays get busy. There's a staff meeting at eleven.
It's very responsible of you"—her tone was admiring and
mildly surprised—"to make the extra effort to locate the
foundation today. I will confess I wasn't sure what to expect
from Chloe's sister. Chloe is"—a pause—"casual about
things."

Nela well understood. Chloe was not only casual, but
slapdash and last minute.

"Though," Louise added hurriedly, "she's a nice girl and
somehow everything gets done."

Nela gave her a reassuring smile. There was no point in taking umbrage because truth was truth. "Chloe moves quickly." That was true, too.

Louise smiled in return. "Yes, she does. I'll show you her office, but first"—she began to walk, gesturing to her right—"these small offices are for summer interns. We also have a new position this year." A faint frown touched her face. "For an assistant curator. The new director thought it would be good to put one person in charge of overseeing artifact donations. Haklo is unusual among foundations because we not only provide grants, we create our own programs to celebrate Oklahoma history. Thanks to Haklo, many schools around the state now have displays that we have provided, everything from memorabilia about Will Rogers to women's roles in early statehood to Indian relics." The frosted glass of the office door read:

ABBY ANDREWS
ASSISTANT CURATOR

Louise moved to the next door. "This is Chloe's office." She opened the door and flicked on the light.

Nela felt her sister's presence as they stepped inside. Chloe had put her personal stamp on a utilitarian room with a gray metal desk and a bank of filing cabinets. There on the bookcase was a picture of Nela and Chloe, arm in arm on a happy summer day at the Santa Monica pier. Four posters enlivened pale gray walls, an aerial view of Machu Picchu, a surfer catching a big one in Hawaii, a tousle-haired Amelia Earhart in a trench coat standing by a bright red Lockheed Vega, and the shining gold-domed ceiling of the Library of Congress.

Louise followed her gaze to the posters. "Has your sister been to all those places?"

"In her dreams." When Chloe was little, Nela had often

read Dr. Seuss to her. She sometimes wondered if a little girl's spirit had responded to the lyrical call of places to go and things to see. If Chloe couldn't go there—yet—in person, she'd travel in her imagination.

"I suppose that's why she went to Tahiti." Louise's voice was almost admiring. "I don't think I'd ever have the courage, but she doesn't worry, does she?"

"Sometimes I wish she would," Nela confided. "She always thinks everything will work out and so far"—her usual quick prayer, plea, hope flickered in her mind—"they have. But I'll be glad when she and Leland get home."

Louise's glance was sympathetic. "I know. I always worried so about my son. I always wanted him safe at home and that's when he died, driving home from college in an ice storm. Maybe Tahiti is safer." Her voice was thin. "Certainly nothing's seemed secure here lately. Chloe keeps telling me not to worry. But I can't help worrying."

Worry.

Nela pictured Marian's brown tabby looking up forlornly. . . . *She was worried . . . She didn't know what to do . . .*

"What's been wrong?"

It was as if Louise stepped back a pace though she didn't move. Her face was suddenly bland. "Oh, this and that. Things crop up. The foundation is involved in so many activities and sometimes people get angry."

Nela was abruptly alert. Someone had been angry last night in Marian Grant's apartment, angry enough to pick up a crystal statuette and fling it at a mirror. Nela wasn't reassured by Louise's smooth response. The intrusion in the dead woman's apartment last night had been wrong, and there seemed to be something wrong here at the foundation, but Chloe's boss obviously didn't intend to explain. Was the search last night related to things cropping up, whatever that meant, at the foundation? The secretary's threat to call the police because of Nela's unexpected arrival had to be based on some definite concern.

"Here is the connecting door to my office." Louise gestured toward an open door. "Unless I'm in conference, I leave the door open between the offices and that makes access easier. Chloe handles my correspondence and takes care of filing. We're having a meeting of the grants committee later this month and Chloe is about halfway through preparing one-page summaries of applications. Tomorrow, you can be sure the conference room is ready for the staff meeting, fresh legal pads and a pen at each place. There's a small galley off the main conference room. About ten minutes after everyone arrives, you can heat sweet rolls and bring them in with coffee. The foundation has the most wonderful cook."

She was now businesslike with no hint of her earlier distress. As they approached the front of the building, the size of the offices grew. Louise walked fast and talked fast. Names whirled in Nela's mind like buzzing gnats. ". . . These offices are provided as a courtesy to the members of the grants committee." She rattled off several names. They reached the front hall.

"The main hallway"—she made a sweeping gesture—"runs east and west. This is the west hall." She pointed across the spacious marble hallway. "The corner office belongs to Blythe Webster. She's the trustee of the foundation."

Louise flicked several switches, illuminating the magnificent main hallway. "There are only two front offices, one at each corner. Now for our beautiful rotunda." She looked eager as she led the way. "I love the fountain behind the reception desk."

Water gurgled merrily, splashing down over blue and gold tiles.

Louise stopped next to a horseshoe-shaped counter opposite the huge oak front door. She patted the shining wooden counter. "This is the reception desk. Rosalind McNeill takes care of the phones."

Nela was pleased to recognize another name. Chloe had mentioned Rosalind in her letter. Rosalind apparently had filled Chloe in on things that had happened at the foundation.

Louise pointed at the high ceiling. "Rosalind has the best view in the building."

Nela looked up at a series of huge frescoes, magnificent, fresh, and vivid.

Louise beamed. "The paintings reflect Haklo Foundation's encouragement of crop rotation. The first panel is wheat, the next is canola, and the third is sesame."

Nela felt swept into a new world as she admired the vivid frescoes, the three distinctly different crops, grazing cattle, a champion bull, an old field with ranks of wooden derricks.

"We're very proud of the frescoes. They were painted by one of our very own scholarship students, Miguel Rodriguez. The sculptures on either side of the fountain"—she pointed to alcoves in the stuccoed walls—"are members of the Webster family. That's Harris Webster's grandmother, Mary Castle, who was a Chickasaw. The Webster family goes way back to Indian Territory days when Caleb Webster married Mary Castle. Mr. Webster—"

There was reverence in her voice and Nela had no doubt she referred to the foundation's benefactor, Harris Webster.

"—honored his Chickasaw heritage when he named the foundation Haklo. That's Chickasaw for *to listen*. That's what we do. We listen to the requests from our community and respond. Our grants fund agricultural research, rancher certification programs, wildlife and fisheries management, biofuel studies with an emphasis on switchgrass, seminars of interest to farmers and ranchers, and, of course, we support the arts, including grants and scholarships to students, artists, musicians, a local nonprofit art gallery, and particular programs and faculty at Craddock College. And we have our wonderful outreach with the historical exhibits that we create ourselves."

Pink tinged her cheeks. Her eyes glowed with enthusiasm. She gestured at the east wing. "That way is the director's office and conference rooms and the foundation library. The catering office and kitchen are at the far end. The other staff offices and an auditorium are upstairs. Aren't the stairs beautiful?"

Twin tiled stairways with wrought iron railings curved on either side of the fountain area.

They left the rotunda and walked toward the end of the main cross hall. "In the morning, I'll take you around early to meet—"

A rattle of footsteps clicked behind them on one of the curving stairways.

Louise stiffened. Her eyes flared in alarm.

Nela realized the executive secretary was afraid. Louise had said she was alone in the building.

A man spoke in a high tenor voice, the ample space of the rotunda magnifying the sound. ". . . don't know what the bitch will do next."

Louise exhaled in relief but again bright pink touched her cheeks, this time from dismay.

A softer, more precise male voice replied. "Let it go, Robbie."

"I won't let it go. I won't ever let it go."

Louise gripped Nela's elbow, tugged, and began to speak, lifting her voice, as she hurried Nela back toward the reception desk. "I forgot to show you the sculpture of Mr. Webster."

Two men came around the curve of the stairwell. The older man's silver hair was a mane, matched by an equally dramatic silver handlebar mustache. A black cape swirled as he moved, accentuating the white of a pullover sweater and matching black flannel trousers and black boots.

Nela was reminded of a drama professor from summer school between her junior and senior years. When he quoted from a play, a character came alive, robust, individual, memorable. He had been fun and she'd enjoyed every moment of the class.

His companion was younger, with perfectly coiffed thick blond hair and a smoothly handsome face now soured by a scowl. He was more conventionally dressed in a black turtleneck and blue jeans.

Nela knew instantly that they were a couple. There was that sense of physical connection that imbued all unions, whether heterosexual or homosexual.

Louise bustled forward to meet them at the foot of the stairs. She smiled at the older man. "Erik, it's wonderful to see you." She gestured toward Nela. "I want you to meet Nela Farley. She's taking her sister's place this week while Chloe is on her great adventure. Nela, this is Erik Judd and Robbie Powell." There was the slightest hesitation and a flick of a glance at Erik, then Louise said hurriedly, "Robbie is our director of public relations." She looked at the younger man. "Robbie, you scared me. I didn't know anyone else was here. I didn't hear your car come into the lot."

"We're in Erik's Porsche. He insisted on parking in the visitors' lot." Robbie's tone was petulant.

Louise looked dismayed. "Oh, Erik, you are always welcome here."

Erik smoothed back a silver curl. "Since we're in my car, I thought it was more appropriate to park in the visitors' lot. I use the visitors' lot now when I do research here." But his smile was friendly. "It's good to see you, Louise, and to meet Nela." His nod was gracious.

Robbie managed a smile for Nela. "Thanks for filling in for Chloe. I hope you'll enjoy your time with us."

The two men walked toward the front doorway, Robbie leading. As Robbie opened the heavy door, a gust of cold air swirled inside. Erik Judd's cape billowed.

Louise turned back to Nela and picked up their conversation as if there had been no interruption. "Rosalind will buzz you about midmorning Monday to deliver the mail. She'll have everything sorted. Start with Miss Webster."

Clearly, Louise had no intention of discussing Erik and Robbie or explaining the odd emphasis on the visitors' lot.

"Now"—Louise sounded brighter—"let's look at the east wing."

Nela's grasp of who worked where was hazy. However, there was no doubt of the pecking order. Miss Webster had the big front office at the west end of the central hall. Whoever worked in the east front office must also be a major player.

Nela gestured at the door. "Is that the director's office?"

Louise drew in a sharp breath. "That was the office of our chief operating officer. She passed away last week. A dreadful accident."

Nela felt a moment of surprise that Marian Grant had outranked the foundation director in status. "Miss Grant's office?"

Louise stared at her, eyes wide.

Of course, Chloe hadn't bothered to explain where Nela would stay so Louise was startled by Nela's knowledge. "I spent the night at Miss Grant's apartment. Since Chloe e-mailed with Miss Grant's sister in Australia about arranging matters here, Chloe volunteered to stay in the apartment and take care of Miss Grant's cat until a home is found for him. I'm there while Chloe's gone." *Unless,* she qualified in her mind, *someone tries to break in again.* Nela almost told Louise about the entry in the night, but the secretary was staring at the office door in such obvious distress Nela didn't want to add to her unhappiness. Certainly if she grieved for her lost coworker, it would upset her more to think the dead woman's home had been invaded. And it would be unkind to ask Louise to take care of the Coach bag. A woman's purse is very personal and Louise would have seen the bag many times.

"Her belongings"—Louise's voice shook a little—"need to be gathered up. Perhaps you can take care of that for us. I'll arrange for some cartons. I can't bear to think about it. Her personal trinkets . . ." She stopped and pressed her lips together. Louise cleared her throat. "We need to find out if Marian's sister wants to have everything stored or shipped to her or perhaps disposed of." She paused, said dully, "Disposed of . . . It's dreadful to talk of Marian's belongings that way. She was such a competent person. She knew everything. I don't know how the foundation will manage without her. Her death is a huge loss. And to think of Marian of all people falling from her stairs! Marian skied and jogged and climbed mountains. She wasn't the least bit clumsy." Her voice quivered with emotion, almost a touch of anger, as if Marian Grant had let them down. "But there's nothing we can do about it."

S teve Flynn slid into the last booth in a line of red leather-ette booths at Hamburger Heaven. On a Sunday night, choice for dinner in Craddock was limited to the usual suspects: McDonald's, Sonic, Braum's, Applebee's, Olive Garden. The hometown restaurants closed after Sunday brunch except for Hamburger Heaven.

The crowd was sparse. Sunday was a family evening. Steve was getting used to eating out alone. He dipped a French fry in the side of ranch dressing that he always ordered with his cheeseburger. He felt a flicker of amusement. Living on the wild side, ranch dressing instead of Heinz. His hand froze midway to his mouth.

A dark-haired woman in her early twenties slipped onto a wooden seat at a nearby table. She was a stranger. Not that he could claim to know everyone in Craddock, but he knew most of her age and class. He had never seen her before, of that he was certain. He would not forget her. She wasn't conventionally pretty. Her face was too thin with deep-set eyes, narrow nose, high cheekbones, and a delicate but firm chin. There were smudges beneath her brilliantly dark eyes. She carried with her an air of melancholy.

She sat at a table close to him, but he had no doubt that though she was physically present, her thoughts were far away.

His image and hers were reflected in the long mirror behind the counter, two people sitting by themselves, a burly redheaded man in an old sweater, an aloof and memorable dark-haired woman in a thin, cotton blouse.

He didn't know if he'd ever felt more alone.

— 4 —

Nela used to love Monday mornings, especially a Monday when she was on her way to work. Since Bill died, the world had been gray. She did what she was supposed to do. Sometimes she was able to plunge into a task and forget grayness for a while. Maybe taking over Chloe's job, doing something different, would brighten her world. Sunday had been a long, sad day. She'd wandered about Craddock, ended up at Chloe's Hamburger Heaven. But sitting there, eating food that she knew was good but that had no savor, she'd accepted the truth. Old sayings didn't lie. Wherever you go, there you are. It didn't matter if she was in LA or a small wind-blown town half a continent away, there she was, carrying with her the pain and sadness. At least today she had a job waiting for her among people with tasks and accomplishments. She would concentrate on the people she met, think about the things they did, push sadness and pain deep inside. She turned into the Haklo grounds, following a short line of cars.

In the lot, she parked next to a sleek blue Thunderbird. At the same time, an old beige Dodge sputtered to a stop on the other side of the VW.

"Good morning." A plump sixtyish man with a mop of untidy white hair stepped out of the Dodge and bustled toward her, blue eyes shining.

Nela waited behind the Thunderbird. She noted the tag: ROBBIE.

Her welcomer's genial face reminded her of Edmund Gwenn in *The Trouble with Harry*. "You must be Nela, Chloe's sister. You look just like your picture."

Nela knew her dark curls were tangled by the wind. The day on the pier had been windy, too.

"Welcome to Haklo." He spoke as proudly as a man handing out keys to a city. "I'm Cole Hamilton." He spoke as if she would, of course, know his name.

Nela responded with equal warmth. "It's a pleasure to meet you, Mr. Hamilton."

"Oh, my dear, call me Cole. Everyone does."

Heavy steps sounded behind them. A deep voice rumbled, "Good morning, Cole." Despite his size, well over six feet and two hundred plus pounds, the huge dark-haired man moved with muscular grace. "Francis Garth. Good morning, Miss Farley. I knew you immediately when you pulled up in that car. It's good of you to help us out while Chloe is gone."

They were moving toward the walkway to the building, an oddly assorted trio, Francis Garth towering above Nela and her bubbly new friend. Cole was chattering, ". . . Chloe told us you were a reporter. That must be an exciting life. But the pressure . . ."

Nela had thrived on deadlines. It was the only life she'd ever wanted, talking to people, finding out what mattered, getting the facts right. She'd written everything from light

fluffy features to a series on embezzlement at the city trea-
surer's office. She'd learned how to dig for facts. More
importantly, she'd learned how to read faces and body language. She wasn't a reporter now. She'd lost her job more
than six months ago. Last hired, first fired. Print journalism
jobs were as scarce as champagne-colored natural pearls.
She'd once done a story about a woman who had spent a lifetime collecting pearls of many shades, white, black, green,
purple, and greatest prize of all, the golden tone of champagne. After her last newspaper job, Nela had waited tables
at a swell café on Melrose Place in Hollywood. That job, too,
was gone. But someday she would find an editor who would
give her a chance . . .

Immersed in her thoughts, she'd taken a good half-dozen
steps before she realized that Cole's high tenor had broken
off in midsentence.

Voices rose on the sidewalk from the cabins and around
a curve came a very pretty girl and a lanky man in a light
blue cashmere sweater and gray slacks. Nela knew him at
once. Chloe's description had been right on. *The director's
kind of like James Stewart in* The Shop Around the Corner *. . . He's tall and angular and has this bony appealing
face.* His companion looked up at him with a happy face
and her words came quickly. ". . . I haven't seen the Chihuly
exhibit either. That would be such fun."

Perhaps it was the stillness of the trio standing by the
building steps that caught their attention. Abruptly, light
and cheer fled from her delicate features. The director's face
reformed from boyish eagerness to defensive blandness.
Nela wasn't personally attracted, but many women would
find his cleft-chinned good looks irresistible.

Nela sensed antagonism in the men beside her, though
outwardly all was courtesy and good humor.

"Good morning." Francis Garth's deep voice was

pleasant and impersonal. "Nela, here is our director, Hollis Blair, and"—his dark eyes moved without warmth to the blonde's delicate face—"our new assistant curator, Abby Andrews."

In the flurry of greetings, Cole Hamilton hurried up the steps, held the door. "Almost eight o'clock. We're all on time this morning." The dumpy little man with thick white hair suddenly looked as if his blue suit was too large for him.

As the door closed behind them, Hamilton veered toward a door marked STAIRS. "Have to see about some things." He was subdued with no echo of the pride that she'd heard when he'd greeted her in the parking lot.

The new grant applications are in the first filing cabinet. The applications are made online but we print out copies for our records"—Louise gestured at the filing cabinet—"and we make copies for the members of the grants committee. Marian says they can look at them online but as a courtesy we also provide printed copies. The committee meets every fourth Thursday of the month. We have fifteen new applications to consider. Whenever a new application is received, Chloe prepares a one-page summary. I placed the remaining applications that need summaries in Chloe's in-box. The top folder holds one Chloe had already prepared and you can look it over for the format. You can—"

"Louise." The deep voice was gruff.

Francis Garth stood in Nela's doorway, making it look small. His heavy face was stern. He held up several stapled sheets. "There is an error in today's agenda."

Louise's face registered a series of revealing expressions: knowledge, discomfort, dismay, regret.

Francis raised a heavy dark eyebrow. There was a trace of humor in a sudden twisted smile, but only a trace. "I take it there was no mistake. Why was the proposal removed?"

Louise cleared her throat. "I understand the director felt that opposing the wind farms was at odds with the foundation's support of green energy."

"Wind farms can ruin the Tallgrass Prairie ecosystem. Isn't that a green"—it was almost an epithet—"concern? Hasn't Haklo always respected tribal values? The Tallgrass Prairie is the heart of the Osage Nation."

"Oh, Francis, I know how you feel about the Tallgrass Prairie. But Hollis persuaded Blythe that it was important for Haklo to rise above parochial interests to fulfill its mission of nurturing the planet." Clearly Louise was repeating verbatim what she had been told.

"Nothing in this world should be permitted to defile the Tallgrass Prairie." He spoke slowly, the words distinct and separate. He didn't raise his voice but there was no mistaking his passion. He turned, moving swiftly for such a big man.

Louise stared at the empty doorway, her face troubled.

Nela had no idea what the Tallgrass Prairie meant. But whatever it was, wherever it was, Francis Garth was clearly furious.

Louise took a deep breath. "Let's make the rounds, Nela. I want to introduce you to everyone."

"I met several people coming in this morning, the director and the assistant curator and Mr. Hamilton and Mr. Garth. I met Miss Webster Friday night at the apartment." It wasn't necessary to explain the circumstances.

"Wonderful. We'll run by all the offices so you'll know where to take the mail and we can drop in and say hello to Peter and Grace."

As they reached the cross hall, Louise slowed. She looked puzzled. "Blythe's door is closed. Usually everyone keeps their doors open. Webster wanted everyone to feel free and easy at Haklo." She looked forlorn. "That's the way it used to be."

Nela doubted Louise realized how revealing her

statement was. So Haklo was not a happy place. Not now.
Was Louise's dismay because of the death of a colleague?
Nela wished that Chloe had been more attuned to the place
where she worked, but Chloe was Chloe, not self-absorbed
in a selfish way but always focusing on fun. Nela knew her
sister well enough to be sure that all kinds of emotions
would have swirled around Chloe without leaving any
impression.

"But we still"—and now she was walking faster—"make
such a wonderful difference in so many lives."

They reached the horseshoe-shaped reception desk in
the rotunda.

A plump woman with a round cheerful face beamed at
them. "Hi, Louise. And you must be Nela. I'm Rosalind
McNeill." She eyed Nela with interest. "You sure don't look
like Chloe." There was no hint of disparagement in the soft
drawl, simply a fact mentioned in passing.

Nela smiled at the receptionist. "That's what everyone
says."

Rosalind's brown eyes sparkled. "Chloe's very nice. You
look nice, too."

Nela imagined that Rosalind always found her glass half
full and that her presence was as relaxing to those around
her as a sunny day at the beach. In contrast, tightly coiled
Louise exuded tension from the wrinkle of her brows to
thin shoulders always slightly tensed.

"I'm taking Nela around to introduce her. If the mail's
ready, we can deliver it."

Rosalind shook her head. "I'm about half done. Lots of
calls for Miss Webster this morning. Something's got the
members of the grants committee riled. They called, bang,
bang, bang, one after the other. I've heard happier voices at
wakes. I don't think Miss Webster was hearing love notes.
If I had one, I'd toss in a bottle of bath salts with her letter
delivery." She grinned. "I've been rereading Victorian

fiction. Ah, the days when gentle ladies fainted at the drop of a handkerchief to be revived by smelling salts. Did you know they're really a mixture of ammonia and water? That would revive anybody. From the tone of the callers, I'm betting Miss Webster could use a sniff."

Louise looked ever more worried. "I'd better see what's happened. Rosalind, you can finish sorting the mail, then give Nela the room numbers." She turned to Nela. "I'm sorry you haven't met some of the staff yet."

"Meeting new people has always been what I enjoy most about working on a newspaper. I'll be fine."

Louise gave her a quick smile, which was replaced almost immediately by a furrow of worry as she turned and hurried toward the trustee's office.

Rosalind's glance was admiring. "Chloe said you were a reporter. That must be exciting."

"It can be. I'm looking for a job right now." She refused to be defensive. Everybody knew somebody who'd lost a job. She didn't mind waiting tables in the interim, but someday, somehow she would write again. Bill wouldn't want her to give up. The only happiness she'd known in this last dreary year was when she was writing. That became a world in itself, arranging facts, finding words, creating a story.

Nela came behind the counter. A vase of fresh daisies sat on the corner of Rosalind's desk. A foldout photo holder held pictures of three cats, a bright-eyed calico, a thoughtful brown tabby, and a silver gray with a Persian face.

Rosalind saw her glance. "My gals, Charlotte, Emily, and Anne. They can't write, but they snuggle next to me when I read. Funny thing"—there was an odd tone in her voice—"and you probably won't believe me, but every time I sit down with *Jane Eyre*, Charlotte rubs her face against the book. Of course, she's making it hers, but it's only that particular book. Go figure." As she talked, she flicked envelopes with the ease of long practice into a long plastic tray. Dividers were marked with recipients' names. "I've added the mail for Miss Grant to Dr. Blair's stack. I guess Chloe told you about the accident. That was a shocker." She slapped the last of the letters in place. "The trustee's mail is always delivered first."

When Nela lifted the plastic tray, Rosalind gave a half salute. "If you need reinforcements, I'll be at The Office."

Clearly Rosalind's tone was wry, but Nela dutifully inquired, "The Office?"

"That's Craddock's home-away-from-home watering hole. Coldest beer, hottest wings." A grin. "When things get too hairy here at Haklo, we always kid around and say you can find us at The Office." A sigh. "In my dreams."

Blythe Webster's door was still closed.

Nela shifted the tray on her hip. She'd been instructed to deliver the mail. She would do so. She knocked lightly on the panel, turned the knob, and pushed the door open.

". . . have to investigate." The man's voice was loud, stressed.

The door made a sighing sound.

Nela immediately realized she'd intruded at a stressful moment. Blythe Webster stood behind her desk, face drawn down in an intense frown. Louise Spear stood a few feet away. Eyes huge in a shocked face, Louise twisted her hands around and around each other. The lanky director moved back and forth, a few steps one way, then back again, clearly distraught.

Nela obviously had interrupted a grim conversation. The sooner she departed, the better. "Excuse me. I have the morning mail for Miss Webster." She remained in the doorway, poised for a quick withdrawal.

Blythe lifted a hand to touch a double strand of pearls. Her face was set and pale. "Put the letters in the in-tray."

Nela quickly crossed to the desk, deposited several letters and mailers.

Blythe managed a strained smile. "Nela, this is Dr. Blair,

director of the foundation. Hollis, this is Nela Farley, Chloe's sister. Nela is taking Chloe's place while she's on her holiday."

"Thank you, Miss Webster. I met Dr. Blair earlier." She began to move toward the door.

"Wait a minute." Blythe's tone was sharp. She glanced at a diamond-encrusted watch. "It's almost ten. We must deal with this immediately. Nela, as you deliver the mail, inform each staff member that the meeting has been moved to ten o'clock. Attendance is mandatory."

—5—

Louise looked at the grandfather clock in the corner of the conference room. The minute hand stood at twelve minutes past ten. The golden oak of the clock matched the golden oak paneling. In the glow of recessed lights, the granite conference tabletop added more serene colors, streaks of yellow and tangerine against a wheat background.

A sense of unease pervaded a room where no expense had been spared to create a welcoming environment. In the mural on one wall, monarchs hovered over reddish orange blooms on waist-high grasses that wavered in a wind beneath a cloudless blue sky. On the other wall, a buffalo faced forward, dark eyes beneath a mat of wiry black curls in a huge head framed by curved horns, massive shoulders, short legs, and shaggy brown hair.

Nela sat to one side of the conference table in a straight chair. Six black leather swivel chairs were occupied, leaving a half dozen or so empty at the far end of the table. The delivery of the mail had given her the chance to meet both

Grace Webster, Blythe's sister, and Peter Owens, the director of publications. It had been interesting when she issued Blythe's summons to each staff member to be in the conference room at ten o'clock instead of eleven. She would have expected surprise. There had been wariness, but no surprise.

In what kind of workplace was a peremptory summons treated as if it were business as usual?

She looked with interest around the room. Cole Hamilton fiddled with a pen, making marks on the legal pad. Francis Garth sat with his arms folded. He reminded her of the buffalo in the far mural. All he lacked were horns and short legs.

Her gaze paused on Abby Andrews. Nela thought that Chloe's description of the new assistant curator didn't do her justice. Abby was a classically lovely blonde with perfect bone structure. Her brows could have used a bit of darkening, but her deep violet eyes were striking. At the moment, she sat in frozen stillness as if she might shatter if she moved.

Why was she so tense?

Nela had no doubt that Blythe's younger sister Grace was trouble waiting to happen. Grace tapped her pen on the tabletop. *Tap. Tap. Tap.* Her rounded face was not unpleasant, but she was clearly combative.

The quarter hour chimed.

Robbie Powell brushed back a lock of brightly blond hair.

Nela made a quick link. Tab Hunter in *Damn Yankees* but with longer hair. She knew Chloe would agree.

"I'm expecting a call from a Dallas newspaper. I may be able to place a feature story on that research into antibiotic overuse in stock. I had to change the time. And now we're sitting here, waiting." Robbie kept his tone light. "I assumed something important had occurred, but neither the trustee nor the director have shown up after the imperial summons." Robbie straightened a heavy gold cuff link in his blue oxford cloth shirt. His blue blazer was a perfect fit. He had the patina of a man at home in meetings, always sure to know everyone's name, quick with a smile and compliment.

Nela was good at reading moods, and beneath Robbie's surface charm, she sensed anger.

Louise was placating. "They'll be here soon. There's been an upsetting development."

The faces around the table were abruptly alert. There was unmistakable tension.

Francis cleared his throat. "What development?"

Louise didn't meet his gaze. "It will be better for Blythe to explain."

Peter Owens shifted in his seat. "Ah, well, we're on company time." His comment was smooth, but he, too, looked uncomfortable. A lean man with black horn rims perched in wiry dark hair, he had wide-set brown eyes, a thin nose, and sharp chin. His good quality but well-worn tweed jacket with leather elbow patches made him look professorial. "How about some of Mama Kay's sweet rolls? A little sugar will lift your spirits, Robbie."

Louise looked at Nela. "Please serve the sweet rolls and coffee now. Except for Blythe and Hollis."

Nela warmed the sweet rolls and carried the serving plate to Louise. Nela poured coffee into Haklo Foundation mugs, gold letters on a dark green background, and served them.

Peter nodded his thanks, then lifted his mug. "Ladies and gentlemen, a toast to our newest addition. Welcome to Haklo Foundation, Nela. We enjoy your sister. She's definitely a breath of freshness in this fusty atmosphere. Have you heard a report from Tahiti?"

Nela responded to his genuine interest. "Just a call Friday

night to say they arrived safely and everything was fantastic."

"Fantastic in all caps?" But his voice was kind.

Nela smiled. "Absolutely."

He nodded toward her chair. "Pour yourself some coffee, too. I highly recommend Mama Kay's raspberry Danish. The foundation is beyond good fortune to have her as our chef."

Nela glanced at Louise, who nodded.

Nela settled at her place with a plate. The sweet roll was indeed excellent, the flaky crust light, the raspberry filling tart and perfect.

Peter spoke in a mumble past a mouthful of pastry. "Speaking of travelers, I suggest we vote on a staff conference in Arizona. Surely there is something useful we could survey there. Or possibly Costa Rica. Francis, you're very good at sniffing out development prospects for Oklahoma beef. How about Costa Rica?"

Francis turned his heavy head. He looked sharply at Peter's smiling face, then said quietly, "In the past we've done good work gaining markets for Oklahoma beef. But the new budget doesn't support that kind of outreach."

Peter shrugged. "Your office has had a very good run." His face was still pleasant, but there might have been a slightly malicious curl to his crooked lips.

As he drank from his mug, Nela wondered if she had imagined that transformation.

Francis folded his arms. "Things change." His deep voice was ruminative. "I played golf with Larry Swift the other day. You know him, Swift Publications. He's pretty excited to be invited to submit a bid to handle the design of a pictorial history of Carter County."

Peter's face tightened. "I've been talking to Blythe. I think she understands that in-house design is cheaper and, of course, better quality."

"Does she?" Robbie's tone was ingenuous. "She asked me about Swift Publications the other day. I had to say they do swell work."

"Nela, please take the carafe around, see if anyone wants more coffee. My, I hope the weather doesn't turn bad . . ." Louise chattered about the awfully cold weather, and had they heard there was a possibility of an ice storm?

Nela poured coffee and wondered at the background to the ostensibly pleasant but barbed exchanges.

The door swung open. Blythe Webster hurried inside. Her fine features looked etched in stone. Hollis Blair followed, his lips pressed together in a thin, hard line. He was Jimmy Stewart after he lost his job at the little shop around the corner.

Chairs creaked. There was a general shifting of position.

"My, my, my. What's happened?" Cole Hamilton's rather high voice quavered. Francis Garth's heavy bushy eyebrows drew down in a frown. Abby Andrews's lips trembled and she seemed even more fragile. Grace Webster's blue eyes narrowed as she studied her sister's face. Robbie Powell looked apprehensive. Peter Owens leaned back in his chair, gaze speculative, arms folded.

Nela half expected Louise to dismiss her from the meeting. This no longer seemed an occasion for her to serve pastries and coffee. But the secretary never glanced her way. In the stress of whatever prompted the earlier meeting, Louise wasn't thinking about Nela and her function. It wasn't Nela's job to remind her.

Blythe Webster stopped behind the end chair. "Sit down, Hollis."

Nela thought her tone was brusque.

Hollis Blair dropped into the empty seat to her right. He hunched his shoulders like a man preparing to fight.

Blythe remained standing, resting a green folder on the

chair back. She made no apology for their late arrival and gave no greeting. "This morning I received calls from Alice Garcia, Kay Drummond, and Jane Carstairs. In today's mail, each informed me she had received a letter on Dr. Blair's letterhead which contained obscene material." She looked toward the director. "I immediately spoke with Hollis. He assures me he had no knowledge of the letter." The words were spoken evenly, suggesting neither acceptance nor denial of the director's involvement.

Hollis Blair's head jerked up. "Obviously I didn't send the letters. I know nothing about them. Someone obtained my letterhead and used it without permission."

Robbie Powell flapped his well-manicured hands. "We have to get those letters back. This could be a nightmare. Can't you see the headline in the *Oklahoman*? *Prurient Letter Linked to Haklo Director.*"

"It isn't his fault." Abby blurted out the words angrily, a flush staining her pale cheeks.

Hollis looked toward her, his blue eyes suddenly soft. "It's all right, Abby. We'll find out who's responsible."

Peter Owens spoke quietly. "If there's no proof Dr. Blair sent the letters, the foundation can disclaim any responsibility. Since there have been other random acts of vandalism—"

It was like a picture that had been askew righting itself. Now Nela understood the reason why Louise spoke nostalgically about happy times at Haklo. Moreover, none of the staff had seemed surprised at a peremptory summons.

"Doesn't sound too damn random." Francis's voice was gruff. "Obscene letters sent to members of the grants committee suggests the recipients were chosen quite specifically. Of course"—he looked at Blythe—"you may soon be receiving other calls."

Blythe shook her head. "I don't think so. The calls came

ping-ping-ping as soon as the morning business deliveries were made. I checked with Bart Hasting's secretary. He has a letter from the foundation from Dr. Blair. I asked her not to open it. Bart and his family are skiing at Vail. If anyone else in town had received a letter, I'd know by now. So, the damage can be contained. Since no one on the committee wishes harm to the foundation, they will keep this confidential." She glanced at the wall clock.

Cole Hamilton looked distressed. "This is a serious matter. A suggestion of immorality could taint the foundation forever."

"I'm afraid women with a juicy bit of gossip never keep it to themselves." Robbie shook his head in regret.

Nela wondered if there was a hint of malicious amusement in his light voice.

"Really?" Grace was dismissive. "I'm sure you never gossip, do you, sweetie?"

Robbie stared at her. For an instant, the handsome youngish man looked old and beaten. "I was misquoted, my words taken out of context."

"Grace, that matter is closed. Robbie apologized." Blythe's tone was sharp.

Grace laughed aloud. "Oh, my charitable sister. No matter if an employee is overheard describing her as Head Bitch at the foundation. But maybe truth is a defense."

For a long instant, the sisters stared at each other.

Cole Hamilton fluttered his hands. "Girls, girls. I know your father would move swiftly to correct the current dreadful situation here." His eyelids blinking rapidly, he spoke in a rush. "It is shocking how calamities have engulfed the foundation since Dr. Blair took over last fall."

Peter Owens cleared his throat. "Let me see, we had some roadkill out in front of the foundation last week. I guess that's Hollis's fault as well."

Cole's face creased in stubborn lines. "You can't pretend there aren't problems."

Blythe made an impatient gesture. "No one is pretending there aren't problems. Hollis has instituted inquiries into each incident."

Robbie raised a thick blond brow. "What has he found out? Who set that girl's car on fire? Who destroyed the Indian baskets? Who set off the indoor sprinklers and drenched my office? Who turned on the outdoor fountain and the pipes froze and it's going to cost thousands to fix it? Who took the skateboard from Abby's porch? Next thing you know, the vandal will strap a bomb to it and roll it up the main hall one night. Who stole your necklace? I find it puzzling"—his green eyes flicked toward Hollis—"that our director didn't call the police, and that necklace must be worth thousands of dollars with those heavy gold links and those diamonds. And now these letters . . ."

Nela remembered too clearly the heavy weight of the necklace, the glitter of the stones. Somehow she managed not to change expression. She had the same sense of unreality that an earthquake brought, jolted by one shock and then another. A missing skateboard. A stolen necklace. She pushed aside thoughts of a skateboard. That was her invention, extrapolating what a cat meant by a rolling board. But the gold necklace heavy with diamonds that rested at the bottom of Marian Grant's purse was real, not an invention. Up to this moment, she had been engaged as an observer. Now, with abrupt suddenness, she was as intensely involved as any of the Haklo staff.

"I"—Blythe's tone was imperious—"instructed Hollis to arrange for a private investigation about the necklace. I do not want the disappearance of the necklace to become a police matter. Inevitably, if there is a police report, there would be a story in the *Clarion*. We've had enough stories. I'm still getting questions about that car fire and the fountain.

However"—she glanced at her watch—"if all of these incidents are connected, the person who wishes harm to the foundation may have been too clever. Within a few minutes, I expect to know whether one of our computers generated the message. Obviously the writer would have deleted the file but IT assures me that any deleted file can be found. At this moment, our IT staff is checking every computer. Penny Crawford will bring the results to me. As we wait, we will proceed with our regular meeting. Hollis."

Dr. Blair gave an abrupt nod. "I will be sending out a memo to staff today in regard to our annual . . ."

The words rolled over Nela without meaning. How many heavy gold-link necklaces studded with diamonds could be floating around Craddock? But if the jewelry had been stolen, why was it in Marian Grant's purse? From everything she'd heard about Marian Grant, the idea that she'd commit a theft was preposterous. But the necklace was in the purse.

Maybe that's what the intruder was looking for Friday night. Yet the person who entered had ignored Marian Grant's purse, instead slammed through her desk.

Whatever the reason for the search, Nela knew she had to do something about the purse that now rested behind a stack of cat food in Marian Grant's kitchen cabinet. Nela's situation was untenable. If she admitted she'd searched Miss Grant's purse and not mentioned to anyone what she'd found, it would be difficult to explain the fact that she'd hidden the purse. If she kept quiet, it would be devastating if anyone found the hidden purse.

A knock sounded on the door.

"Come in." Blythe spoke firmly.

The door opened and a dark-haired young woman stepped inside. She kept her gaze fastened on Blythe's face. "Miss Webster, I found the file."

Blythe's fingers curled around the double strand of pearls at her throat. "Which computer, Penny?"

The young IT tech looked uncomfortable. "The computer is in the office assigned to Abby Andrews."

Abby gave a choked cry. Her face flushed, then turned pale. She came to her feet, held out a trembling hand. "I never wrote anything like that. Never. I wouldn't hurt the foundation." She ignored Blythe, turned instead toward Hollis Blair, her gaze beseeching.

Hollis stood, too. His bony face flushed. "Of course you didn't. Someone else used your computer, Abby."

Blythe studied Abby. Her gaze was interested, neither supportive nor accusing. "Sit down, Abby, Hollis." She waited until both of them took their seats. Blythe's cameo-perfect face was composed.

Nela wondered if it was inherent in Blythe's nature to exercise control. She also wondered if the trustee knew that she was diminishing both Hollis and Abby with her cool instruction. *Sit down, children.*

Blythe continued in a measured voice. "Remain calm. There's no proof Abby created the file. There's no proof Abby didn't. Let's explore the possibilities." She nodded at the IT staffer. "When was the file created?"

"Thursday at eleven oh eight p.m." Penny Crawford carefully did not glance toward Abby.

"I was in my cabin." Abby's voice was defiant. "I was by myself. I had no reason to come here at night."

Cole Hamilton peered at the assistant curator. "It requires a password to access a computer." The question was implicit.

Robbie looked relieved, almost complacent. "They say you always leave an electronic footprint. This may explain all the trouble we've had this winter."

Abby swung toward him, her thin face stricken. "I didn't create that file. It's a lie. Why would I do something like that? If anyone had reason to cause trouble for Dr. Blair, it's you. You and your boyfriend."

Nela realized that the usual office veneer had been stripped away. It was an unpleasant scene, but she watched each one, hoping that one of them might reveal something to explain the necklace in Marian's purse.

Robbie's smooth face turned to stone. "If Cole's worried about the taint of immorality, maybe we should start at the top. With our new director and his girlfriend."

"Let's all stop saying things we'll regret." Peter Owens's voice was calm.

"Don't be a bore, Peter." Grace was amused. "This is more fun than *The View*. What's wrong with some home truths? Everybody knows Robbie's as inflated with venom as a puff adder since Erik got canned. The psychology's a little twisted to tag Abby as the villainess but these days nothing surprises. She's the director's adoring slave even though the rest of us aren't sure he's up to the job. Of course, he responds. Maybe Abby caused the troubles so she could console him." She turned to Abby. "You are living in one of the foundation's guest cabins. I saw his car there very late one night. I told Blythe. But she didn't do anything about it. Of course"—she shot a questioning look at her sister—"you were hell-bent to hire Hollis and you never, ever make a mistake, do you, Sister?" Grace didn't wait for an answer. "It's too bad Dad isn't still around. Dad always had a rule about women in his office. He told everyone, 'Don't fool with the working stock,' and in case you want to know what that means, a man in charge doesn't screw the secretaries. They didn't have assistant curators in those days. But the rule should be the same."

Hollis's voice grated. "My private life and Abby's private life have nothing to do with you or with the foundation. The suggestion that she'd create any kind of situation that would harm the foundation is absurd. That's a nasty, twisted idea. If we're going to consider who might be angry with the foundation or"—his glance at Blythe was measuring—"with Blythe, we don't have far to look." He looked directly at Robbie Powell.

Robbie's boyish face hardened. "What's that supposed to mean?"

Grace laughed. "Come on, Robbie. Skip the hurt innocence. Be a big boy." Her tone was chiding. "You started the toe-to-toe with Hollis when you suggested Abby was vandal-in-chief. Our director may not be able to keep his pants zipped, but he's not a fool. If anybody wants to make a list of people pissed off at Blythe, you and your boyfriend clock in at one and two. Speaking of, how is our former director?"

Robbie's voice was clipped. "Erik's working diligently on a definitive history of the foundation."

Nela sorted out the players in her mind. It was Erik in the cape who had opted to park in the visitors' lot. Now she knew why.

Robbie looked at Blythe. "The foundation should be ready to sign a contract for its publication."

Grace gave a hoot. "Don't be a pushover, Blythe. Robbie's trying to make you feel guilty because you booted Erik."

"Grace, please." Blythe frowned at her sister. "It was time for the foundation to have younger leadership, a more forward-looking vision." The words were smooth, automatic, meaningless.

Robbie was strident. "Erik gave the best years of his life to the foundation. What thanks did he receive?"

Grace looked amused. "I rest my case. Who hates you the most, Blythe? Erik or Robbie? I'd say it was a tie. We know Robbie can get in and out of the building. You can bet Erik still has his keys. Or he could easily filch Robbie's."

"You have keys." Robbie's tone was hard. "You've been furious ever since Blythe vetoed the grant to the Sutton

Gallery. The vandalism began the very next week. I hear the gallery might have to close down."

Nela moved her gaze from one cold face to another.

"The gallery won't close." Grace spoke with icy precision. "I will make sure of that."

Blythe was impatient. "I insist we remain on topic. We have to deal with the file in Abby's computer." She turned toward the assistant curator. "An emotional response isn't helpful. We will deal with facts."

Abby sent a desperate glance toward Hollis. She looked helpless, persecuted, and appealingly lovely.

Nela didn't know these people but the idea seemed to be that Abby and Hollis were lovers. If ever anyone had the aura of a heroine adrift on an ice floe, it was Abby. Her need for support could be genuine or could be calculated to bring out the defending male response of chivalry. There was no doubt the handsome, lanky director was charging to Abby's defense. He gave her a reassuring smile. "We'll get to the bottom of this. It's unpleasant, but it has nothing to do with you, Abby."

Abby's eyes never left his face.

A skateboard disappeared from Abby's porch. Whose skateboard? When did it disappear? Before Marian Grant fell to her death?

Blythe wasn't deflected. She tapped the folder. "Who knows your password?"

Abby's voice shook. "I don't know. Someone must have gotten it somehow."

Blythe's gaze sharpened. "Did you tell anyone your password?"

"Never. Someone got it somehow." Her violet eyes were dark with misery.

Blythe looked skeptical. "How?"

Francis Garth shifted his big body, rumbled, "Stop badgering her, Blythe."

Blythe massaged one temple. "My password's written on a slip of paper in my desk drawer. Maybe—"

Louise clapped her hands together. "Don't you remember, Blythe? Marian kept a list of current passwords in case a computer needed to be accessed." Louise looked excited. "We can check." She turned to Nela. "Go to Marian's office. She kept a small notebook with tabs in her right-hand desk drawer. Marian was always organized. Look under *p*s for password."

Nela closed the conference room door behind her. It was a relief to be outside that emotionally charged atmosphere. Maybe she would find an answer that would help Abby. The assistant curator was upset for good reason. To be accused of sending out a sleazy message on the director's letterhead was bad enough, but obviously she and Hollis were more than employer and employee. All the dictums of good sense warned against an office romance, but dictums didn't matter to love. A casual friend had warned her against dating Bill, pointing out, for God's sake, he's in the army, and what kind of life is that? Good advice, but her heart didn't care. Bill hadn't planned to stay in the army. He was going to go back to school . . .

Nela jerked her thoughts back to Abby. Abby's wavering denials did nothing to prove her innocence. Nela walked faster. Abby couldn't prove her innocence and Nela couldn't prove she'd had good intentions when she found that necklace in Marian's purse.

In the main hall, Rosalind looked up from the reception desk. "Hey, is the meeting over? I've got a backlog of calls."

It wasn't Nela's place to say the meeting might go on forever and all hell was breaking loose. She forced a smile. "Still going. They sent me for something from Miss Grant's office."

She felt hopeful when she reached the office door. Maybe she would find the notebook and possibly offer at least a sliver of succor to Abby. If Marian had indeed recorded computer passwords, someone might have obtained Abby's password. The sooner Nela returned, the sooner the meeting would end. By then it would be nearing lunchtime. She'd go back to the apartment and do something about that damned necklace.

She opened the door to chaos. One word blazed in her mind. *Fury.*

— 6 —

"Why didn't you ask?" Blythe Webster flung out a hand. "I should have been consulted." Her face was tight with anger.

Rosalind McNeill looked upset and uncertain. "I'm sorry, Miss Webster. Nela stopped in the doorway and I knew something dreadful had happened. I hurried over there. When I saw the mess, I raced to my desk and called nine-one-one. Then I ran to tell you and now you're all here." She gestured toward the staff members, who milled about near Marian's office.

The sound of approaching sirens rose and fell.

Blythe pressed her lips together, finally said brusquely, "I understand, Rosalind. Of course you did the right thing." The words clearly came with an effort at civility. "It's just that we've had so much dreadful publicity. Now there will be more." She turned away, moved toward the front door.

Rosalind looked after her with a worried face.

"You did the right thing." Nela doubted her reassurance

brought much comfort to Rosalind. "It's against the law to conceal a crime."

Nela stepped a little nearer to the open office door.

Hollis Blair stared into the trashed office with a tired, puzzled expression. Abby looked relieved. Perhaps she thought the violent destruction—drawers' contents flung on the floor, filing cabinets emptied, computer terminal smashed, art work broken or slashed, chairs overturned—benefited her. Certainly the file on her computer was no longer the center of attention.

Nela caught snatches of conversation.

Cole Hamilton paced back and forth. ". . . grounds need to be patrolled . . ."

Francis Garth massaged his heavy chin. ". . . obviously dealing with an unbalanced mind . . ."

Grace Webster jangled silver bracelets on one arm. ". . . I heard last week that Erik still hadn't found a job . . ."

Peter Owens looked worried. ". . . suggest care in publicly discussing any grievances . . ."

Robbie Powell was businesslike. ". . . essential to prepare a press release . . ."

Outside, the sirens shrilled, then cut off.

Hollis Blair braced his shoulders, moved to join Blythe.

The heavy main door opened. A fast-moving, dark-haired woman in street clothes was followed by two uniformed officers, a thin wiry blonde and a large man with a balding head.

Nela was glad it wasn't the same pair of officers who had been at Marian Grant's apartment. Even the most incurious of police might wonder that she had called for help Friday night and today she had found a vandalized office. Logic denied a link, but swift judgments often had little connection to logic. Happily, she'd never seen either the dark-haired woman or the uniformed officers before.

Blythe was gracious. "Thank you for responding to our

call." She looked past the detective and the uniformed officers. Her face stiffened at the approach of a burly redheaded man in a worn pullover sweater and shabby gray corduroy slacks. The sweater looked very old, several threads pulled loose near one shoulder. The shirt beneath the sweater had a frayed collar. Blythe's tone was sharp. "The foundation is private—"

Robbie Powell moved past her to clap the redhead on the shoulder. "Hey, Steve. We don't have a statement yet. Apparently we've had some serious vandalism but let's see what the police can discover. Guess you picked up the call on the *Clarion* scanner?"

Wiry red hair flamed above a broad, pleasant, snub-nosed face spattered with freckles. His gaze stopped when he saw Nela.

Nela felt her lips begin to curve upward, then controlled her face. It was as if she'd looked into the blue eyes of an old friend, but her reaction to the redheaded man was nothing more than a funny link, half glad, half sad, to her past. It was as if Gram were beside her, describing happy summer nights watching first-run movies outside on a moonlit pier in Long Beach with the sound of the ocean as a backdrop. Gram's favorite movie star had been Van Johnson, a chunky, appealing redhead.

Nela put the pieces together. *The Clarion.* Statement. Police scanner. He was a reporter. A print reporter obviously, because he carried a laptop and no cameraman trailed him. Maybe her instinctive positive attitude toward him was as much a recognition of a mind-set like hers as a legacy of long-ago movies.

She wondered if the stocky reporter, who had given her one last searching glance before following a clutch of police officers, would ever have heard of the boy-next-door movie star so famous in the 1940s and '50s? Nela had managed to find DVRs of all of Van Johnson's films for Gram and they'd been a great pleasure to her those last few months.

"Nela, are you coming?"

She looked up, startled.

Louise gestured toward the hallway. "Detective Dugan will report on the progress of the investigation in half an hour. Then she will interview each of us individually. Blythe has arranged for lunch to be served in the conference room while we wait."

Conversation was disjointed. No one spoke to Nela. The staff seemed oblivious to her presence and that suited her fine. She tried to maintain a grave but disinterested expression even though she was focused on a matter that each of them would find supremely interesting, the diamond-and-gold necklace in Marian Grant's purse. It was too late to explain that she'd found the necklace. Perhaps after work she'd pretend she'd been curious, wondered if the purse held a clue, and immediately call the police upon her "discovery" of the necklace. That seemed like a sensible course. But the weight of her knowledge wouldn't be lifted until she could finally hand the purse over to someone in charge.

The conference room door opened and the redheaded reporter stepped inside. He nodded at the large policeman who stood near the buffalo mural, then walked casually toward the far end of the table. If he was attempting to be inconspicuous, he didn't succeed. He was too burly, too vigorous, too intense to miss. His flaming red hair could have used a trim, curling over the rim of the collar that poked above his worn sweater.

"Excuse me." Clearly Blythe addressed him. "This is a private meeting, not open to the press."

"I'm covering the police investigation into a possible theft, possible breaking and entering, possible vandalism at the foundation." He nodded toward the policeman. "It's standard procedure for officers at the scene to sequester possible witnesses. The public portion of police investigations are open to the press."

"Hey, Steve, take a seat." Robbie Powell shot a quick warning look at Blythe. "The foundation always welcomes public scrutiny. From a quick survey, it appears the foundation has been subjected again to pointless vandalism. This probably won't be of much interest to you."

Blythe pressed her lips together. She said nothing further but her irritation was obvious.

The reporter's blue eyes checked out everyone around the table, lingering for a moment when they reached her.

Again she fought an urge to smile.

His gaze moved on. "Thanks, Robbie. You may be right." He strolled around the end of the table, dropped into the chair next to Nela. She noticed that he unobtrusively carried a laptop. When he was seated, he slid the laptop onto his knees, flipped up the lid. He did all of this without dropping his eyes to his lap. His fingers touched the keyboard as he made notes.

Without warning, he looked at her. Their gazes met.

Nela gazed at his familiar, unfamiliar face, broad forehead, snub nose, pugnacious chin. Once again, she fought a deep sense of recognition. She was the first to look away.

The foundation chef, a mountainous woman with blue-white hair and three chins that cascaded to an ample bosom, seemed unfazed by the request for an unexpected meal. Within twenty minutes, she had wheeled a cart into the conference room. Nela and Louise bustled to help and soon an attractive buffet was set on a side table. Louise looked pleased at the array of food: chilled shrimp with cocktail sauce, mixed green salad, crisply crusted ham and cheese quiches, steamed asparagus with a mustard and butter sauce, chocolate cake, coffee, iced tea.

The large police officer remained standing by the door,

declining an offer of food. With a balding head but youthful face, Sergeant Fisher might have been an old thirty or a young fifty.

The staff members returned to the seats they'd taken that morning. The meal was eaten quickly and in almost complete silence.

Francis Garth pushed back his plate and glanced at the grandfather clock. "Sergeant"—he turned to the end of the table—"will we be seen in a particular order? I need to leave for Stillwater by one o'clock. I have a meeting with a researcher on switchgrass production."

Sergeant Fisher's voice was as unrevealing as his face. "I will inform Detective Dugan."

Cole Hamilton's face once again furrowed in worry. He shot a sideways glance toward the policeman. "I'm sure all of us wish the police the very best, but why talk to us? What do we know that would be helpful? Someone broke in."

"Did someone break in?" Grace's tone was silky. "I suppose the police are checking all the ground-floor windows and doors. Of course, if any had been smashed, the alarm would sound." She flicked a glance toward the large square windows. "It would take a crowbar and maybe a sledgehammer to break in through these windows."

Nela's glance flicked to the swiftly moving fingers on the laptop.

Grace smoothed back a lock of strawberry blond hair. "It's the same in all the conference rooms and offices. Dad built this place like a fortress. The only windows that might be vulnerable are the French windows in the main rotunda. Funny thing, though. Nobody"—she looked from face to face—"noticed anything out of the ordinary when they came to work this morning. It's a little hard to believe Rosalind crunched through broken glass when she opened the French window blinds this morning and neglected to mention it."

Peter Owens poked his horn rims higher on his nose. "Your point?"

"If nobody broke in, how did the office trasher get inside?" Grace looked at each face in turn.

No one spoke.

Nela glanced around the room. Blythe looked grim, Hollis thoughtful. The reporter's freckled face was bland. His eyes never dropped beneath the rim of the table. The unobtrusive note-taking continued.

Grace's smile was sardonic. "My, what a silent class. It looks like teacher will have to explain. A key, my dears."

Beside Nela, those broad freckled hands moved silently over the electronic keypad.

Blythe's tone was cold. "It's better to let the authorities reach their own conclusions."

Hollis Blair rubbed knuckles on his bony chin. "We have to provide them with anything pertinent."

Blythe slowly turned toward Nela. There was a welter of conflicting expressions on her usually contained face: uncertainty, inquiry, and possibly suspicion.

Sergeant Fisher's curious gaze moved from Blythe to settle on Nela.

Nela's chest felt tight. She knew what was coming. These police officers hadn't connected Nela to Friday night's 911, but Blythe Webster had heard the sirens and hurried to see. Obviously Blythe was making a connection.

Nela lifted her head, spoke quickly. "Friday night someone broke into Miss Grant's apartment. The sounds of a search woke me up. I was staying there to take care of Miss Grant's cat." She heard the exclamations from around the table. Only Blythe was unaffected. Beside her, the reporter's face remained bland and interested and knowledgeable. He would have seen the police report about Friday night's break-in. Nela had herself looked at a lot of police reports.

It had never occurred to her that one day her own name would be included in one.

Hollis Blair's frown was intense. "Why wasn't I told about this?"

Blythe made a dismissive gesture. "It didn't occur to me to mention it, Hollis. Friday night the investigating officers believed someone saw the obituary and thought the apartment would be empty. Marian's desk was searched."

"Searched for what?" Grace's tone was flat.

Nela shrugged. "I suppose for valuables of some kind. But I wonder if there is a connection to the search of her office." She tried to block from her mind the heavy gold necklace in the black Coach bag.

"That makes sense." Blythe suddenly sounded cheered. "Perhaps the thief went from the apartment to the foundation. This must be attempted robbery."

"I hate to throw darts at your trial balloon"—Grace was sardonic—"but there's still a pesky little question: How did a thief get into Marian's apartment and how did a thief get inside the foundation and what the hell was he trying to steal? Or she."

"That's for the police to determine." Blythe was impervious to her sister's attack. "Nela probably forgot to lock the apartment door. One officer said old door locks are easy to jiggle open and maybe someone opened it with a credit card."

Grace folded her arms. "Not even an American Express Platinum could budge a foundation door."

Francis Garth looked thoughtful. "As Grace points out, gaining access to the foundation would be challenging for someone without a key. Does anyone have any ideas?"

Louise shifted uneasily in her chair. Her hand trembled and she hastily placed her fork on her plate. "I don't see how any of us can have any information that would help the police."

Francis added a packet of sugar to his iced tea. "It may be helpful to determine when the vandalism occurred. Marian's funeral was Thursday. Friday morning I went into her office. I was looking for a file on the Rumer Co-op. I found the file. At ten forty-five Friday morning, her office was fine. Who has been in her office since that time?" He looked inquiringly around the table.

Abby Andrews, violet eyes huge, looked terrified but spoke steadily. "Friday afternoon I returned some papers that I'd borrowed the week before. It was probably about two thirty. The office hadn't been disturbed."

Louise twined the red and gray scarf at her throat around one finger. "I was in her office a few minutes before five Friday. I checked to see if she'd finished the direct bank deposits before"—she swallowed—"before she died." Quick tears misted her eyes. "They were all done. Marian always took care of things on schedule."

Francis reached for the legal pad Nela had placed on the table that morning. The big head once again rose like a buffalo surveying the plain. "Anyone else?"

Silence.

He made quick notes. "How about this morning?"

Silence.

· Francis tapped his pen on the legal pad. "Her office was entered after five p.m. Friday and before approximately eleven twenty this morning when Nela"—he nodded toward her—"was sent to look for password information." His face corrugated in thought. "Marian died a week ago today. Why did the searches occur this past weekend?"

Blythe was impatient. "You'd have to ask the thief."

Nela wasn't sure it was her place to speak out, but maybe this mattered. "Chloe exchanged e-mails with Miss Grant's sister. Her sister asked Chloe to stay in Miss Grant's apartment to take care of Jugs. Chloe was there until she left town

Friday. I don't think anyone knew I was going to be there Friday night."

Cole Hamilton's round face was puzzled. "How would a thief know that your sister was there during the week or that she left on Friday?"

Grace clapped her long slender hands together. An emerald gleamed in the ornate setting of a ring on her right hand. "Cole"—her tone was a mixture of amusement and affection but her eyes moved around the room, steely and intent—"do you realize what you just said?"

He turned to Grace. "I fail to see anything odd. It seems to me that some thief reading the newspaper couldn't possibly know . . ." His words trailed away.

"Bull's-eye. But there's no bull about it." Grace's eyes were hard. "Only someone associated with the foundation would know that Chloe had been staying in Marian's apartment or that Chloe left Friday."

Nela quickly looked around the room.

Blythe's brows drew down in a sharp frown. Hollis Blair appeared startled. Eyes wide, Abby Andrews pressed fingers against parted lips. Robbie Powell's handsome face smoothed into blankness. Louise Spear shook her head, lips pressed together in negation. Peter Owens looked quizzical, his horn-rimmed glasses gently swinging from one hand. Cole sat with his mouth open, a picture of befuddlement. Francis Garth's heavy face closed into an unreadable mask.

Francis cleared his throat. "We're a long way from determining who might have known what and how either of these crimes occurred. I suggest we remain focused on timing."

"Anybody—with a key—could easily visit the foundation over the weekend. Nobody's here unless we have an event." Grace's tone was musing.

Louise looked uncomfortable. "I wish we'd gone inside Marian's office Saturday. Then we'd know if her office was entered Friday night."

Peter Owens raised an eyebrow. His glasses ceased to move. "You were here Saturday? With someone?"

Louise's thin face stiffened. "I don't have a computer at home. I was doing some genealogy research. It wasn't on foundation time. I'd already cleared it with Blythe."

Blythe waved a hand. "Of course you can use your computer on your free time. Who else was here?"

Louise nodded toward Nela. "Nela came to be sure she knew her way for Monday. I showed her around the building. And Robbie and Erik were here, too."

Robbie spoke quickly. "I can assure you that Erik and I had no occasion to enter Marian's office."

Nela saw a flurry of quick, covert glances. "I wanted to be sure I knew the way Monday." She was aware of a distancing by the staff members, as if each drew back a little, considering, thinking, wondering.

Francis's big chin poked forward. "Did you knock on the door? Or do you have Chloe's keys?"

"I have her keys." Nela lifted her chin, tried not to sound defensive. "I didn't use them. Louise came to the door."

Grace's chair creaked as she leaned back, apparently completely at ease. "Nela, you look like somebody in the water with circling sharks. I fail to see why you'd stage a break-in at Marian's apartment or trash her office. Unless Chloe asked you to do more than sub for her, I'd say you're the original innocent bystander."

Heavy braided gold necklace with diamonds . . .

The door opened. Detective Dugan strode inside and the spotlight turned. She was perhaps in her early forties. Short dark hair faintly streaked with gray framed a broad face. She wore a wine-colored cable-knit turtleneck, moderate-length black wool skirt, and black penny loafers. She might have been a Realtor or a secretary or a shop owner except for an underlying toughness evident in the dominance of her gaze and the set of a strong chin. She carried an aura of competence, suggesting she could handle anything from gang members to a sexist cop in the break room.

Nela's tense shoulders relaxed. She gave a little sigh of relief. She was no longer the center of attention. Then she felt an intent gaze. She looked at the reporter.

His bright blue eyes watched her, not the police officer.

— 7 —

Nela was the last person to be summoned from the conference room to a small adjoining office.

Detective Dugan gestured toward a straight chair in front of the borrowed desk. "Thank you for your patience, Miss Farley." She spoke in a cool voice, rather deep for a woman. Sergeant Fisher sat to one side. He held an electronic notepad.

Nela took her seat and smiled. Her smile fled when the officer's face remained unresponsive.

Dugan glanced at a second electronic pad, read in silence. When she looked up, her gaze was sharp. "When the first responders arrived Friday night, you unlocked the front door. Investigating officers found no sign of a forced entry." She tilted her head. "With Miss Webster's permission, an officer visited the apartment a short while ago."

Nela's hands clenched. Had they found the purse? She felt a pulse flutter in her throat.

"I have a report here." Dugan tapped the screen. "An

officer made several attempts to engage the lock and open the door with a credit card. He didn't succeed. However"—her tone was judicious—"an intruder equipped with a plastic strip or a lock pick would likely gain entry."

"Friday night an officer told me that when the housekeeper found Marian Grant's body, she hurried upstairs and entered the apartment with a card from a playing deck." Nela felt triumphant.

There might have been a flicker of admiration in Dugan's eyes. "It isn't commonly known, but a laminated playing card is more supple than a credit card and more likely to succeed. Most people don't carry an extra playing card with them. Are you suggesting the housekeeper was the intruder Friday night?"

Nela's response was quick. "I have no idea who broke in."

"No one 'broke' in." Dugan spoke with finality. "If there was an intruder, the means of access hasn't been determined." She tilted her head to one side, like a cat watching a sparrow. "How do you think the intruder gained entry?"

"I don't know any thieves. I don't know what they carry or how they get in. I locked that door Friday night." Nela looked into Dugan's suspicious face. "Someone came in. I think they used a key."

"A key." Oddly, there was a note of satisfaction in Dugan's voice. "You have a key, both to the apartment and to the foundation."

Nela sensed a threat.

"You arrived Friday afternoon. You called nine-one-one at one thirty-five a.m. claiming the apartment of the late Marian Grant had been entered. Officers found much of the living room in disarray, suggesting an intense search. There was no sign of forced entry. Moreover, you had to unlock the front door to admit the officers. It is rare"—the detective's tone was dry—"for a fleeing intruder who has presumably jiggled a lock with a credit card or some other tool to carefully close and lock a door. That takes time. Fleeing criminals find time in short supply. Today police were summoned to find evidence of a search at Miss Grant's office." Dugan shifted forward in her chair, her brown eyes cold. "Let's say someone plans to search Miss Grant's office. There may be information in that office that someone cannot afford to be found."

Nela listened with increasing alarm. She didn't know where Dugan was going, but the detective's gaze was hard and searching.

The detective's eyes never left Nela's face. "The searcher might be aware that the foundation could not easily be broken into. In fact, the searcher must have known that no alarm was triggered by the use of a key after hours. Miss Spear reassured you about that when you came on Saturday."

Nela had thought Louise Spear liked her. But maybe she'd innocently told the detective about their conversation on Saturday.

The detective continued, her tone brusque. "It appears the searcher used a key to enter the foundation. There are a limited number of persons who have keys to Haklo Foundation. What steps could be taken by a possessor of a key to suggest innocence?" The question was as smooth as a knife sliding into butter. "Any ideas, Miss Farley?" Dugan's broad face looked heavy, formidable.

"I don't know anything about Marian Grant or her work at the foundation." But she knew Marian's purse held a stolen necklace. The necklace had to be the reason for the search. Maybe if she told the detective . . . Nela pictured Dugan's response—suspicion, disbelief, accusation.

Dugan spoke in a quick cadence. "Your sister, Chloe Farley, arrived in Craddock last September."

Nela was puzzled. What did Chloe's arrival have to do with a search of Marian Grant's apartment and office?

"The week after your sister arrived, a foundation

employee's car was set on fire." Dugan leaned forward. "Gasoline was poured inside, ignited. The employee quit. The next week Chloe Farley was hired by the foundation."

Nela controlled a hot flash of anger. The interview with the detective had turned ugly. She had to think fast, try to reason with this woman. "Are you claiming that Chloe set fire to somebody's car on the chance that the woman would quit and Chloe would get her job? That's absurd. Chloe would never burn up someone's car. And how could she know the girl would quit or, if she did, that Chloe could get the job?"

The detective continued in the same clipped voice. "Your sister came to Craddock with Leland Buchholz. His father is a financial adviser who has worked with foundation investments. People get jobs because they know people. Jed Buchholz spoke to Miss Webster the week before"—she paused for emphasis—"the car fire. Miss Webster told him if they had any openings, she'd be happy to hire your sister. Let's review what has happened since Chloe Farley started to work at the foundation." Her eyes dropped to the notepad. She brushed a finger on the screen. "Tuesday, November fifteen, Indian baskets being photographed for publication were found hacked to pieces. Monday night, December five, activated sprinklers in Mr. Powell's office flooded his desk and damaged a sofa and chair. The flooring and rug had to be replaced. Friday, December sixteen, outdoor fountains were turned on, allowed to run for some period of time, then turned off, causing the pipes to freeze and break. Up to this point, everything appears to be vandalism for the sake of destruction. Then what happens? Something entirely different." A flicker of irritation creased her face. "The police should have been immediately notified when Miss Webster's necklace—valued at two hundred and fifty thousand dollars—was stolen from her desk drawer. She discovered the theft Thursday morning, January five. However, now that we have been informed, it seems clear what happened."

Nela's voice was equally clipped. "What does any of this have to do with Chloe?"

"She's the only new employee." Dugan flung out the words like a knife thrower hitting a target.

Nela didn't try now to keep the hard edge of anger from her voice. "That's no reason to suspect her. Moreover, she isn't the only new employee. The foundation has a new director." She wasn't sure when Dr. Blair came to work but she didn't think he'd been there much longer than Chloe.

The detective was unimpressed. "This is Dr. Blair's first post as a foundation director. Should he someday seek to move to a larger foundation, his résumé will have to include a description of these incidents and his inability to protect the foundation. Miss Andrews is also a new employee this fall. However, no one thinks"—her tone was bland—"that Miss Andrews would in any way jeopardize Dr. Blair's job. That leaves your sister."

"You're wrong. Besides, how could Chloe steal Miss Webster's necklace?"

"Miss Webster informed me today that it was common knowledge around the foundation that she kept the necklace in her desk drawer. The necklace was a gift from her father and a sentimental favorite. She made a point to wear it during the Monday-morning staff meetings." Dugan's face folded in disgust. "A quarter million dollars in an unlocked drawer. She might as well have hung up a sign with an arrow: Get rich here."

Nela couldn't imagine carelessly leaving a necklace worth—to her—a fortune in an unlocked desk. "She kept the necklace in her desk? That's crazy."

"Yeah. You got that right. But here's the point. That necklace rested safely in that drawer until your sister came to work here."

"Detective"—Nela's voice was icy—"you have no right to accuse Chloe. Where's your proof?"

"I don't have proof." Dugan's voice was dour. "I feel it in my gut. Your sister comes to town. She needs a job. Miss Webster says she can have the first opening. The next week, a fire scares off Louise Spear's assistant. There's a job available and your sister gets it. Nothing more happens until she's been here long enough to find out about a necklace worth big bucks. Now, if the necklace disappeared right after she came, there might be some suspicion. So she muddies up the water with vandalism. When the necklace is stolen, everybody chalks it up to just another crazy thing by somebody who has it in for the foundation. I don't buy that scenario. It stinks. Something's out of kilter here. All the vandalism accomplished was fouling up Dr. Blair's record and upsetting Miss Webster. The necklace is different. That's money. Lots of money. I checked out your sister. She's never had a regular job—"

Nela looked at Dugan. She would read the police office as steady, contained, purposeful. She had probably never had a flaky moment in her life. Would she understand that Chloe never lived for regular? Chloe frosted cupcakes, helped raise rabbits, parked cars at charity functions (*Nela, I got to drive a Jag today!*), was a magician's assistant, tracked island foxes on Catalina Island as part of an effort to protect the endangered species, worked as a kitchen hand in a gourmet restaurant.

"—and she doesn't have any money. We're checking everything out. I saw the feature in the *Clarion* about her boyfriend winning a free trip for two to Tahiti. Maybe that's phony. We'll find out. Maybe she's got a lot of money now."

"Chloe has no money. Neither do I. Does that make us thieves?" Nela's voice was tight with fury.

Dugan's jaw set in a stubborn line. "She comes to town. All of this follows."

"She wasn't here Friday night. She wasn't here this weekend."

Dugan's hard stare was accusing. "You're here."

It was like coming around an outcrop on a mountain trail to find a sheer drop.

Dugan's stare didn't waver. "I understand you talked to her Friday night."

In high school, Nela had once gone to Tijuana with a bunch of kids. She'd not realized they were going to a bull-fight. She'd hated watching the bull pricked by tiny barbs. She'd bolted from the stands, waited on a hot dusty street until the others joined her. Now she felt one sharp jab after another and, like the bull, there was no escape for her from the arena. The detective must have quizzed each of the staff members about Chloe and Nela. Louise had been kind and welcoming but it was she who must have told Dugan that Nela had a key and knew there was no burglar alarm. Even though the director of publications had seemed genuinely interested in Chloe, Peter Owens must have revealed that Chloe called Nela Friday evening. Dugan was taking inno-cent pieces of information and building a case against her and against Chloe.

"You know how I see it, Miss Farley? The necklace was stolen before Miss Grant's accident. What if Miss Grant knew Chloe took the necklace? What if she had some kind of proof? What if she told Chloe she was keeping that infor-mation in a safe place away from the foundation? But Miss Grant's unexpected death made things tricky."

. . . board rolled on the second step . . .

The detective's accusatory words jabbed at Nela as her thoughts raced. Nela heard them, understood them, but she grappled with a far more deadly understanding. Marian Grant either stole the necklace herself or she knew who took the necklace. It had to be the latter. That's why Marian Grant died. She must have told the thief that she had the necklace, that she'd put it in a safe place. She had not summoned the police. Perhaps she wanted to avoid more disturbing headlines

about the foundation. Perhaps she wanted to use the possession of the necklace to block future attacks against the foundation. Perhaps she saw the necklace as a means of making
the thief accede to her demands, whatever they might be.
Perhaps she set a deadline for the thief to quit or confess.
What if the deadline was Monday morning?

  . . . board rolled on the second step . . .

Dugan threw words like rocks. "Maybe Chloe thought
the information was in the apartment and that's why she
volunteered to take care of the cat. Maybe she looked and
looked with no success. Maybe she worried all the way to
Tahiti and called you and said you had to look for her. Once
again we get the pattern. You dial nine-one-one and claim
a break-in and that sets it up for the office search to look
like someone else must have done it."

Nela wanted to shout that Dugan had everything wrong.
She was looking for a vandal and a thief. She should be
looking for a murderer.

Marian Grant had been murdered.

Nela opened her lips, closed them. What was she going
to tell this hard-faced woman? That she'd looked into a cat's
eyes and seen his thoughts? *. . . board rolled on the second
step . . .* She could not claim to have special information.
She could imagine Dugan's response to a claim that a cat
had seen a skateboard. Yet now she felt certain that she
knew the truth of that early-morning fall.

Nela wasn't ready to deal with the reality that she knew
what was in a cat's mind, if reality it was. Not now. Maybe
never. However the vivid thought had come to her—a psychic intimation, a reporter's intuition, a funny split instant
of a memory of a teenage Bill and his skateboard tangling
with her climb up steep steps to a dead woman's apartment—
she couldn't share that knowledge.

Yet she had to face the truth that a skateboard on the steps,
removed after Marian's fall, inexorably meant that Marian

Grant's death was no accident. But if Nela suggested murder, Dugan would likely add murder to the list of Chloe's supposed crimes.

Dugan was quick to attack. "You have something to say?"

"Yes, I do." Nela spoke with determination and confidence. "Chloe is innocent. I am innocent. I don't know what's behind the things that have happened at the foundation. Chloe never even mentioned the vandalism except for the girl's car. She seemed surprised that she quit."

Dugan raised a skeptical brow. "Your sister never mentioned the vandalism to you?"

Nela wondered how to explain a free spirit to the fact-grounded detective. "She talked about Leland and what they were doing. Chloe never thinks about bad things. She's always upbeat. You're right that something bad is going on at the foundation, but it doesn't have anything to do with Chloe or me. I agree"—her tone was grave—"there's something very wrong here. I think the theft of the necklace was part of the other things, not because it was worth a lot of money." And Marian Grant died because she knew the identity of the thief. But that she couldn't say, not without admitting she could, at this very minute, lead police to the necklace, which would likely result in her prompt arrest.

Dugan looked sardonic. "Nice try. Turning on a sprinkler system isn't in the same league as heisting jewelry worth a couple of hundred thou. Besides, if the necklace wasn't stolen for money, why take it? I've been a cop for a long time and, like a good coon dog, I know the real scent when I smell it."

Nela shook her head. "It isn't just the necklace. There was too much destruction in Miss Grant's office."

Dugan looked puzzled.

"There was fury. It wasn't just a search."

Dugan's smile was bleak. "Camouflage. Just like the baskets and the sprinkler and the fountains."

— 8 —

Steve Flynn's strong stubby fingers flew over the keypad.
He was nudging the deadline, but he still had ten minutes. He'd fallen back into the routine as if he'd never been
away, the early pages locked down around two, late-breaking
news up to four. His six years on the *LA Times* until he was
let go in one of the wholesale newsroom firings seemed like
a mirage. Maybe they had been. Most of that life had been
a mirage. Especially Gail. He felt the familiar twist, half
anger, half disbelief. So much for 'til death us do part. Maybe
that phrase ought to be dropped from modern weddings.
Maybe the vows should read, *I'll stay until something better
comes along.* Or, *been good to know you, but my way isn't
your way.* When the call came about his dad's stroke, he had
told her he needed to go back to Craddock to run the *Clarion.*
Somebody had to do it unless they sold the newspaper that
had been founded by his great-grandfather. His brother Sean
was a surgeon in Dallas. Sean had never been drawn to the
business while Steve had grown up nosing around the

newsroom. He tried to explain to Gail about the paper and family and keeping a flame alight in the little town they loved. Gail stood there within his reach, close enough to touch, but she receded like the tide going out. Oh, she'd been kind. Or thought she had, her words smooth . . . *felt us growing apart for a while now . . . have such a great future here . . . got a callback today . . . The producer wants to see more of me . . . wish you the best of luck . . .*

He'd been back a little over a year and the divorce had been final for six months.

He returned to the screen, his fingers thumping a little too hard on the keyboard. He finished the story, glanced at the time. Four more minutes. He scrolled up.

A gold and diamond necklace valued at approximately $250,000 was stolen from the desk of Haklo Foundation Trustee Blythe Webster sometime between Jan. 4 and 5, according to Craddock Police Detective K. T. Dugan.

Detective Dugan said the necklace was an original work of art created by Tiffany & Co. for Miss Webster's father, Harris Webster, who established the foundation.

The theft was revealed Monday when police were called to the foundation to investigate a possible break-in. Detective Dugan said the foundation had been entered, apparently over the weekend, and the office of late employee Marian Grant vandalized.

Detective Dugan said Miss Webster had not previously reported the theft of the necklace because she wished to avoid further negative publicity for the foundation, which has been attacked by vandals several times, beginning in September. Incidents include a car set afire in the foundation employees' parking lot; destruction of valuable Indian baskets; activated fire sprinklers in an office resulting in property damage; and water turned on, then off in an outdoor fountain, causing frozen pipes. The car fire occurred Sept. 19 during office hours. Other incidents occurred after hours.

According to the police report, the office vandalized this weekend had been occupied by Grant, who was chief operating officer at the time of her death, Jan. 9. Miss Grant, a jogger, was found dead at the foot of her apartment stairs, apparently the victim of a fall. Police said the fall may have been caused by new running shoes. Police said Miss Grant customarily jogged early every morning.

Police received a 911 call at 11:40 a.m. Monday from Rosalind McNeill, Haklo Foundation receptionist. In the call, Mrs. McNeill reported that an office was trashed, papers thrown everywhere, file cabinets emptied, the computer monitor cracked, and furniture overturned.

According to police, Mrs. McNeill said the office had not been emptied of Miss Grant's belongings and there was no way to determine if anything was missing.

Detective Dugan declined to suggest a motive for the invasion of the office.

The detective also declined to speculate on whether the damage to Miss Grant's office was connected to a reported break-in early Saturday morning at the dead woman's apartment at 1 Willow Lane. A 911 call was received at 1:35 a.m. According to the police report, the call was placed by Cornelia Farley, a temporary employee of the foundation who was staying at the apartment to care for the late resident's cat. Miss Farley told police she awoke to hear sounds of a search in the apartment living room. She called 911. When police arrived, no trace of an intruder was found, but Detective Dugan said a desk had been searched and the living room was in disarray. Detective Dugan said it was unknown if anything had been removed from the apartment.

The Haklo Foundation issued a statement: "Operations at the Haklo Foundation remain unaffected by the series of unexplained incidents, which apparently are the work of vandals. Blythe Webster, foundation trustee, announced today a reward of $100,000 for information leading to the apprehension and conviction of the vandals. Miss Webster will personally fund the reward. No foundation monies will be used. Miss Webster emphasized that she and all the employees will not be deterred from the execution of their duties by this apparent vendetta against the foundation."

Detective Dugan said the investigation is continuing.

W hen he came home to the *Clarion*, Steve had insisted he was a reporter. There were five of them in the newsroom. He glanced around the room, gray metal desks, serviceable swivel chairs, maps of the county on one wall, a montage of early-day black-and-white photographs of Craddock on another.

At the far desk, Ace Busey looked older than Methuselah, with a lined face and drooping iron gray mustache. Ace still smoked, but he covered city and county politics like a burr on a horse's back, darting out of meetings long enough to catch a drag when he was certain nothing was going to pop. He'd never been wrong yet.

Freddi Frank nibbled on a cinnamon bun as she made notes. Freddi ran the Life section: houses, gardens, recipes, and women's groups, any spare inches allotted to wire coverage of the glitterati currently atop the celebrity leaderboard. Freddi was unabashedly plump and amiable, and her Aunt Bill's candy was the centerpiece of the staff Christmas party.

The sports desk was unoccupied. Joe Guyer could be anywhere: at a wrestling match, covering a high school basketball game, adding clips to his old-fashioned notebook. Joe worked on a laptop but he continued to distrust the electronic world. Balding, weedy, and always in a slouch, he had an encyclopedic memory of sports trivia, including facts large and small about the Sooners football team. He could at any time drop interesting tidbits: the first OU football game in September 1895 was played on a field of low prairie grass near what is now Holmberg Hall; the Sooners beat the Aggies seventy-five to zero on November 6, 1904 in their first contest; 1940 quarterback Jack Jacobs was known as Indian in a tribute to his Creek heritage; in 1952 halfback Billy Vessels was the first OU player to win the Heisman Trophy.

Jade Marlow rounded out the lot. Steve didn't glance toward her desk. He was aware of her. Very aware. The new features reporter, Jade was a recent J-school grad, good, quick, smart, glossily lovely, a tall slender blonde, curvy in all the right places, sure she was going big places. She'd been inviting, but he had simply given her a cool blue look and walked away and now she avoided him. That was good. He looked at her and he saw Gail—beautiful, confident, blond, smart, and a producer wanted to see more of her. How much more? Did she get the role? Or was she playing a different kind of role? He didn't give a damn. Not anymore. He wrenched his mind back to the newsroom.

Around the corner from the sports desk was the lair of the *Clarion* photographer, Alex Hill. Pudgy and always disheveled, Alex handled a Nikon D3S as delicately as a surgeon with a scalpel.

Steve felt pumped. It wasn't the *LA Times* newsroom, but, in its own way, it was better. That's why he didn't mind spending part of every day in the publisher's office. Maybe Dad would come back. Right now he still had only a trace of movement on his right side and his speech was jerky and sometimes unintelligible. It was up to Steve to make sure the *Clarion* kept on keeping on. Ads were the paper's life-blood. He went to all the service clubs meetings. He renewed old friendships, made new ones. He rode herd on ads and circulation and the aged heating system and the printing press that might need to be replaced. A memo from the business office recommended switching paper purchase to a mill in India. He'd worry about that tomorrow. Right now he was pleased with his afternoon. A good story, would probably run above the fold.

Steve clicked send and looked across the room at a trim, white-haired woman. As the file arrived, she half turned from her computer screen to give him a thumbs-up. Mim Barlow, the city editor, had worked at the *Clarion* since Steve was a little boy. She knew everyone in town, insisted on accuracy, and sensed news like a hawk spotting a rabbit. She was blunt, brusque, stone-faced, and scared the bejesus out of kid reporters. She was tough, but her toughness masked a crusader's heart. She'd helped break a story about abuse at a local nursing home that resulted in two criminal convictions and the closure of the home. The night Mim received the Oklahoma Press Association's Beachy Musselman Award for superior journalism, she'd walked back to the table carrying the plaque and taken her seat to thunderous applause. She'd bent closer to him. "If I'd sent the reporter out a month sooner—I'd heard some stuff at the beauty shop—maybe that frail little woman wouldn't have died. Good, Steve, but not good enough. I was busy with that series on the county commissioners and that road by the Hassenfelt farm. I let little get in the way of big."

Maybe it was being around Mim that made him look at people's faces and sometimes see more than anyone realized. He'd looked at a lot of faces today. One stood out, a face he wouldn't forget. He'd seen her last night at Hamburger Heaven. He'd watched her leave with regret, wishing that someday, somehow he would see her again, damning himself as a fool to be enchanted simply because a beautiful, remote woman sat at a nearby table and her loneliness spoke to his.

Today he had seen her again.

He reached for his laptop, checked his notes. Cornelia Farley, called Nela. Pronounced *Nee-la*. Pretty name. Glossy black hair that looked as if it would be soft to the touch, curl around his fingers. He'd known last night that he wouldn't forget her face and bewitching eyes that held depths of feeling.

She'd been the last to be interviewed by Dugan. As staff members exited the police interview, Steve queried them. All had "no comment" except Robbie Powell, who promised to provide an official statement. Powell refused to confirm or deny that Blythe Webster had declared a news blackout. Steve remained in the hall asking questions, though now he knew there would be no answers.

When Nela came out of the room, she'd walked fast, never noticed him standing nearby. Her cheeks were flushed, her eyes bright. She moved like a woman in a hurry.

Last night she'd been ice. This afternoon she was fire.

He wanted to know why.

She'd moved past him. He would have followed but he had a job to do. Brisk steps sounded and he'd turned to Dugan.

"Hey, Katie." He'd known Katie Dugan since he was a high school kid nosing after the city hall reporter and she was a new patrol officer. "Let's run through the various incidents here at the foundation."

The blockbuster was the revelation of the theft of Blythe Webster's two-hundred-fifty-thousand-dollar necklace. Katie had been grim about the fact that no report had been made at the time. She'd related the disparate incidents, including a somewhat vague reference to misuse of foundation stationery. She'd balked at explaining how the stationery had been used, but she'd provided a detailed description of the necklace: diamonds set in eighteen-karat gold acanthus leaves connected by gold links. He'd come back to the office knowing he had a front-page story.

Now he'd finished his story but he couldn't forget Nela Farley. He had seen her in profile as he left Haklo, sitting at her desk, working on a computer, but her face spoke of thoughts far afield. There was a determined set to her jaw. Now he looked across the room at the city desk, gave an abrupt nod, and came to his feet. As he passed Mim's desk, he jerked a thumb in the general direction of Main Street. "Think I'll drop by the cop shop."

Mim's sharp gray eyes brightened. "You got a hunch?"

"Maybe." Maybe he felt the tug of a story behind a story. Nela Farley's interview with Katie Dugan had transformed her. As a newcomer to town, her involvement at Haklo should have been peripheral. But he knew he cared about more than the story. He wanted to know Nela Farley. Maybe he was not going to let the little get in the way of the big.

At four thirty, Louise stepped through the connecting door. Her frizzy hair needed a comb. She'd not bothered to refresh her lipstick. Her eyes were dark with worry.

Nela watched her carefully. Had the detective told Louise that Nela and Chloe were her number-one suspects? Since the brutal interview with Dugan, Nela had made progress on the stack of grant applications while she considered how to combat the accusations against her and Chloe. It was essential that she continue to work at the foundation. It came down to a very clear imperative. She had to find out who was behind the vandalism, including the theft and likely the murder of Marian Grant, to save herself and Chloe. But first she had to get rid of the necklace.

Since Dugan hadn't returned with a warrant for her arrest, Nela felt sure that the purse still remained hidden behind the stacked cans of cat food. Would it occur to the detective that the search of the apartment and the office might be a search for the necklace? Right now, Dugan was convinced of Chloe's guilt and believed the necklace had already been sold and the proceeds pocketed. That's why Dugan questioned the expensive trip to Tahiti. An investigation would prove that there had been a contest and that Leland won. No doubt inquiries were being made into Chloe and Nela's finances as well. If poor equaled honest, she and Chloe had no worries. Unfortunately, the fact that Chloe's bank account and Nela's had lean balances didn't prove their innocence.

Louise gave a huge sigh. "What a dreadful day. That horrible letter . . . At least it wasn't sent to anyone other than members of the grants committee. That's a huge relief. But I don't know what to think about Marian's office. There doesn't seem to be any point other than making a mess. Of course there wasn't any point to any of the other vandalism. And you must have been very upset when someone broke into the apartment." Her glance at Nela was apologetic. "I'm afraid I've been so busy thinking about the foundation, I didn't even stop to think how you must be feeling." Louise came around the desk, gently patted Nela's shoulder. "A young girl like you isn't used to these sorts of incidents." Louise was earnest. "I don't want you to think things like this happen much in Craddock. I've been at the foundation for twenty-three years and we never had any vandalism before September. Poor Hollis. The car was set on fire only a month after he came. What a way to begin your first big job. He'd only been an assistant director at a foundation up in Kansas for two years, and it was quite a plum for him to become head of the Haklo Foundation. Of course, it was real hard on Erik, our former director. But anyone who works for a family foundation has to remember that the family runs everything. Blythe's the sole trustee and she has complete power over the staff."

"Why did she want a new director?" Nela knew the question might be awkward, but she was going to ask a lot of awkward questions.

"Oh." It was as if a curtain dropped over Louise's face. "She met Hollis at a big philanthropy meeting in St. Louis. We attend every year. Hollis made a good impression. Fresh blood. That kind of thing." She was suddenly brisk. "Here I am chattering away. You go home early and get some rest."

As Nela left, Louise was sitting at her desk, her face once again drawn with worry. Nela forced herself to walk to Leland's VW even though she felt like running. The sooner she reached the apartment, the sooner she could decide what to do about the damnable necklace.

S teve Flynn ignored his shabby leather jacket hanging on the newsroom coat tree. He rarely bothered with a coat. Oklahomans weren't much for coats even on bitter winter days. Hey, maybe it was in the twenties today. By the end of the week, it would be forty and that would seem balmy. He always moved too fast to feel the cold, thoughts churning, writing leads in his head, thinking of sources to tap, wondering what lay behind facades.

He took the stairs down two at a time to a small lobby with a reception counter. A gust of wind caught his breath as he stepped onto Main Street. Craddock's downtown was typical small-town Oklahoma. Main Street ran east and west. Traffic was picking up as five o'clock neared. Most buildings were two stories, with shops on the street and offices above. Craddock had shared in the prosperity fueling the southwest with the boom in natural gas production, especially locally from the Woodford Shale. New facades had replaced boarded-up windows. Some of the businesses had been there since he was a kid: Carson's Drugs at the corner of Main and Maple, Walker's Jewelry, Indian Nation Bank,

Hamburger Heaven, and Beeson's Best Bargains. There were plenty of new businesses: Jill's Cupcakes, Happy Days Quilting Shop, Carole's Fashions, and Mexicali Rose Restaurant.

It was two blocks to city hall. He walked fast, hoping he'd catch Katie before she went off duty. Again he didn't use an elevator. The stairwells were dingy and had a musty smell. He came out in a back hallway and went through an unmarked frosted door to the detectives' room.

Mokie Morrison looked up from his desk. "Jesus, man, it's twenty-two degrees out there. That red thatch keep you warm?" Mokie wore a sweater thick enough for Nome.

Steve grinned at Mokie, who had three carefully arranged long black strands draped over an ever-expanding round bald spot. "Eat your heart out, baldie." He jerked his head. "Dugan still here?"

"She's got a hot date with her ex. Better hustle to catch her."

At Katie's office door, he hesitated before he knocked. Katie and Mark Dugan's on-off relationship evoked plenty of good-natured advice from her fellow officers. Katie blew off comments from soulful to ribald with a shrug. Steve was pretty sure Katie would never get over her ex. Mark was handsome, charming, lazy, always a day late and a dollar short. Like Mokie had told her one night as he and Steve and Katie shared beers, "Katie, he's not worth your time." Good advice but cold comfort in a lonely bed on a winter night. Just like he told himself that he was better off without Gail and then he'd remember her standing naked in their dusky bedroom, blond hair falling loose around her face, ivory white skin, perfect breasts, long slender legs.

He knocked.

Katie looked up as he stepped inside. "Yo, Steve." She glanced at a plain watch face on a small black leather band.

"Just a few questions." He turned a straight chair in front

of her desk, straddled the seat. "I was out in the hall at Haklo when you talked to the staff. I timed the interviews."

She raised a strong black brow. "That's anal. Even for you."

"Sometimes I pick up a vibe in funny ways. That's what happened today." His gaze was steady. "Some interviews lasted a few minutes, several ran about ten. You spent thirty-one minutes talking to Miss Farley."

Not a muscle moved in Katie's stolid face.

"Come on, Katie." His tone was easy. "I picked up some stuff at Haklo. Nela Farley's been in town since Friday afternoon. She's subbing for her sister, Chloe, Louise Spear's assistant. Why the inquisition?"

Katie massaged her chin with folded knuckles, an unconscious mannerism when she was thinking hard.

Steve kept his face bland.

Katie chose her words as carefully as a PGA player studying the slope of a green. "I thought it was proper to discuss her nine-one-one call from Miss Grant's apartment Friday night."

Not, Steve thought quickly, to talk about a break-in or even a *purported* break-in, but the placement of a 911 call. He kept his voice casual. "Yeah, the report said she awoke to find an intruder in the living room."

"She said"—slight emphasis—"she heard someone in the living room. She appeared to be upset." Kati's tone was even. "She unlocked the front door when the investigating officers arrived. That's the only entrance to the apartment. No windows were broken. Officers found no sign of a forced entry."

He frowned. "How did an intruder get inside?"

Katie was firm. "Investigating officers found no evidence of an illegal entry at Miss Grant's apartment."

He raised an eyebrow. "Are you saying Miss Farley lied?"

"I am saying no evidence was found to suggest a forced entry." She glanced again at her watch. "If that's all—"

He was running out of time. Work was fine but other people's problems never beat out sex, and Katie was impatient to leave. He spoke quickly. "The apartment appeared to have been searched. Miss Grant's office was searched. Do you believe both incidents are part of the pattern of vandalism, including the missing necklace?"

"Yes." Clipped. Definite. One word. *Nada mas.*

"How can Miss Farley be involved since she arrived in Craddock Friday?"

"The investigation is following several leads." Katie came to a full stop, pushed back her chair.

Steve was exasperated. "That's no answer. You talked to Miss Farley for thirty-one minutes. Is she a person of interest?"

Katie came to her feet. "At this point in the investigation, there is not a single suspect. No premature announcement will be made." She pulled out a lower drawer, retrieved a black shoulder bag, stood.

He rose and turned the chair to once again face the gray metal desk.

Katie was already out the door.

In the hall, he watched her stride toward the exit. Katie had been careful, circumspect, cautious, but when he connected the dots, he understood why ice had turned to fire. Nela Flynn was in big trouble.

J ugs followed Nela into the kitchen, chirped impatiently as she closed the blinds. She put the McDonald's sack on the counter. He jumped up and sniffed. "Not good for you, buddy. I'll get yours in a minute."

With the blinds closed, no one could see her. The front door was blocked by the safety wedge. She dropped to one knee by Jugs's cabinet, pushed aside the stacked cans of cat food, felt weak with relief. The black leather bag was there.

She started to reach, quickly drew back her hand. If ordinary criminals were careful about prints, she wasn't going to be mutt enough to leave hers on Marian Grant's purse.

Once again attired in the orange rubber gloves, she edged out the purse, pulled the zipper, held the sides wide, moved the red leather gloves, saw the glitter of gold and diamonds. So far, so good. She took comfort that the police hadn't entered the apartment, found the stolen jewelry. But safety was illusory. She had to get rid of the necklace. ASAP.

Jugs stood on his back paws, patted at the shelf. "I know, buddy. It's suppertime and you think I'm nuts." She returned the purse to the cabinet, knowing any casual search would find it. But for now, that was the best she could do. She dished up Jugs's food, placed the bowls on the newspaper, provided fresh water.

Jugs crouched and ate, fast.

She found a paper plate for herself, opened and poured a Coke. By the time she settled at the kitchen table, Jugs was finished.

The lean cat padded to the table, jumped, once again settled politely just far enough to indicate he wasn't encroaching upon her meal. He gazed at her with luminous green eyes. "*. . . miss Her . . .*"

Nela stared into those beautiful eyes. For now, she would accept that whenever she looked at Jugs, she moved into his mind. She took some comfort from that rapport, whether real or imagined. "I'm sorry." And she was. Sorry for Jugs, grieving for lost love. Sorry for everyone lost and lonely and hurt in an uncaring world. Sorry for what might have been with Bill. Sorry for herself and Chloe, enmeshed in a mess not of their making. Sorry and, more than that, determined to do what she had to do to keep them both safe. It was, she realized, the first time since Bill died that she'd felt fully alive.

She looked into Jugs's gleaming eyes.

". . . *You're mad . . .*"

She pulled her gaze away from his, unwrapped a double cheeseburger, began to eat. She felt a flicker of surprise. Yeah. Jugs had it right. She was mad as hell. So many paths were blocked. It was too late to report finding the necklace. She could claim it occurred to her to wonder if anything had been taken from the bag so she opened it . . . She shook her head. Nice try, but it wouldn't fly. The detective would never believe she'd found the necklace in the purse. Detective Dugan would see that claim as a lie and be convinced Chloe had stolen the necklace and left it in the apartment for Nela to keep safe. The necklace had to go.

Throw it away?

It would be her luck to toss the jewelry in a trash bin and be seen.

How about taking a drive, tossing the necklace into the woods? Two hundred and fifty thousand dollars flung into underbrush? Probably a birdwatcher would ring the police before she drove a hundred yards. If she parked and walked into the woods, maybe dug a hole, she'd leave footprints.

What did you do with something that didn't belong to you?

She ate, dipping the fries in pepper-dotted ketchup, drank the Coke, and made plans.

At Hamburger Heaven, Steve stirred onions and grated cheese into chili and beans. He spread margarine on a square of jalapeño-studded cornbread. He once again sat in his usual booth. Beyond the tables, every space was taken at the counter. A roar of conversation competed with Reba McEntire's newest country music hit. Steve shut out the lyrics about love gone wrong, picked through the nuances of his exchanges with Katie.

When he'd asked if Nela Farley was a person of interest,

Katie could have made several replies. She was never shy about barking, "No comment." However, he could then have written a story saying that Detective K. T. Dugan declined to reveal whether Nela Farley was a person of interest. Any reader might reasonably assume, as he did, that Dugan's reply definitely indicated Farley was indeed a person of interest.

That wasn't the only red flag. Instead of discussing a break-in at Marian Grant's apartment, Katie talked about the 911 call and the fact that there was no proof anyone had broken in. If no one broke in, either Nela Farley had searched the room, then placed a fake 911 call—she had permitted someone to enter and leave, then ditto—or someone with a key to Marian Grant's apartment was the intruder.

If there wasn't an intruder . . .

Steve knew he wanted to believe Nela's story. But Katie was a good cop and she'd lined up Nela Farley in her sights. Why did he want to defend the girl with the intelligent, sensitive face? He knew better than most that beauty didn't count for much and a woman could look at you with love in her eyes one minute and it's-time-for-you-to-go the next. Women lied.

Why would a girl who'd never been to Craddock want to plow through the desk in a dead woman's apartment?

He always thought quickly and the answer was waiting in his mind. Nela Farley had a connection to Craddock. Her sister, Chloe, worked at Haklo. In fact, Nela was in town to sub for her sister while Chloe and her boyfriend were on a two-week freebie to Tahiti. Freddi had written a fun feature for the Life section about Leland Buchholz's contest win and his and Chloe's plans for the Tahiti holiday. Alex took some great shots, capturing the couple's happy-go-lucky attitude.

Nela could be acting on behalf of her sister. However, her sister had been in the apartment for several days and surely had time for a thorough search. Even if Chloe asked Nela to search again, Nela had no need to create an intruder. She was staying in the place as a caretaker for a cat. She could search anything at any time she wished and no one would be the wiser.

Steve ate his chili without noticing the taste.

So he didn't get Katie's emphasis on the 911 call . . .

And then he did.

If it was absolutely essential to remove something from Marian Grant's office, a paper, a file, maybe a link to the theft of a two-hundred-fifty-thousand-dollar necklace, a previous search of the Grant apartment by an unknown intruder pointed away from Nela Farley.

But not if the police thought the 911 call was phony.

Steve pushed back the bowl. He lifted his Dr Pepper and drank.

Katie believed the apartment break-in was fake. She linked both searches to the vandalism and the theft of the necklace.

Steve gave a soundless whistle. Now he understood why Katie refused to name a person of interest. Clearly, following Katie's reasoning, the vandalism and theft had been committed by Chloe Farley and now Nela Farley was desperately trying to protect her sister.

He finished the Dr Pepper, but without his usual pleasure in the tingly burn of the pop. Katie Dugan always spoke carefully. Her final comment had been bland until he parsed the words: *At this point in the investigation, there is not a single suspect. No premature announcement will be made.*

He knew every word was true. There was no single suspect. There were two suspects, Chloe Farley and Nela Farley. There would be no premature announcement because Chloe Farley was in Tahiti, a nice place to hang out to avoid prosecution in the U.S.

Steve recalled the feature story written by Freddi. Leland

was part of a prominent Craddock family. Though Freddi wrote with humor and enthusiasm, Leland and his girlfriend came across as flakes. Nice flakes, but flakes. Had a quarter-million-dollar necklace been too big a temptation?

Steve realized he'd crushed the empty Dr Pepper can. *Ease up, man. You don't know her.* But she looked like a woman of courage touched by sadness. Her image haunted his mind.

She could be innocent . . .

Or guilty.

— 9 —

Nela, wearing the orange rubber dishwashing gloves, carefully positioned Marian Grant's purse on the bookcase by the door. A casual observer would never suspect the purse had been moved since Marian placed it there. Nela opened the purse and fished out the necklace. The diamonds glistened in the living room light. Nela dropped the necklace into a clear quart-size plastic bag and placed the bag also on the bookcase. The plastic bag, carefully eased by gloved fingers from the middle of its box, was fingerprint free. She felt a spurt of satisfaction as she returned the gloves to the kitchen. She was turning into an old pro at avoiding fingerprints. That was easy. Now came the challenge. She would be safe and so would Chloe if she could follow—sort of—in the footsteps of Raffles, one of Gram's favorite fictional characters. Nela doubted if Detective Dugan had ever heard of Raffles. Gram had loved the short stories as well as the movies, especially the 1939 film with David Niven as the gentleman thief. Tonight, Nela pinned her hopes on doing a reverse Raffles.

She ran through her plan in her mind. She'd leave about ten. She glanced at her watch. Almost two hours to go. She was impatient. There was so much she needed to do. She'd already tried to use Marian's home computer but there was no handy password in the desk drawer. Nela didn't have a laptop. If she did, she could seek information about the staff at Haklo. Still, she could use this time profitably.

She settled on the sofa with a notebook. Jugs settled beside her. She turned to a fresh page. She always traveled with a notebook. She might not be able to dig for facts and figures, but she could sum up her impressions of the people she'd met. She didn't doubt that the vandal/thief and possible murderer was among that group. Only someone with intimate knowledge of Chloe's schedule would have been aware of her departure Friday for Tahiti, leaving Marian Grant's apartment unoccupied for the first time since her death.

Nela wrote fast.

Blythe Webster—Imperious. Possibly spoiled. Accustomed to having her way. A woman with her emotions under tight control. Attractive in a contained, upper-class way, large intelligent eyes, a rather prim mouth. Seems on good terms with everyone at Haklo.

Louise Spear—Eager to please, thoughtful, a perfect assistant. Her eyes held uncertainty and worry, a woman who wanted someone else to lead. Distress about vandalism appears genuine. No discernible animus toward anyone.

Robbie Powell—Obviously resents the new director. Emotional. Angry enough at his partner's firing to vandalize Haklo?

Erik Judd—His flamboyant appearance said it all. He lived in bright colors. No pastels for him. How much did losing his post at Haklo matter? Probably quite a lot. He had swept out the door, cloak flaring, but there was a sense of a faded matinee idol. Did parking in the visitors' lot reveal festering anger? Vandalism on a grand scale might amuse him.

Cole Hamilton—She'd had only a glimpse of him in his office but he hadn't looked as though he was engaged in any work. His round face was not so much genial as lost and bewildered. He had an aura of defeat. What was his function at Haklo?

Francis Garth—Big, powerful, possibly overbearing. Not a man to cross. The thought was quick, instinctive. Though he'd remained calm about the agenda item, clearly the Tallgrass Prairie mattered more to him than a matter of business. Did he have other disagreements with the trustee and director?

Hollis Blair—Boatloads of aw-shucks, Jimmy Stewart charm but he had run into a situation where charm didn't matter. Was someone jealous of his apparent affair with Abby Andrews? Or was his assumption of the directorship offensive to more than just Robbie Powell and Erik Judd?

Abby Andrews—She would have looked at home in crinolines holding a parasol to protect her alabaster complexion from too much sun. Was she a clinging vine or a scheming woman who engineered problems for Hollis so that she could be there to offer support?

Grace Webster—To say there was an undercurrent between the sisters was to put it mildly. Grace was by turns combative, difficult, chiding, hostile. Grace struck Nela as reckless, daring, and impulsive. Several times

she had been darkly amused. Maybe she thought vandalism was a joke, too.

Peter Owens—He'd seemed like a tweedy intellectual,
but she didn't think she'd imagined his pleasure in tweak-
ing Francis Garth. There—

Jugs lifted his head. He listened, came sinuously up on
his paws, flowed to the floor. He moved toward the front
door.

She spoke gently. "Ready for a big night?" Words didn't
matter to a cat. Tone did.

Jugs stopped a few feet from the door, stood very still.

The staccato knock came with no warning.

Nela jumped up and bolted to the bookcase. She used
the edge of her sweater to pick up the plastic bag. Heart
thudding, she opened Marian's purse, using another edge
of the sweater, and dropped the bag inside.

The quick, sharp knock sounded again.

Nela moved to the door, taking a deep breath. She turned
on the porch light, but she couldn't look out to identify the
visitor. The door lacked a peephole. She opened it a trace.
"Who's there?"

"Steve Flynn. *Craddock Clarion*." His voice was loud,
clear, and businesslike.

Nela's tight stance relaxed. Steve Flynn, the redheaded
reporter who could have been a double for Van Johnson.
She'd almost smiled at him when their gazes first met. But
he wasn't the boy next door.

Why had he come?

"Miss Farley, may I speak with you for a moment? About
the break-in Friday night."

Nela's thoughts raced. The detective didn't believe there
was a break-in. Would it be suspicious if she refused to talk
to the reporter? She didn't need anyone else suspecting her

of a crime. She glanced at the Coach bag, hesitated, then turned the knob.

The wind stirred his short red hair. The glare of the porch light emphasized the freckles on his fair skin. Steady blue eyes met hers. "I've been looking over the police report on the attempted burglary here. Can I visit with you for a minute?"

Cold air swirled inside. He stood hunched with his hands in his pockets, his only protection an old pullover sweater.

She held open the door.

As she closed it, his eyes noted the door wedge. He raised them to look at her.

Nela saw a flicker of interest. He didn't miss much.

She led the way into the living room, once again saw him scan the surroundings, taking in the scrape on the back of the desk chair, the discoloration that marked where a mirror had once hung.

He declined coffee. "I don't want to interfere with your evening."

"I don't have anything planned." Other than transporting a stolen necklace as far away as possible.

"Then"—his smile was quick and charming—"if you don't mind, fill me in on what happened Friday night."

On closer view, his boy-next-door face was older, more appraising, less ingenuous than she'd first thought. There was depth in his blue eyes and a hard edge to his chin. She was also suddenly aware of being near him, of his stocky build, of his maleness.

Jugs padded toward him, raised his head.

The reporter nodded at the cat. "You have to have attention first, huh? No entrance without showing proper respect, right?" A broad hand swung down to stroke Jugs's fur. He straightened. "My mom's cat was a big tabby. He thought he was the man of the house along with my dad. What's his name?"

"Jugs."

He grinned. "Those are big ears, that's for sure. Now, about Friday night—"

Nela wondered if he was one of those reporters who always takes a cop's view. It was natural. She'd been there, too. Reporters understood the hard, tough, dangerous world cops face every day. Reporters admired courage masked by black humor. Good reporters never slanted a story, but they listened when a good cop spoke.

"—what happened?"

The cat moved toward her, looked up. *". . . wants to know you . . . not sure about you . . . doesn't trust women . . . women lie . . ."*

Nela jerked her gaze away from Jugs. "I was in the guest room. I'll show you." She turned to lead the way. Jugs padded alongside. Nela struggled for composure. What was wrong with her? Jugs couldn't know anything in the mind of this man who meant nothing to her—except that he might pose a danger.

As she opened the bedroom door and half turned toward him, their eyes met. "I was asleep."

He looked past her toward the bed.

She was intuitively aware of him, of his nearness, of the tensing of his body, of a sense of uncertainty, of a man who had been hurt and was still angry, of longing and wariness. She steeled herself. The emotions of the day had fogged her reason.

"Noise woke you?"

"Yes. Then I saw the line of light beneath the door." She shut the bedroom door, gestured toward the living room. "Come sit down and I'll tell you." She chose the easy chair, waited until he settled on the sofa opposite her. She spoke at a quick clip, wished her voice didn't sound breathless. ". . . bangs and crashes . . ." She described everything. "I yelled the police were coming. I heard someone leave. I didn't come out until the police knocked. Then I ran to open the door."

Those clear deep blue eyes never left her face. "The police said the door was locked when they arrived."

"The thief locked the door behind him. I think whoever came had a key."

He looked puzzled, his gaze flicking across the room toward the door. "How about the doorstop? A key doesn't do any good if that's in place."

"I bought the wedge Saturday morning. Somebody had a key Friday night. Somebody still has a key. I shove the wedge under the door now at night."

"What were they looking for?"

The necklace. She felt the answer deep in her gut. She stared at him and realized her peril. The quick sharp question had caught her unaware. Unless she knew more than she had revealed to the police, she should have quickly said she didn't know or suggested they must have been looking for money. She had remained quiet too long. When she spoke, she knew her answer was too little, too late. "I suppose whatever thieves look for. Money, valuables of some kind."

He didn't change expression, but he wasn't fooled. He was well aware that she had knowledge she had not revealed. He folded his arms, that classic posture of wariness. "Somebody with a key wouldn't be your run-of-the-mill thief."

"If you say so." She suddenly felt that they looked at each other across a divide. "I don't have any experience with thieves."

"A key makes everything different. Either someone knew her and had a key or someone knew her well enough to know, for example, that she tucked an extra key in a flowerpot."

"Flowerpot?"

For an instant, he was amused. "Metaphorically

speaking. Somewhere. Under a flagstone. In the garage. People do things like that around here."

Nela considered the possibility. "If someone knew where Miss Grant kept an extra key, they must have known her pretty well. What do you know about her?"

"Smart, hardworking, type A, absolutely devoted to Haklo. She came to Craddock twenty years ago as Mr. Webster's executive secretary." He paused, gave a small shrug. "In any little town, the leading lights, and that's spelled *people with money*, are the focus of gossip. Everybody thought she was his mistress. Maybe she was, maybe she wasn't. Webster's wife was reclusive. Again it's all gossip but people said he and his wife didn't share a bedroom. In any event, Marian was a good-looking woman who never exhibited any interest in anybody else—man or woman—so the gossip may have been right. Haklo was definitely Webster's baby and pretty soon she was running it. All she cared about was Haklo, especially after Webster died. Maybe she saw Haklo as a monument to him. Maybe she felt closest to him out there. Anyway, Haklo was her life. Everybody knew better than to cross her, including the Webster daughters. Both of them were always charming to Marian but I don't think there was any love lost between them, which figures if she slept with their dad. Marian was always in charge. Anyone who opposed her ended up backed against a wall, one way or another. Marian maneuvered money and pressure from money to get the best deal possible for Haklo."

"If she found out who was behind the vandalism, she'd make them pay?"

"With a pound of flesh and smile while she was doing it." His eyes narrowed. "What are you suggesting?"

Her gaze fell. She hoped she hadn't looked toward the door. This man saw too much, understood too much. How would he feel if she blurted out that somebody put a skateboard on the second step and that's why Marian Grant died?

He would demand that she tell him how she knew. She spoke hurriedly. "Nothing. I just think someone had a key to get in." Nela felt certain she had met the late-night intruder today at Haklo. "Maybe Miss Grant's office was wrecked before the thief came here. Maybe she kept a key lying in the front drawer of her desk. Maybe it had a tag on it: *Extra front-door key.*"

"That's possible. It certainly explains how someone got in here." He spoke in a considering tone. "Somebody has a key. They come in . . ." His gaze stopped at the purse on the bookcase. "Is that your purse?"

She should have put the hideous purse away. She deliberately kept her eyes away from the bookcase.

He waited for her answer.

"Miss Webster said the purse belonged to Miss Grant."

"Miss Webster?"

"She heard the sirens and came."

"Was the purse there Friday night?"

She tried to sound as if her answer didn't matter. "Yes."

"A thief walked right by the bookcase and ignored the purse?" He looked skeptical.

"I shouted that the police were coming." She had to convince him. "I heard running steps. He didn't take time to grab the purse."

"He took time to push the door lock."

"Maybe not, then. Maybe when he first came it, he locked the door so no one could surprise him." Nela figured that's what must have happened. "It's the kind of lock that has to be disengaged. It doesn't pop out automatically."

"That may be right."

"I think the thief went straight to the desk. It was a mess. Somebody was looking for something in her desk."

"Have you checked the purse? Maybe the answer to everything is there." He rose and took a step toward the bookcase.

Nela popped to her feet, caught up with him, gripped his arm. "We can't do that. We have no right. Tomorrow I'll take the purse to the foundation and ask Miss Webster to take charge of it." She pulled her hand away from his arm, remembering the muscular feel of his forearm beneath the sweater.

He remained midway to the bookcase. "I suppose you have a point there." But he still gazed at the black leather bag.

She had to get rid of him.

"That's all I have to say, Mr. Flynn. If you don't mind, I'm rather tired. It's been a long day." She opened the door.

He stared at her for a long moment.

Nela felt an odd sadness. If she didn't know better, she would think she'd seen a flash of disappointment in his eyes, disappointment and regret.

"Yeah. I'll bet you are. Thanks." He turned away, crossed the small porch in a single step, started down the stairs.

She closed the door, leaned against the cold panel, and stared at the purse.

A t the bottom of the stairs, Nela waited for her eyes to adjust to the darkness. She wore Chloe's big coat and her brown wool gloves. In one pocket she'd stuffed a pencil flashlight she'd found in a utility drawer in the kitchen. The plastic bag with the necklace was in the other pocket. She'd tucked her driver's license in the pocket of her jeans along with a ten-dollar bill and Chloe's key to the employee entrance.

She gazed at the back of the Webster house. Light seeped from the edges of curtains, but there was no movement in the long sweep of gardens or on the terrace. Time to go. There could be no safety until she disposed of the necklace. She hurried down the steps. The wind was up. Knife-sharp air clawed at her face.

The garage door lifted smoothly. As she backed the VW from the garage, she clicked on the headlights. She made no effort at stealth. She had every right to run out to a 7-Eleven and pick up something. She left the car door open as she closed the garage door.

At the end of the drive, she turned left instead of right. She drove three blocks until she was out of the enclave of expensive homes. She entered a convenience store lot. As she locked the VW, one car pulled out from a line of pumps, another pulled in. She hurried inside, bought a six-pack of Cokes. In the car she placed them on the floor in front of the passenger seat.

She glanced at her watch in the splash of light from the storefront. Twenty after ten. In her mind she traced her route. She'd studied the Craddock city map Chloe had included in the packet with one of her usual sticky notes. A thin squiggly line appeared to reach the main grounds of the foundation from a road on the west side. That would be safer than using the main entrance.

The drive didn't take long. Traffic was light. There was one set of headlights behind her when she turned onto the road that ran in front of the foundation.

Nela drove around a curve and jammed on her brakes. A doe bounded across the road, her fur a glossy tan in the wash from the headlights. In another bound, the deer cleared a fence and disappeared into a grove of trees. A car came around the curve behind her, slowed.

Nela started up again. She was aware of the headlights in her rearview mirror. The car pulled out to pass, roared around the VW, and now the road was dark behind her. She continued for about a hundred yards and turned right onto a narrow blacktop road with a thick mass of trees on one side and a fenced field on the other. The VW headlights seemed frail against the country darkness. She peered into the night. If the thin line on the map indicated a road into the Haklo property, it should soon come into view on her right. She saw a break in the woods. Slowing, she swung onto a rutted dirt road. The headlights seemed puny against the intense darkness, but she dimmed to fog lights, affording her just enough illumination to follow the ruts.

A hundred yards. Another. She reached an open expanse. Dark buildings loomed to her left. Light filtered through a grove of trees to her right. That would be light from the occupied Haklo guest cabin. Nela turned off the fog lights and coasted to a stop by a long low building. Her eyes adjusted to night. She rolled down the window. She was parked next to a galvanized steel structure, which probably housed equipment and supplies for the upkeep of the foundation and its grounds. Straight ahead was the line of evergreens that marked the staff parking lot. Quietly she slipped from the car. She looked again toward the cabin. Though light glowed from the windows, there was no movement or sound.

Except for the occasional *whoo* of an owl, reassuring silence lay over the dark landscape ahead of her. Once past the evergreens, she tried to walk quietly, but the crunch of gravel beneath her feet seemed startlingly loud. It was better on the sidewalk leading to the staff entrance. She took her time, using the pencil light to light her way. All the while, she listened for sound, movement, any hint that she had been observed. Surely if the police had left a guard, someone would have challenged her by now. Every minute that passed increased her confidence that only she moved in the stillness of the country night.

The building itself lay in total darkness.

At the staff entrance, Nela held the pencil flash in her gloved left hand, used Chloe's key. In an instant she was inside, safe in a black tunnel of silence. She ran lightly up the hallway, using the tiny beam to light her way. She was almost there, almost safe. In only a moment she'd be free of the incriminating necklace.

She opened the door to Blythe's office and dashed across the room. She pulled out the plastic bag, emptied the necklace onto the center of the desktop. The stones and precious metal clattered on the wooden surface. In the light of the flash, diamonds glittered and gold gleamed.

She whirled away from the desk. In the hall, she shut Blythe's office door behind her. The tiny beam of light bouncing before her, she again ran lightly down the hallway, not caring now at the sound of her sneakers on the marble. She felt exultant when she reached the exit. She and Chloe were safe. As soon as she reached the car and drove away, there was nothing to link her and Chloe to that damnable, gorgeous, incredibly expensive necklace.

She pulled open the heavy door at the end of the hall and stepped out into the night. The door began to close.

A quick bright light blinded her.

"The image also records the time. *Temporary Employee Exits Haklo After Hours.* Interesting headline, right?" His tenor voice was sardonic. "Care to comment?" He came quickly up the steps, used a broad hand to hold the door open. "Why don't we go inside?"

Once Nela had seen a bird trapped inside an enclosed mall, flying up, seeking, not finding. Sometimes there is no escape. Numbly, she turned and stepped inside.

He followed close behind her.

When the door closed, she lifted the pocket flashlight, held the beam where she could see his face.

He squinted against the light, his freckled face grim, his gaze accusing. He looked big, tough, and determined. He cupped a cell phone in his left hand. "What's your excuse? Forgot your hankie?"

His tone hurt almost as much as the realization that she had failed Chloe. She should have done something, anything, to be rid of the necklace. Instead, she'd tried to return the stolen jewelry to its owner and now she—and

Chloe—were going to pay the price. She was cornered but she wouldn't go down without a fight. "Why are you here?" But she knew the answer. He was after a story and he couldn't have any idea just how big it was going to be. "Do you make it a practice to follow women you don't know?"

If she had no right to be here, certainly he didn't belong either. So he was a reporter. So he looked like Van Johnson, an older, tougher Van Johnson. Maybe Gram would have loved him, but his presence here was as unexplained as hers. Maybe he knew much more about what had happened at Haklo than she could ever imagine. "How did you know I was coming here?"

His mouth twisted in a wry half smile, half grimace. "Pirates used to fly the skull and crossbones to scare the hell out of ships. You sent plenty of signals tonight. You're as wary as an embezzler waiting for the bank examiner. You know more—a lot more—than you want to admit. You might as well have marked Marian's purse with a red X. Once I got outside, I decided to hang around, see if anything popped. I didn't know what to expect, maybe someone arriving. Instead, you slipped down the steps like a Hitchcock heroine." There was an undertone of regret mingled with derision.

"You followed me? But I went to the Seven-Eleven . . ." Her voice trailed off.

His gaze was quizzical. "For a Hitchcock lady, you aren't very savvy about picking up a tail. Once you left the Seven-Eleven, you were easy meat. When you turned on Pumpjack Road, I knew you were going to Haklo. I was right behind you. I passed you, went around a curve, and pulled off on the shoulder. When you didn't come, I knew you'd taken the back entrance." His eyes were probing. "Not a well-known route. Clever for someone who's new to town. So, shall we take a tour? See if there are any other offices trashed?"

"Would you like to hear the truth?" She flung the words at him. "Or are you enjoying yourself too much?"

His face changed, disdain melding into combativeness. "Yeah. I'd like to hear some truth from you."

In his eyes, she saw disappointment and a flicker of wariness: *Fool me once, shame on you; fool me twice, shame on me.*

She met his gaze straight on. Maybe truth would help. Likely not. But truth he damn well was going to get. "Friday night somebody searched Marian's living room. Saturday I had the same thought you did. Why hadn't the thief taken the purse? I looked inside. I found an incredibly beautiful diamond-and-gold necklace in the bottom of the bag. I left it in the purse. I knew nothing about the theft of a necklace at Haklo. Chloe never mentioned the theft when we talked. All she cares about is Leland and fun and adventure. She told me about Turner Falls and Bricktown and the Heavener Runestone. I didn't know the necklace was stolen until the staff meeting this morning."

He listened with no change of expression.

"If you want more truth"—anger heated her voice—"I found out a stranger in town makes an easy target. The detective made it clear that Chloe is suspect number one as the thief, with me busy covering up for her. I knew Dugan wouldn't believe I found the necklace in the purse. Tonight I brought the necklace here and put it on Blythe Webster's desk."

"You put the necklace in Blythe's office?" His broad face reflected surprise, uncertainty, calculation, concentration. He stared at her for a long moment, then slid the phone into his pocket. "Show me."

The heavy silence of an empty building emphasized the sound of their footsteps on the marble floor. At Blythe's office, he opened the door and flicked on the lights. The necklace was starkly visible in the center of the desk, the diamonds glittering bright as stars.

Steve Flynn walked slowly to the desk. He stared down at the magnificent diamonds in the ornate gold settings. "I'll be double damned." He pulled his cell from his pocket. A tiny flash flared. He looked for a moment at the small screen. "You can tell the damn thing's worth a fortune even in a cell phone picture." He closed the phone, turned, and looked at Nela. Finally, he shook his head as if puzzled. "Why didn't you throw it away?"

"It would have been smarter." But nobody gets second chances.

"Why didn't you?" He was insistent.

"It wasn't mine." It was ironic that basic honesty was going to put her in jail. "The more fool I."

"Yeah. There's a small matter of property rights." He sounded sardonic. "All right, I may be a fool, too, but everything in here"—he waved his hand around the office—"appears to be in place. You came in, you dropped the necklace, you left. Come on."

"Aren't you going to call the police?"

"No. For some crazy reason, I believe you." He jerked a thumb at the door. "Let's get out of here. We need to talk."

$-10-$

Steve leaned back against the plumped pillow, legs outstretched, and listened. Pretty soon he had a sense of how Haklo appeared to her: Blythe Webster imperious but shaken, and staff members who weren't just names but individuals with passions. Louise Spear grieved over Marian and Haklo's troubles. Francis Garth was furious at a threat to his beloved Tallgrass Prairie. Francis was proud of his Osage Heritage—the preserve was the heart of the Osage Nation—and Francis was a formidable figure. Robbie Powell and his partner, Erik Judd, bitterly resented the new director. Hollis Blair was in a situation where aw-shucks charm didn't help. Abby Andrews was either a wilting maiden or a scheming opportunist. Cole Hamilton appeared subdued and defeated, but his comment that emphasized the necessity of a key to Haklo might be disingenuous. Grace Webster was at odds with her sister. Peter Owens was affable but possibly sly.

When Nela revealed the existence of the obscene letters

sent out on the director's letterhead, he saw another link in
the chain of ugly attacks on the foundation. But this one
appeared tied directly to Abby Andrews, which might tilt
the scale toward schemer instead of victim.

Steve liked Nela's voice. Not high. Not low. Kind of soft.
A voice you could listen to for a long time. She looked small
in an oversize chintz-covered chair, dark hair still tangled
by the wind, face pale, dark shadows beneath her eyes. But
she no longer seemed remote as she had in his first glimpse
at Hamburger Heaven.

His eyes slid from her to a photograph on the table next
to her chair. A dark-haired laughing man in a tee and shorts
stood near an outcrop of black rocks on a beach, the wind
stirring his hair. Across the bottom of the photograph was
a simple inscription: *To Nela—Love, Bill.* A red, white, and
blue ribbon was woven through the latticed frame.

Steve was accustomed to figuring from one fact to
another. The picture had to belong to Nela. To carry the
photograph with her as she traveled meant that the man and
the place mattered very much to her. He was afraid he knew
exactly why the ribbon was in place and that would account
for the undertone of sadness that he'd observed.

But tonight, she was fully alive, quick intelligence in her
eyes, resolve in her face, a woman engaged in a struggle to
survive. The brown tabby nestled next to her. One slender
hand rested on the cat's back. As she spoke, she looked at
him with a direct stare that said she was in the fight for as
long as it took.

When he'd caught her coming out of Haklo, he'd felt a
bitter twist of disappointment, accepting that Katie had been
right, that she was covering up for her light-fingered sister.
At that point, he had a picture of her leaving Haklo, the time
electronically recorded. She was cornered. All he had to do
was tie up the loose ends. It was like ballast shifting in a

hull. When the heavy load tipped to one end, the ship was sure to go down.

Now the ballast was back in place. He was pretty good at keeping score and she had two heavy hits in her favor: the return of the necklace and the door wedge. Sure, she could have found the necklace at the apartment, maybe not in the purse as she claimed, decided her sister was the thief, and returned the necklace to protect her. But the smart decision would have been to fling the necklace deep into woods on the other side of town. She could easily have found some woods and jettisoned the jewelry. She took a big chance bringing the necklace to Haklo tonight, which argued she not only wasn't a thief, she was too honest and responsible to throw away a quarter of a million dollars that didn't belong to her. That was one home run. The second hinged on one small fact: The morning after her 911 call, she went out and bought a wedge to shove under the door.

She turned her hands palms up, looked rueful. "I understand if you decide to call the detective. You're a reporter. You have to be honest with the cops you know. I was a reporter, too. Trust is a two-way street."

He wasn't surprised. She had the manner of someone who was used to asking questions, looking hard at facts, winnowing out nonsense. She'd showed she was tough when he confronted her at Haklo. She'd asked if he would listen to truth. Truth was all that mattered, all that should matter to a reporter. Maybe that was why he'd felt a connection to her right from that first look. They might have lots of differences in their backgrounds, but they would always understand each other.

"If you call Dugan"—her voice was calm—"I'll tell her what I've told you. Someone came here hunting for the necklace and that's the reason her office was searched. Unfortunately, Dugan won't believe me."

He didn't refute her conclusion about Katie Dugan. If Katie learned the necklace had been in Nela's possession, she'd be sure her judgment was right. As soon as Chloe returned from Tahiti, they'd both be booked.

"Let me be sure I get it." He watched her carefully. "You arrived here Friday afternoon. Everything was fine. You went to bed, somebody got inside, hunted in the desk. You called nine-one-one. When the cops came, you had to unlock the front door. You believe someone entered with a key. That likely comes down to a small list. Marian's life was centered at Haklo. Either someone knew where she kept an extra key or maybe the intruder entered Haklo first and found a key to the apartment in her office and came here when the necklace didn't turn up in the office. Saturday morning you checked Marian's purse and found the necklace. You didn't do anything about it because you had no business snooping and no reason to think she shouldn't have a necklace in her purse. You hid the purse to protect the necklace. You went to Haklo Saturday, Louise took you around. Monday you heard about the vandalism, including the obscene letters. But that receded into the background after you found Marian's office trashed. Then you learned that the necklace was stolen property. Katie Dugan believes your sister heisted the necklace after puffing up a smokescreen with the vandalism and you are covering up for her. Tonight you decided to put the necklace on Blythe's desk. That's everything?"

She hesitated, frowning. Her gaze dropped to the cat nestled close to her.

Why wasn't she looking at him? What else did she know? Steve came upright, leaned forward, his eyes insistent. "I've gone out on a limb for you. I know you went in Haklo after hours. I know where the necklace is. If this all came out, I could be charged as an accessory. I need to know what you know."

Slowly she looked up.

He stared into dark brilliant eyes that held both uncertainty and knowledge.

"I don't have proof." Her gaze was steady.

"Tell me, Nela." He liked the sound of her name, *Nee-la*. "I'll help you. All I ask is that you don't lie to me. I've heard too many lies from beautiful women." He stopped for a long moment, lips pressed together. "Okay. I want honesty. I'll be honest. I heard too many lies from one particular beautiful woman, my ex-wife. I'm telling you this because I want you to know where I'm coming from. I'll help you—if you don't lie to me. You have to make a choice. If you can't—or won't—be honest, tell me and I'll walk out of here and tonight never happened. I never came here, I never went to Haklo, I don't know anything about a piece of jewelry."

"I won't lie to you. I may not be able to tell you everything." She was solemn. "Whatever I tell you will be the truth. I think I do know something." She glanced again at the cat, then said, almost defiantly, "I can't tell you how I know."

He wanted to believe her, wanted it more than he'd wanted anything in a very long time. *Steve, you damn fool, women lie, don't let her suck you into something screwy. Why can't she tell how she knows whatever it is that she knows? Protecting somebody?* He almost pushed up from the chair. He could walk away, avoid entanglement. But he was already speaking. "All right. Keep your source."

As for how she obtained a piece of knowledge, the possibilities were pretty narrow. Either she or her sister had seen something that Nela now believed to be important in the saga of Haklo and its troubles. He'd bet the house she was protecting her sister. He was putting himself in a big hole if he didn't report her entry into Haklo and the necklace on Blythe Webster's desk. He needed every scrap of information to dig his way out. He would be home free—and so would Nela and Chloe—if the jewel thief was caught. "What do you know?"

"Marian Grant was murdered."

The words hung between them.

Steve had covered the story. Marian Grant was a prominent citizen of Craddock. Her death was front-page news. Marian's accident had been a surprise. She had been in her late forties, a runner, a good tennis player. However, accidents happen to the fit as well as the unfit. For an instant, Nela's claim shocked him into immobility. Then pieces slotted together in his mind—vandalism at Haklo, a missing necklace in Marian's purse, a thief fearing arrest, Marian's death—to form an ugly pattern, a quite possible pattern. Still . . .

"Are you claiming somebody was here and shoved her down the steps?"

"No. I have reason to believe"—she spoke carefully—"that someone put a skateboard on the second step."

"A skateboard?" He pictured that moment, Marian hurrying out the door for her morning jog, taking quick steps, one foot landing on a skateboard. Hell yes, that could knock her over a railing. "If somebody knows that for a fact, the cops have to be told."

"They would want to know how I know. I can't identify the source."

He liked piecing together facts from a starting point. "You arrived here Friday, right? You can prove you were on a certain flight and that you were in LA until you took that flight?"

"Absolutely."

"You've never been to Craddock before?"

"No."

"Therefore, you couldn't know about a skateboard on the steps from your own knowledge. Who told you?" The list had to be short. Her sister, Chloe, had to be the only person Nela knew before she arrived.

Nela brushed back a tangle of dark hair. "I promised the truth. I'm telling you the truth. No one told me."

"If"—he tried to be patient—"no one told you and you weren't here, how do you know?"

"All I can say is that no one told me." She spoke with finality, looked at him with a faint half smile.

He understood. She wasn't going to budge. There had to be a strong reason for her silence. But she had nothing to gain from making a claim that Marian Grant had been murdered. If anything, turning the search for the necklace into a murder investigation might place her and Chloe in more peril. Once again Nela was making a moral choice: Return a quarter-million-dollar necklace. Expose murder.

"Steve—"

It was the first time she'd ever said his name. Someday would she speak to him, call him by name, and be thinking of him and not stolen jewels or murder?

"—you said I could keep my source. But we need to tell the police. Sometimes I got anonymous tips on stories. Will you tell the police you got a tip, an anonymous tip? Can't you say that somebody said"—she paused, then began again, this time in a scarcely audible wisp of sound—"Marian Grant was murdered. She knew who took the necklace. Someone put a skateboard on the second step of the garage apartment stairs . . ."

C raddock had few public pay phones left. In the parking lot of a Valero filling station, Steve stood with his back to the street, his shoulders hunched against the cold. He not only didn't have his jacket, he didn't have gloves. In fact, he didn't own a pair of gloves. He'd found a shammy crammed in the glove compartment. He dropped in the coins, pushed the buttons. The phone was answered after five rings. He listened to the entire message, waited for his extension number, pushed the buttons. He heard his own voice, waited again, finally whispered, repeating Nela's words. He hung up and used the shammy to clean the receiver.

N ela looked down at the muscular cat stretched out with his front paws flat on the surface of the kitchen table. "You look like one of those stone lions that guard the New York Public Library."

Jugs regarded her equably. *". . . You're happier today . . ."*

Yes, she was happier today. Removing the necklace from the apartment was like kicking free of tangled seaweed just before a big wave hit. "That's just between you and me, buddy. Thank God cops don't read cat minds. I'd be in big trouble."

Jugs continued to stare at her. *". . . You're worried . . . She was worried . . ."*

As she sipped her morning coffee, a faint frown drew her eyebrows down. Although she felt almost giddy with relief every time she thought about the necklace now in Blythe's office, the removal of the jewelry didn't solve the main problem. Maybe that's why her subconscious, aka Jugs, was warning her.

She pushed away the quicksilver thought that her subconscious could not possibly have known if someone had rigged the step to make Marian Grant fall. But something had to account for that searing moment when she'd looked at Jugs and imagined his thoughts. . . . *board rolled on the second step* . . . When she thought of a rolling board, the image had come swiftly, a skateboard. Saturday morning when she'd looked at the banister, a streak of paint was just where a skateboard might have struck if tipped up. That was confirmation, wasn't it? Something had hit that banister. They said violence leaves a psychic mark. Who said? Her inner voice was quick with the challenge. All right. She'd read somewhere that there was some kind of lasting emanation after trauma. If Marian had been murdered, if someone left a skateboard on her steps, that certainly qualified as a violent act. When Marian plunged over the railing, did she have time to realize what had happened?

Nela shook her head. She might as well believe in voodoo. But some people did. Maybe she'd had a moment of ESP. But she'd never had any use for so-called psychics. The explanation had to be simple. There was that gash in the stair rail. Maybe subconsciously she'd noticed the scrape when she first arrived and the shock of confronting Jugs stirred some long-ago memory of a skateboard.

She looked at Jugs, but his eyes had closed. When he'd looked at her Friday night, other thoughts had come to her mind. . . . *She was worried . . . She didn't know what to do . . .*

About a stolen necklace?

Nela thought about the last few days in the life of a woman she'd never known, a smart, intense, hardworking woman who had devoted her life to Haklo.

A vandal struck Haklo again and again.

Blythe's necklace was stolen.

The necklace was in Marian Grant's purse that she placed atop the bookcase the last night of her life.

Did Marian steal the quarter-million-dollar adornment?

The violent searches of her office and apartment after her death appeared almost certainly to be a hunt for the necklace. Dumped drawers indicated a search for some physical object, not incriminating papers suggested by Detective Dugan. The destruction in her office reflected a wild and dangerous anger on the part of the searcher when the effort to find the necklace failed. From everything Nela had been told about Marian, there was nothing to support the idea that Marian could have been a thief. Instead, it was much more likely that Marian had discovered the identity of the thief and obtained the necklace. However, she didn't contact the police. She kept the necklace in her purse.

Why hadn't she called the police?

As Steve had made clear, Marian always protected the foundation. Her decision to handle the theft by herself meant that a public revelation would create a scandal. She was a confident, strong woman. Perhaps she insisted the thief had to confess or resign or make restitution. Perhaps she said, "I've put the necklace in a safe place and unless you do as I say, I will contact the police." Perhaps she set a deadline.

Had the thief killed her to keep her quiet?

She died early Monday morning. The funeral was Thursday. Chloe had stayed in the apartment since Monday night to take care of Jugs. Whether Marian's death was accident or murder, the presence of the necklace in her purse was fact. The thief's first opportunity to search the apartment had been Friday night after Chloe had left town.

Nela welcomed the hot, strong coffee but it didn't lessen the chill of another pointer to someone on the Haklo staff. All of them knew about Chloe's trip to Tahiti. Chloe hadn't mentioned that Nela would stay in the apartment until Chloe's return. As for access to Marian's apartment, perhaps a key was, as Steve suggested, secreted in some simple place known to the searcher. Or perhaps the office was searched before the apartment and a key found in that desk.

Whatever the order, the searches were fruitless because the necklace was in Marian's purse. The treasure wasn't hidden. The necklace had simply been dropped to the bottom of a Coach bag, a safe place in the eyes of its owner. A killer scrabbled through drawers, dumped files, and all the while the necklace was within reach.

Detective Dugan's instinct was good. The necklace was the crux of everything. But Dugan was convinced that Chloe was the clever thief who'd created the vandalism as a diversion and that Nela was covering up for her. When Steve reported a tip about murder, Dugan might tab Chloe as a murderer as well as a thief.

Nela put down her mug. She couldn't count on the police investigation. But she wasn't blinded by hometown loyalties. If Dugan wasn't willing to look at the Haklo staff members as suspects, Nela was.

D etective Dugan stood with arms folded. "All right."
Steve flicked on the speakerphone, punched for messages. He listened with a sense of relief. His whisper had been very well done, the faintly heard words sexless, unaccented wraiths that couldn't be grasped. "Message received at eleven forty-two p.m. Monday: . . . Marian Grant was murdered . . . A skateboard on the second step . . . threw her over the railing . . . She knew who took the necklace . . ."

Detective Dugan touched a number in her cell phone directory. "Mokie, get a trace on a call received at the *Clarion* last night at eleven forty-two. Send out a lab tech to One Willow Lane. Marian Grant died in a fall down the garage apartment stairs. Check for possible damage to the railing. Look for scratches, paint traces. If there is damage, get forensic evidence. Also measurements and photos. Thanks."

She turned to Steve. "Play the message again." She listened with eyes half closed. At its end, she shook her head. "Can't tell whether the caller was a man or a woman. Could have been anybody. No discernible accent." Her eyes opened, settled on Steve. "Why you?"

Steve was unruffled. "Goes with the territory. If you have a tip, call a reporter."

"Why last night?"

Steve kept his expression faintly quizzical. "A big story

in yesterday afternoon's *Clarion*. It probably caught some-one's attention."

Katie's face wrinkled in concentration. "I want to talk to that caller. Murder." Her tone was considering. She squeezed her eyes in thought. "I figured all along that the necklace was the key and that Grant knew who took it. That explains the search of her office. The searcher messed every-thing up to try and make it look like more vandalism. The point has to be the necklace. A quarter of a million dollars is serious money. Let's say Grant threatened to name the thief. People around her knew she jogged every morning. A skateboard on the steps couldn't guarantee she'd be killed but the probability was good. Okay, the thief puts a skate-board on the steps then shows up around six fifteen, taking care not to be seen. If she was still alive, pressure on the carotid would dispatch her pronto. If she's already dead, pick up the skateboard and melt away. Now, how could any-one except the murderer know about a skateboard on the steps? If someone did know, why keep quiet until now? Scared? Not sure? Maybe saw a skateboard in a weird place and decided Marian was too athletic to fall accidentally?" Her chin jutted. "I've got to find who made that call."

Steve felt uneasy. Murder made all kinds of sense, but he couldn't figure out how Nela knew. If her sister had sto-len the necklace and committed murder, Nela would never in a million years have told him about the skateboard. That she had revealed the skateboard affirmed her and Chloe's innocence for him. But Nela had spent only one day at Haklo. Certainly no one would confide that kind of infor-mation to her. How the hell did Nela know?

"Maybe"—and he knew he was dealing with his own worries—"you should hunt for somebody who has a skateboard."

Katie looked sardonic. "Who on the Haklo staff does wheelies? I'll ask around."

* * *

In the Haklo staff lot, Nela felt a tiny spurt of amusement as she parked once again between the snazzy Thunderbird and the old Dodge. The Thunderbird, psychedelic VW, and prim Dodge surely made some kind of statement. But grim worry returned when she reached the walkway to the staff entrance and saw a police officer waiting there. Even though she knew the police would be called when the necklace was found, her stomach tightened. She walked a little faster. Anyone would be curious, right? She came to a stop and looked up the shallow flight of steps.

Officer Baker's faded red hair curled becomingly under her cap. "Good morning, ma'am." She held the door open. "Please go directly to the conference room in the east wing."

Nela stopped and stared. Any innocent person would. "What's happened?"

Officer Baker was pleasant. "Miss Webster has asked that everyone report to the conference room. Detective Dugan wishes to speak with staff members."

In the conference room, Louise Spear stood at the head of the table, her brown eyes anxious. "Nela, please make coffee for us. I suppose the police know something now about Marian's office."

As Nela measured beans, placed them in the grinder of the coffeemaker, she heard low voices around the edge of the partition, several asking Louise about the purpose of the meeting. She listened, making out what words she could. So far, no one had mentioned the necklace. Nela was surprised that Blythe Webster hadn't told Louise of her discovery. Perhaps Louise knew and had been told not to mention the necklace.

While the coffee was brewing, Nela glanced around the

partition. In addition to the staff members present yesterday, Rosalind McNeill, eyes bright with excitement, sat toward the end of the table next to the imposing white-haired chef. The receptionist was clearly delighted by the change in routine. The chef's brown eyes had the remote expression of someone in attendance but thinking of something else. A difficult recipe?

Nela added two more mugs. When the coffeemaker pinged, Nela filled mugs and carried the tray around the table. When she'd served those who accepted, she returned the tray and the carafe to the kitchenette, then settled on the straight chair a little to one side of the long table.

Once again Haklo staff was in place. She had a quick memory of *Casablanca*, another of Gram's favorite movies, and Captain Renault's wry, "Major Strasser has been shot. Round up the usual suspects."

Blythe Webster looked like a woman who had received shocking news, her eyes wide and staring. The fingers of one hand plucked at the pearl necklace at her throat. Cole Hamilton's aging Kewpie doll face wavered between indignation, worry, and perplexity. Francis Garth looked immovable as a monolith, his gaze somber, his heavy shoulders hunched. Abby Andrews twined a strand of blond hair around one finger, her violet eyes uneasy as she looked from the detective to the director. Hollis Blair gave Abby a swift, warm look before his bony face once again settled into ridges of concern. Grace Webster noticed the exchange with cool disapproval. Robbie Powell wasn't as youthfully handsome this morning. His green eyes darted around the room. His face thoughtful, Peter Owens propped an elbow on the table, gently swung his horn rims back and forth. Rosalind McNeill had the air of a woman awaiting the start of a performance. The chef stared unseeingly toward the buffalo mural.

The door opened and Detective Dugan entered, trim in a stylish white wool blazer and black wool slacks. Detective

Morrison followed, tape recorder in hand. In comparison with his fashionable superior, he looked down-at-the-heels in a baggy gray sweater and too large plaid wool slacks. He closed the hall door. Dugan stopped a few feet from the table and turned her gaze to Blythe.

Blythe looked at her with hollow eyes and nodded.

Dugan looked around the room, waited for silence. "Ladies and gentlemen." Her voice was smooth with no hint of threat. "We are continuing our investigation into a series of events at the foundation, including vandalism and theft. However, our investigation has taken a much more serious turn. We have received a report on good authority"—Dugan paused for emphasis—"that Marian Grant was murdered."

Louise Spear gave a cry. "That can't be." She touched her throat with a shaking hand.

"Murdered?" Grace Webster's round face was incredulous. "She fell down the stairs."

Dugan stared at the younger Webster sister. "It may be that a device placed on the stairs caused her to fall. Therefore, when I ask questions, I want each of you to understand that we are seeking information leading to a murderer. It is the duty of the innocent to answer truthfully and accurately. Detective Morrison will record this meeting. When you respond to a question, please preface your answer with your name."

If possible, Abby Andrews shrank even farther into her chair. Hollis Blair looked dazed. Cole Hamilton's face screwed up in dismay. Robbie Powell sat rigid in his chair. The horn rims in Peter Owens's hand came to a stop, remained unmoving. Rosalind's mouth curved in an astonished O. The chef remained imperturbable.

"Murder?" Cole's voice rose is disbelief. "That's impossible. How can you make such a claim? It was dark. Marian had on new running shoes. She fell."

"Forensic evidence supports the claim that her fall may

have been caused by a foreign object placed on the second step." Dugan's gaze briefly touched each face.

Nela pictured that telltale scrape on the baluster. Dugan had wasted no time. Obviously, she had already received a report. Had a police officer viewed the scarred surface, possibly brought a skateboard, experimented to see if pressure on one end tilted the board enough for the tip to strike at that level?

Francis Garth cleared his throat. "Detective Dugan, I'd like to clarify our position. Is there a presumption by police that those present in this room are considered to be suspects in the as yet unproven murder of Marian Grant? If so, please explain how that conclusion has been reached."

Nela sensed both fear and indignation in the room.

"This investigation is focused"—Dugan's tone was firm—"on those who have keys to Haklo Foundation. Significant force would be required to break into Haklo. Yesterday when police arrived to investigate the search of Marian Grant's office, there was no evidence of forcible entry. We believe the search of her office was connected to the theft of Miss Webster's necklace. We believe Miss Grant had proof of the identity of the thief. This information may have led to murder. Miss Grant may have said the incident would be overlooked if the necklace was returned and the vandalism ceased. From what we understand, Miss Grant was always mindful of the Haklo Foundation's stature in the community. We think she was trying to protect the foundation. Possibly she told the thief that she had evidence hidden away and gave the thief a deadline. Since there is now evidence that her death was not an accident, we can reasonably assume a connection between her death and the search of her office."

Nela spoke out forcefully. "Someone also searched the living room of her apartment Friday night."

The detective's cold eyes paused at Nela.

Nela understood that Dugan still thought it was possible that the 911 call from Marian's apartment was phony. Dugan included Nela and Chloe among possible suspects. But if Nela and Chloe were the main suspects, what was the point of this inquiry? Did Dugan hope for some kind of damaging information about Chloe to surface? And why hadn't Dugan mentioned the return of the necklace? Nela clenched her hands, saw Dugan take note. She forced her hands to go limp, knew that movement had been cataloged as well.

Dugan continued smoothly. "We believe the person who took the necklace either searched Miss Grant's office or arranged for such a search." Again a quick glance at Nela. "That person had a key to the foundation." She glanced down at a note card. "I have here a list of every person who has a key. Three people with keys are known to have been out of town this past weekend and their absence has been confirmed. Everyone in this room has a key. The final person who may have a key or access to a key"—she glanced at Robbie Powell—"is the former director, Erik Judd."

Robbie frowned. "Erik would never use his key to enter for any reason other than work."

"He has a key?"

Robbie was bland. "Yes. He's engaged in research here at Haklo for his history of the foundation."

"I understand Mr. Judd resented being fired."

Robbie shook his head. "Actually, he's welcomed the time to be able to concentrate on his writing."

"Why was he fired?" Dugan's tone was pleasant but her eyes sharp.

There was an uncomfortable pause.

Dugan's cool gaze moved to Blythe.

Blythe looked stubborn. "Erik was getting old and he wasn't very exciting. After all, he's in his fifties." She spoke as if it were a greatly distant age. "I wanted someone to lead Haklo to a new level, give us vision. I know Erik was disappointed, but he has a pension. And we'll publish his history."

Robbie said nothing.

Nela saw the twitch of one eyelid. Robbie was keeping anger over his lover's dismissal under wraps, but she had no doubt that beneath his smooth surface he harbored intense dislike for Hollis. She needed to find out more about both Erik and Robbie.

Cole brushed back a white curl. "Erik dealt with problems quickly. I think it's disappointing that Hollis hasn't made any progress on clearing up these matters." There was a flash of malice in his eyes.

"Erik could not have done more than Hollis has, Cole." There was an edge to Blythe's voice. "Hollis is in no way responsible for the dreadful things that have happened. His energy and enthusiasm have inspired us all." Blythe gave Hollis Blair a reassuring nod. "Anyway, vandalism doesn't matter now. If someone hurt Marian, we have to find out what happened. As for that necklace, I don't care if I ever see it again."

Nela was puzzled. The necklace was on Blythe's desk this morning. Had she turned the jewelry over to the police? Was that her meaning?

"I've told Detective Dugan that we will do everything we can to find out the truth of this"—she paused—"anonymous call that claims Marian was killed. I have to say it doesn't seem likely to me. But it is now a police matter." She was somber but there was no suggestion of personal distress.

Nela studied Blythe's composed face. Where was sorrow? Where was outrage? Blythe spoke like a woman directing a meeting and a troublesome issue had arisen. Marian Grant had been a part of Haklo since its inception. She had been important to Webster Harris . . .

Nela looked toward Grace Webster. She appeared shocked and uneasy, but again there wasn't the flare of sorrow and anger that would follow after learning of a cherished friend's murder.

Louise held tight to the gold chain at her neck. "This is dreadful. Nothing matters except Marian. Marian was part of our lives, the heart of Haklo. There's a picture in her office of Webster breaking a champagne bottle on the front pillar when the building was first opened and Marian clapping and laughing out loud. When I was with her, I almost felt that Webster would walk in the room any minute." Louise's face crumpled in misery. She looked up and down the table. "All of us have to answer the detective's questions. We have to tell the detective everything we know. For Marian."

"Of course we will," Francis responded.

Nela looked at the Webster sisters. Neither Blythe nor Grace spoke. Nela knew then that Steve had been right when he spoke of a small town's suspicion of an affair between Harris and Marian. It would be interesting to check the oil man's will. Nela had no doubt that Harris had made certain that Marian would remain as chief operating officer. Blythe and Grace had very likely long lived with hidden resentment.

Grace gave her sister a searching look, then said rapidly, "If anyone knows anything, speak up."

Blythe nodded. "Absolutely. We have a duty to aid the police."

A duty, but no impassioned call for justice from either Grace or Blythe.

The emotion came from Louise Spear. She pressed her fingertips against her cheeks. Her lips trembled. Hollis Blair's bony face looked haggard. Abby Andrews sent quick, panicked glances around the room. Francis Garth's heavy head moved until his dark eyes fastened on Peter Owens. Peter felt the glance and his professorial face hardened. Robbie Powell frowned, seemed to withdraw. Cole

Hamilton was the picture of worried concern. Rosalind placed fingertips against her lips. The chef alone seemed unaffected, though her brown eyes were curious.

"We'll get started." Dugan glanced around the table. "Among those who work in this building, including any not present today, who—"

Nela sensed danger. Dugan wasn't confining her inquiry to this room. Was the expanded field—anyone with a connection to the foundation—a clever way to apply the question to Chloe?

"—possesses a skateboard or has ever been seen with a skateboard?"

Francis Garth's heavy head turned toward Abby Andrews. Peter Owens, too, stared at the assistant curator. Hollis Blair's bony face creased in dismay.

Abby pushed back her chair, came to her feet. She turned toward Hollis. "Someone's—"

"Name first." Dugan was forceful.

"Abby Andrews." She looked at the detective pleadingly. "Someone's trying to get me in trouble. They used my computer for those awful letters. And now a skateboard. Ask anyone. My little brother was here for a visit and he forgot his skateboard. It was on the porch of the cabin. It disappeared last week."

Dugan took a step nearer the table. "Describe the skateboard."

"It's black with orange stripes."

"When did you last see it?" The question came fast.

"The Saturday"—Abby looked frightened—"before Marian died."

"Where?" Curt, short, demanding.

"On the front porch of the cabin. It was propped up by the door."

"There are four cabins on the grounds west of the main

building. You are the only person currently occupying a cabin."

Her violet eyes huge with fear, Abby nodded.

"When did he leave the board on the porch?"

"Craig was here the week before."

"Who would have occasion to see the skateboard on the porch?"

"Anybody. Everybody. Blythe had all the staff members out to the cabin next door to discuss redoing the interiors. They passed my cabin to go inside. The skateboard was right there in plain sight." Her voice wobbled but the challenge was clear.

Dugan turned to Blythe. "Is there anyone in addition to those present who were included in the survey of the cabin?"

Blythe's face creased in thought. "I think that's—oh, of course. Chloe Farley was with Louise."

Nela's glance locked with Dugan's. She hoped the detective read her loud and clear: *Look at these people. They're scared. I'm not. Chloe's innocent.*

The detective's face didn't change. There might have been grudging respect in her dark brown eyes, but the brief silent exchange didn't deflect her from Abby. "When did you notice the skateboard was gone?"

"Sunday afternoon. I'd found a box in the basement and I was going to pack it up to mail to Craig."

Dugan gazed at each person in turn. "Does anyone have knowledge of the skateboard between Saturday and Sunday?"

No one answered.

—11—

Nela's fingers automatically worked the computer keyboard as she prepared a summary of a grant application. Below her surface attention to the task, her thoughts darted as she tried to make sense of the tense meeting with Detective Dugan. Of course murder mattered more than theft, but why hadn't Dugan even mentioned the return of the necklace, especially since she believed the necklace might be the reason for Marian Grant's murder? Why was Dugan keeping that information quiet?

All through the rest of the morning and during lunch and the afternoon, she'd waited for word of the necklace's return to reach her. She had waited for the sound of Dugan's firm steps and the level stare that accused.

It was shortly after three when Louise Spear stood in the doorway between her office and Chloe's. Louise's face was drawn with strain. "Nela, please come here for a moment."

Nela rose and walked into Louise's office. When she

stepped through the connecting door, she expected to see Dugan. Instead, she was alone with Louise.

"Close the door. Sit down."

The door into the hallway was already shut. Louise's office was paneled in gleaming oak. Bookcases filled one wall. A print of a dramatic painting by the Baranovs hung behind her desk, the magnificent colors vibrant and life affirming. Nela loved the glorious colors favored by the Russian artists. The print commanded attention. Nela wondered if, consciously or subconsciously, plain and modest Louise chose the compelling print to make herself less noticeable.

Louise stood to one side of her light oak desk. A shaft of pale winter sunlight emphasized deep lines etched at the corners of her eyes and lips. She looked fatigued and worried.

Nela sat in the plain wooden chair that faced the desk. Had Louise been deputized to fire Nela? Why hadn't the police detective talked to her first? Had the redheaded reporter informed Dugan of her after-hours visit to Haklo?

Louise's brown eyes scarcely seemed to acknowledge her presence. She was turned inward and her thoughts obviously weren't pleasant. Finally, she gazed at Nela. "Tell me about Friday night." She rubbed one thumb along the knuckles of her clenched right hand. "At Marian's apartment."

Nela described the sounds of a search and the light beneath the door and the arrival of the police.

Louise stared at Nela with wide worried eyes. "Did you see anyone when you opened the bedroom door?"

Nela knew abruptly that this was why Louise had called Nela into her office. Louise could have taken the necklace. But she could have taken the necklace many times in the last few years if she had wished. Why this fall? Did she need money? Did she resent Hollis Blair?

"Nela?" Louise appeared tense.

Nela felt suddenly that Louise was afraid of what Nela might say. "I didn't open the bedroom door until the police knocked. The thief was gone by then."

Louise's shoulders slumped. "I was hoping you might have some idea who was there. Well, I suppose if you knew anything you would have told the police."

"Yes. I would have told the police." But perhaps she'd been wiser than she knew when she'd stayed safe in the bedroom waiting until the front door slammed behind the intruder, an intruder who looked everywhere for a hidden necklace and it wasn't hidden at all. "Have the police found out anything more about the necklace?" Why had no one discussed the return of the necklace? Surely its mysterious arrival was another pointer to someone with a key. That hadn't been Nela's intent when she brought it, but maybe underlining the connection to Haklo had been a very good idea.

"Unfortunately they haven't been able to trace it. The detective said they have queries out to pawnshops." She lifted thin fingers to touch one temple. "That will be all for now, Nela."

Nela managed to nod and get up and walk into Chloe's office without revealing her shock. She settled behind Chloe's desk and stared blankly at the computer screen. The necklace was still missing. But she'd left it on Blythe's desk. Nela opened the bottom drawer, pulled out her purse. She reached for her cell, then glanced at the open door to Louise's office. She couldn't afford to be overheard when she spoke to Steve. She had to wait until she left the foundation. She dropped the cell in the purse, closed the drawer.

It was one of those days. A tractor trailer overturned on the exit ramp into Craddock. One of Craddock's leading literary lights, a much-published Oklahoma historian, died unexpectedly. A black Lab saved his family by butting against a bedroom door to awaken sleeping parents in time to gather up their five children and escape a house fire caused by a frayed extension cord on a portable heater. Every winter when the frigid days came, the *Clarion* warned readers to be wary of the dangers of frayed cords and of carbon monoxide from faulty fireplaces and wood stoves and generators. Every winter there were blazes. This one had a happy ending. Some didn't.

Steve Flynn was in and out of the office. Lunch was a Big Mac on the run. It was almost three thirty before he had time to call Katie Dugan. He punched his speakerphone.

"Hey, Steve." Of course she had caller ID.

"Bring me up to date on Haklo."

"I suppose you plan a story on the anonymous call to the *Clarion*?"

He leaned back in his swivel chair, propped his feet on the desk, balanced a laptop on his lap. "We print the news as we get it." His tone was laconic.

"I can always dream, can't I? But probably our inquiries have tipped the murderer. If there is a murderer. Which isn't clear."

"And?"

"On the record, we are pursuing inquiries into the anonymous call to the *Clarion* that claimed the death of Marian Grant was murder."

Steve typed the quote, not that he wouldn't remember. It was stock Katie-speak when she didn't intend to elaborate. "And?"

Silence.

"Come on, Katie. Surely there's movement somewhere in this story. A little bird told me there was a bad"—he drew out the vowel but Katie didn't smile—"letter that went out to members of the grants committee."

She gave a quick little spurt of irritation. He knew she was wondering where he'd picked up that piece of information. "No comment."

"Do you have a lab report on damage to the apartment stairs?"

"No comment."

She hadn't said there was no report, which meant there was a report, but she was unwilling to reveal what had been learned. "Could a skateboard—if one is found—be tested for a match?"

"No comment."

"What's the status of the search for the necklace?" That should flush the fact of its return, although he was puzzled that Katie was playing coy about the jewelry's unaccountable arrival on the desk of its owner. The anonymous tip about murder was the lead of the story he would write, but the necklace would get big play, especially since once again a key had surely been used to enter Haklo. The noose would draw tighter around Haklo employees.

"At this point in the investigation, no trace of the necklace has been found."

Steve felt like he'd been sucker punched. The blow came from nowhere. His feet swung to the floor and he sat up straight. He listened blankly to the rest of Katie's response. "Inquiries have been made and will continue to be made at pawnshops and auction houses. Although Miss Webster has so far declined to request reimbursement from insurance, the insurance company with her permission has supplied photographs and a detailed description of the jewelry. If you ask pretty please, I'll send over a jpeg."

"Yeah." It was like staring at a billboard in Czech. Nothing made sense.

"Hey, I thought you'd appreciate this puppy. Did a sexy broad just walk by your desk? I don't need a swami to tell me you've lost interest in our conversation. Ciao."

The connection ended.

He e-mailed the police department's Public Information office, requesting the jpeg. All the while, thoughts ran and nipped at each other's tails like hungry rats. . . . *She could have gone back to Haklo . . . intelligent eyes, quick on her feet . . . glossy black hair . . . promised not to lie . . . necklace gone . . . Someone took it . . . She could be telling the truth about the skateboard . . . If she didn't trust him, the smart thing was to remove the necklace . . . sure as hell must not have gotten a lot of sleep last night . . . Hurts, doesn't it, buddy? . . .*

He reached out to punch the speakerphone, slowly drew back his hand. What good would it do to call Katie Dugan? He had no proof. Yeah, he could pinpoint Nela in the doorway of Haklo after ten p.m. He had a picture of the necklace on Blythe Webster's desk. But still, it came down to his word against hers. She could swear she left with him and never returned, make it clear that he could as easily have returned for the necklace as she. Katie would believe him. Belief wasn't proof. He glanced at the clock. He had ten minutes to meet his deadline. The dog and the fire would run below the fold today. Murder trumped a feel-good story. Or was Nela's claim of a skateboard as phony as her promise not to lie? Of course, she hadn't lied yet. What would she say when he asked her about her return trip to Haklo? As for the skateboard, damned if there wasn't knowledge of one floating around Haklo. Could Nela have known about the skateboard missing from the cabin? He didn't know. As for now, he had a story to write. He typed fast, his face set in hard, angry lines. When done, he reread the piece.

An anonymous phone call to the *Clarion* Monday night claimed Haklo Foundation Chief Operating Officer Marian Grant was a murder victim. Grant died as a result of a fall down her apartment stairs early on the morning of Jan. 9.

The caller, who has not been identified, said Grant was thrown over the side of the stair rail when she stepped on a skateboard deliberately placed on the second step.

Police who investigated Grant's fall did not find a skateboard on or near the stairs. Police Detective K. T. Dugan was informed of the call by *Clarion* staff. Detective Dugan refused to comment on the investigation into the call.

The anonymous caller said Grant was killed because she had discovered the identity of the thief responsible for the robbery of a $250,000 gold and diamond necklace from the desk of Haklo Trustee Blythe Webster.

Detective Dugan said police are continuing to contact pawnshops and auction houses in hopes of tracing the jewelry. Miss Webster has offered a $100,000 reward for the arrest and conviction of the thief.

The theft of the necklace is one in a series of unexplained incidents at the foundation.

Steve ended up with a summary of the vandalism, a description of Marian's career at Haklo, and the foundation's importance to Craddock.

He finished reading, zapped the article to Mim. He stared at the phone. He didn't like being played for a fool. Besides, he'd picked up a hand to play when he hadn't called the cops last night. Now he couldn't pretend to himself that he didn't know beans about a quarter-million-dollar piece of jewelry. His options were limited. Should he call Nela? Be waiting by the VW when she got off work?

To what purpose?

Ace Busey, his plaid wool shirt emanating waves of old

cigarette smoke, settled one hip on the edge of Steve's desk. "Somebody's ticked you off big time. Must be a gal. Hasn't Papa told you that dames are deadly?"

Steve looked up into Ace's saggy, streetwise face. "Just concentrating."

Ace raised a shaggy eyebrow. "You look like a prune on a hot day. Lighten up. No dame is worth it."

Steve forced a humorless smile. "That's a given."

Ace slouched to his feet. "Got to catch a smoke." As he walked away, he said over his shoulder, "Don't say Papa didn't warn you."

Nela stepped into Louise's office with grant application folders. "I've attached one-page summaries to each application." Dry words for dreams and hopes and visions boiled down to a page. She wished that everything was different, that she could be excited about the foundation's outreach, make a difference for kids at summer camps, for libraries with budgets cut to the bone, for research to help drought-stricken farmers.

Louise looked up. Her thoughts seemed to come from a far distance. "Oh, yes." She gestured at her in-box. "I'll take care of them tomorrow."

Nela placed the folders in the lower receptacle. "Is there anything else I can do?"

Louise slowly shook her head. The movement seemed to take great effort.

Nela understood the burden of grief. "I'm sorry about Miss Grant. She must have been a wonderful person."

"Friday afternoon when I went in her office, I could tell she was upset. I asked if something was wrong. There was an odd look in her eyes. She said"—Louise's face crinkled in memory—" 'There's nothing wrong that can't be fixed.

And I intend to fix it.' Of course, Marian believed she could handle anything." Louise massaged one temple. "Just a few days before she died, she told me she should have done something in St. Louis, that she'd known from the start it was a mistake to bring Hollis here. I knew what she meant. I was there, too. Hollis has too much charm. I know what happens when he walks into a room. Some women are more vulnerable than others." She shook her head. "And that girl chasing after him." Her eyes were huge with distress. "If someone put a skateboard on Marian's stairs and Abby's brother's skateboard is missing, there has to be a connection. Oh, I don't know what to think. I may be all wrong."

Nela looked at her sharply. "Do you have an idea who may have taken the skateboard?"

Louise drew herself up. Her voice was stiff. "I don't know anything about the skateboard." There was a ring of truth in her voice. But her eyes were still dark with worry. "It's just that I keep thinking about Marian. I can't bear to think what may have happened."

Nela knew, better than most, that outsiders couldn't lessen heartbreak. Nothing Nela did would ease Louise's sadness about Marian Grant or restore Haklo to happier days. But she knew, too, that kindness helps. "I'm sorry you're upset."

Louise's face softened. "You're a nice girl, Nela. Just like your sister. None of this has anything to do with you—"

Nela wished with all her heart that Louise was right.

"—and I'm sorry if I've troubled you. Don't worry. I know I'm tired. Things are always worse when you're tired." She glanced at the clock. "You can go home now. Home . . ." For an instant, she pressed her lips together. "You're a long way from home. I don't think I could bear to go to Marian's apartment. Especially after someone coming inside Friday night." Once again lines of worry framed her eyes and lips.

"Thank you for staying there. I know Jugs. He must miss Marian terribly. Go home early and pet Jugs for me. For Marian. Tell him he's a good cat." Louise turned away to look toward the windows.

By the time Nela reached the connecting doorway, Louise appeared lost in her thoughts, her thin face drawn and weary. In Chloe's office, Nela glanced at her watch. Only a few minutes after four. She shrugged into her coat. In the hallway, she walked fast, fumbling in her purse for her cell phone. Steve had to know about the necklace. As soon as she was safely alone in the VW, she'd call him.

S teve glanced at caller ID. He let the phone ring three times before he picked up the hand unit. "Flynn."

"Steve"—the connection was scratchy, obviously a call from a cell—"the necklace wasn't found."

"Yeah." The word was clipped.

She talked fast. "Someone took the necklace from Blythe's desk. What can we do?"

"Someone took it?" His tone was taunting.

There was silence. Finally, she spoke. "What do you mean?"

"Two people knew the necklace was there. You. Me. I didn't take it. Do the math."

"You think—" She broke off. "I see." A pause. "That's a funny thing." Her tone was bleak. "It never occurred to me to think you went back and got the necklace."

The connection ended.

"Nela . . ." He spoke to emptiness.

N ela knew what it was to be alone, to feel separated from the world. There had been a moment with Steve—more than one—when warmth seemed near again. That brief connection was broken. There was no point in wasting time thinking about a stocky man with red hair. He'd been a stranger. He was a stranger again with no reason to share what he knew about people he knew.

It was up to her now to find the devious mind behind the troubles at Haklo and she might have very little time to act. She needed the perspective of someone who knew the staff. Louise not only might wonder if Nela came back inside, but, picturing faces in her mind, Nela had no idea which staff member to contact. What would she say? But she had to do something. She opened the car door, taking care not to let the wind butt the edge against the glossy blue Thunderbird with the personalized license plate: ROBBIE. The car was as slick as the PR director. Definitely he wouldn't be the right person to ask who might have a motive to cause trouble for Haklo. Although he kept his comments within bounds, his dislike of Hollis Blair was obvious. Vandalism might have appealed to Robbie as a way of attacking Hollis.

She'd liked Erik Judd. She had sensed beneath his drama that particular empathy that often belongs to creative people.

Nela stared at the Thunderbird, slowly shut the VW door. She used her iPhone, found an address and directions.

It was a five-minute drive to a quiet neighborhood with older homes, some of them brick duplexes, others 1950s vintage ranch-style houses. A green Porsche sat in the drive of the third house on the left, a one-story rambling brick house with bay windows. The house appeared well kept, no fading paint or cracks in the drive. The window glass glistened.

Nela walked swiftly to the front porch, lifted a shiny brass knocker.

The door opened almost at once. Erik Judd stared out at her, his face anxious. "Has something happened to Robbie?"

Obviously he knew who she was, that she had taken Chloe's place, and her unexpected arrival, certainly something beyond the norm, raised fear that something was wrong.

"He's fine." Nela understood the shock of unexpected arrivals. She still dreamed about the moment that Bill's brother walked in. "The police believe Marian Grant was murdered."

Erik's eyebrows folded into a frown. "Robbie called me. But"—his gaze was suspicious—"what does that have to do with you? Why are you here?"

"Everyone at the foundation is a suspect." She looked at him steadily. Sometimes truth wins the day. If he shut the door in her face, so be it. But he might not. She might have only a little time left to do her best for Chloe. He would do what he could to protect Robbie. "That's why I came. You and I both have someone we love who may be at risk from the police. The police are suspicious of Chloe because she's new to Haklo this fall. But Robbie may have publicly taken too much satisfaction from Hollis Blair's difficulties because of the vandalism."

Erik raised a silver eyebrow. "From a bare acquaintance on Saturday, you seem to have learned a great deal about me and Robbie. But I fail to see why you are standing on our front porch."

"I'm an investigative reporter." She might not have a job right now, but that made no difference. She knew how to ask and probe and seek for a story. Now she would use her skills to save herself and Chloe.

Erik's pale blue eyes studied her. "Why do you want to talk to me?"

"You know everyone at Haklo." She saw a flicker of understanding in his watchful gaze. "I want you to tell me who could have committed the vandalism at Haklo and who would kill to avoid exposure as a vandal and a thief."

He smoothed one curling swoop of his mustache. "Aren't you a bit fearful of a private meeting with the 'disgruntled former director'?" His tone put the description in quote marks.

"Oh"—her tone was careless—"Steve Flynn knows where I am."

He was suddenly amused. "Quick thinking, my dear. But I don't believe that. However"—he held the door wide, made a sweeping bow—"enter my parlor if you desire."

She hesitated for only a moment, then stepped inside.

He led the way into a comfortable, manly den with leather furniture, a wide-screen TV, and Indian blankets hung on the paneled walls.

She skirted an easel with a half-finished watercolor of purple and gold wildflowers in a meadow, chose a cane chair.

Erik sat opposite in a red leather chair that was a dramatic setting for his curling white hair, black silk shirt, and white wide-cuffed wool trousers and black half boots. He listened, nodding occasionally as she marshaled her facts.

When she was done, he nodded approval. "Quite concise and complete. I'm aware of all the incidents. I should make it clear that I am not a recluse brooding over ill treatment. It was"—he paused, seeking the right word—"a shock when Blythe dismissed me, especially for a callow youth with no experience, except perhaps"—his mouth twisted in a wry smile—"in the useful art of charming ladies. I always assumed outstanding leadership was sufficient. I was wrong. However"—and now he sounded quite comfortable—"I have enjoyed thoroughly a return to the life of a writer. In fact, if you'd looked in the Haklo library a half hour ago, you would have found me there. I often spend the afternoon at Haklo with my research on the foundation. Robbie has remained angry even though I've assured him I am content. Now"—he leaned forward—"I want to be clear. Neither Robbie nor I have ever done anything that would be detrimental to Haklo. I devoted the best years of my life to making Haklo one of the finest charitable foundations in the country. I am sickened by the events that have occurred this fall. As for Robbie, I'm afraid he has enjoyed watching Hollis squirm, but Robbie knows that I would utterly oppose any kind of attack on Haklo. Haklo is bigger than Hollis or Blythe or me or Robbie."

"Someone there, someone with a key, must be behind the vandalism and the theft." Nela held his gaze. "If you care about Haklo, help me figure out who is guilty."

Erik frowned. One hand touched the crystal eagle that hung from a leather necklace. "From what you've told me, it does seem likely that the vandal is a staff member." His eyes narrowed. "Not Louise. Not Rosalind. I can't speak to the new director or his girlfriend or your sister." A stop. "Harris Webster used to worry about his daughters. Blythe has always been obsessive. Once she was obsessed with a young man who worked for Harris. Now she's obsessed with Haklo but the vandalism punishes Haklo. Grace is impulsive, a wild thing. She's furious that her father made Blythe the sole trustee. Francis is ruthless. Whatever is important to him is all that matters. Cole used to be a major force at Haklo, Webster's good friend. Now he's yesterday. I think it's broken his heart. Peter is fighting Blythe's ideas of outsourcing. He has a wife who likes money. But that tweedy, casual appearance is misleading. He's climbed Kilimanjaro."

As she drove away, Nela carried with her two impressions. Erik trusted Robbie, truly believed Robbie would never do anything to jeopardize the foundation that Erik loved. No doubt he would describe her visit and emphasize how he had made it clear that both he and Robbie had nothing to do with the attacks on Haklo. But if Robbie had been tempted to cause just enough trouble to harm the new director, exposure meant more than criminal action, it meant breaking the heart of the man he loved. Would Robbie be willing to kill to keep the vandalism from Erik?

—12—

"Have to eat, right?" Nela tried to sound upbeat. She spooned chicken-flavored food into a freshly washed cat bowl.

Jugs looked up. *". . . crying inside . . ."*

Nela put down the bowl. She'd pet Jugs after he ate, tell him Louise said he was a good cat. The words wouldn't matter. The tone would give him comfort. She knew she should eat as well, but her throat was tight and she wasn't hungry. She turned away, walked into the living room, dropped into the easy chair. How long would it take for the police to arrive? By this time, Steve Flynn would have contacted Dugan, showed her the photos in his iPhone.

Nela knew she had few options. Whatever she did, she wasn't going to lie. She would decline to comment and that would probably put her in jail. She glanced at her watch. Dugan was taking her own sweet time in coming. Would it do Nela any good to share Erik Judd's views? Or would Dugan have closed her mind to everyone but Chloe and Nela?

* * *

The hospital bed still looked odd in his parents' spacious
bedroom. His dad was dozing. The home health aide
looked at him eagerly. When Steve came for a visit in the
evenings, she could slip out for a while, a walk in good
weather, now a few minutes in her room, catching up on a
favorite TV show. His dad loathed TV, said if he ever got
bored enough to watch TV, he'd hold a funeral service for his
brain.

Steve stood beside the bed. Sometimes it seemed they
took a little step forward, then two steps back.

His father's eyelids fluttered open. His eyes were as blue
as Steve's. His hair, too, had once been red, but was now
white. His broad face sagged a little on one side, a visible
reminder of the stroke that felled him.

"Hey, Dad." Steve spoke in a normal tone. His dad
despised sickroom whispers. Though his speech was still
somewhat garbled, he'd made it clear to a succession of
helpers. ". . . Still hear . . . Up speak . . ."

Those bright blue eyes were as perceptive as always,
reflecting a quick and facile mind trapped in an uncoopera-
tive body. ". . . 'Rubble . . ."

Yeah, there was trouble. Big-time trouble. Chances were
he'd been a sap over a woman. One more time. But this time,
he wanted to call her. He wanted to believe her. He admired
the way her chin jutted when she faced opposition. He
wanted to plumb the intelligence behind her gaze. He
wanted to know about her. Did she like to go camping? Had
she ever trout fished? He knew some things. She had guts.
She loved words. Her face in repose suggested she knew
sadness. A guy named Bill had loved her. But who else could
have taken the damn necklace? Steve gave a shrug, tried to
appear casual. "Hard day. Lots of stuff happening."

Maybe those blue eyes saw more because they'd had a

glimpse of eternity. Maybe Daniel Flynn knew better than to waste time with niceties. His gaze was sharp, demanding. ". . . You . . ."

Steve pressed his lips together, knew his face was a road map of misery.

His dad lifted his head. ". . . heart . . . listen . . . promise . . ."

Listen to your heart. Maybe it wasn't a smart motto. Maybe he didn't give a damn about being smart. Steve reached out, touched a still muscular shoulder. "I will, Dad. As soon as I think some things through."

Jugs lay at the end of the table in his lion pose, watching as she ate.

It wasn't much of a dinner. A bowl of tomato soup and some dry crackers from a box long past its fresh date. Chloe hadn't been in the apartment long enough to leave a half-empty box of crackers. Nela was eating saltines that had been purchased by Marian Grant. Odd. But Marian wouldn't begrudge crackers to someone taking care of Jugs. Nela looked into watching green eyes and felt certain of that. She wasn't certain of anything else. "Jugs, I don't know what to do."

". . . She was worried . . ."

"So am I, buddy." Oh hell yes, she was worried. She ate and listened for a knock at the door, for the questions she dared not answer. She cleaned up the kitchen in only a moment. In the living room, she dropped into the comfortable overstuffed chair and looked across the silent room at the sofa. Last night he'd sat there and given her a chance. When he'd walked into the main hall of Haklo late Monday morning, wiry red hair, broad open face, bright blue eyes, stocky and muscular, she'd instinctively started to smile. It wasn't until he looked at her late last night and gravely listened to her halting explanations that she'd realized he was a man with a hard edge, a man who had been hurt and was afraid to trust.

He'd trusted her. For a little while. She fought away sudden sharp sadness. What difference did it make? She scarcely knew him. Abruptly, she came to her feet, hurried into the living room. She picked up Bill's picture. She looked at his laughing face, young and strong, alive and loving her. Carrying the picture, she sank onto the sofa. The red, white, and blue ribbon she'd wound through the latticed wood of the frame brought no comfort.

Jugs jumped up beside her, pressed against her thigh.

She massaged behind big ears. "It's up to me, Jugs." She looked again at Bill's photograph and the familiar emptiness echoed inside. Bill wasn't here. Bill wasn't anywhere.

Jugs lifted his head, turned to stare at the front door. His ears flicked forward.

A sharp knock rattled the door.

Nela slowly came to her feet. She'd known this moment was coming. She walked to the door, turned on the porch light, twisted the knob. As cold air eddied around her, she stared, her lips parted.

Once again the wind stirred his short red hair. Once again he wore no coat. Tonight he carried a folder.

She looked past him.

"Just me. Maybe you'll tell me to take a hike. I thought it over. I didn't ask you. That wasn't fair." Now his blue eyes held hers. "Did you go back last night?"

"No."

The look between them was more than a question and answer.

His face softened. "Sorry. Sometimes now"—the words came slowly—"I expect bad outcomes. I shouldn't have jumped to a stupid conclusion. "

"It wasn't stupid. You don't know me. I found the necklace in Marian's purse, but I can never prove that it was there. I tried to see it safely back to Blythe. I feel like I've done every-thing I can do. But thank you for coming. It was very kind." She started to close the door.

He held up the folder. "Can I come in? I've got some stuff that may help."

Nela hesitated. "You've already done more for me than you should." He hadn't called the police when he found her coming out of Haklo. She was sure they'd broken some laws leaving the necklace on Blythe's desk, but he didn't deserve to be in trouble because of her. "I'm afraid it's dangerous to hang around with me."

"That's a chance I'll take."

Nela wanted to let him inside. She wanted him to leave. She didn't know what she wanted, but she was acutely aware of his nearness. He was alive and strong and vital. Bill—

"I don't know." She knew she must sound like a fool. "I'm sorry. I don't want to have anything else to do with what's happened at Haklo. I'm going to be here for Chloe until she returns. But she and I have nothing to do with the problems there. Let's leave it at that." She closed the door.

Now she had lied to him. She'd promised him she wouldn't lie and now she had. She couldn't walk away from the turmoil at the foundation. She was going to find out more, much more, seek the truth. For her and for Chloe.

But she didn't have to involve Steve Flynn.

She leaned against the cold wooden panel and listened to the sound of diminishing steps.

S lanting beams from passing headlights created a silhou-ette of leafless limbs on the bedroom ceiling, jumbled dark splotches that made no sense, formed no coherent pat-tern. Steve always sought a pattern. This time he was out of luck. His thoughts shifted from her rebuff to his damn fool determination to help someone who didn't want help, swung from certainty to uncertainty. Was she honest? Did he care? People did what they thought they had to do. She'd help her sister at all costs. Was that why she sent him away? Or was she running from him because she, too, felt the attraction between them when they stood close together? She carried sadness with her. He thought he knew why. Someday he would ask her about the dark-haired guy standing on a beach and the red, white, and blue ribbon that wreathed the brown wooden frame. Someday. Not now.

His mouth twisted in a wry grin. Big talk on his part. Her good night had been a pretty definite good-bye. One thing was for sure. He'd wanted for months to be free of memories of Gail. Maybe he should have remembered to be careful what he wished for. Was the god of hilarity laughing aloud? Gail was fading. Her name no longer conjured images that excited desire or bitterness. Instead, he saw Nela's intelligent, vulnerable face with lips that he wanted to kiss.

The grin slipped away. She was in trouble. She—and her sister—would be safe only if he discovered the truth behind the vandalism and the theft of the necklace. He'd made a start last evening on figuring out who could have taken the necklace from Blythe Webster's desk. Tomorrow he'd narrow the field. He might not have a white horse to ride to Nela's rescue, but he knew Craddock maybe even better than Katie Dugan.

Though Nela was weary to the bone, sleep was elusive. She kept hearing the sound of Steve's footsteps fading into silence. She pushed away thoughts of Steve. She heard Bill's voice . . . *If I don't come back* . . . Bill had wanted to tell her that if he died, she must live. She had placed her fingers on his lips, warm living lips, to stop the words she didn't want to hear. She had read the message in Bill's eyes just as tonight she'd looked into blue eyes and seen another message: *I want to know you. Give me a chance.*

She turned restlessly, tried to get comfortable. She knew what Bill had wanted for her. But not yet. Not while emptiness filled her heart.

She'd sent Steve away. She wanted him to be safe. As a reporter, he was jeopardizing his job to keep information about a crime from the police. She had involved him in a crime when he learned that she'd returned the necklace to Haklo. Detective K. T. Dugan could charge him with obstruction of justice and possibly conspiracy in regard to transportation of stolen property. Right now there was no reason Dugan should ever learn that Steve had been at Haklo last night. Nela would never tell anyone.

She began to sink into the oblivion of exhausted sleep. Faintly, Nela heard a *click-click-click* on the bedroom door. Her eyelids fluttered open as she turned her head on the pillow. Jugs . . . wanted in . . . good cat . . . lonely . . . Groggily she rolled on an elbow, sat up. *Click-click-click.* She came to her feet, crossed the cold hardwood floor. She'd learned a lesson Friday night. The door would always be locked while she slept. She turned the knob, held the panel open. A dark shape flowed past. When she settled again on the bed, Jugs snuggled beside her, soft and warm. A faint purr signaled his happiness.

— 13 —

Steve took another bite of a glazed doughnut, washed away the sweetness with strong coffee. Not much of a breakfast, but enough. He wrote fast, his printing big and legible on a legal pad. He could have made notes on his laptop. For quick jottings, he still liked real paper. He had been in kindergarten when the *Clarion* installed computers. He remembered thick yellow copy and the clack of Remingtons and an ever-present smoky haze. Now the newsroom was silent, the walls had long ago been repainted to remove years of nicotine scum, and the copy spike on Mim Barlow's desk was a memento. He was finishing his third cup of coffee when Mim's brisk steps sounded in the newsroom.

She stopped beside his desk. "Something big?" She sounded hopeful.

"Background."

Her glance was sharp. "Let me know if I should hold space."

"Not today."

"Right. Do a follow-up on the missing necklace."

"Already sent it over."

"If everyone was as efficient . . ." She turned toward her desk.

Steve put the legal pad to one side of the screen, ready now for a summation that he could print out. He wanted to have a copy for Nela. Stubby fingers flew over the keys.

HAKLO TIMETABLE

1. *September 19.* Car set afire in employee parking lot. 1995 Camaro destroyed. Unsolved. No suspects. Anne Nesbitt, 23, owner of car, relocated to Norman, now works at the Sam Noble Museum of Natural History. No record of troubled relationships in her personal life. Police investigation concluded the fire was randomly set and not directed at Nesbitt personally.

2. *November 15.* Nine Chickasaw baskets found hacked to pieces in exhibit room.

3. *December 5.* Sprinklers activated in Robbie Powell's office.

4. *December 16.* Courtyard fountain turned on, frozen pipes.

5. *January 5.* Necklace missing from desk of Blythe Webster.

6. *January 9.* Marian Grant died from a fall down garage apartment stairs.

7. *January 14.* Nela Farley called 911 to report intruder in Marian Grant's apartment.

8. *January 14.* Nela Farley found expensive necklace in Marian Grant's purse.

9. *January 16.* According to Nela, members of Haklo grants committee received obscene material on Haklo Director Hollis Blair's letterhead.

10. *January 16.* Ditto, letter traced to file in computer of Assistant Curator Abby Andrews. Andrews denied creating file.

11. *January 16.* Search of Marian Grant's office discovered by Nela Farley. Office searched sometime after 5 p.m. Friday and before late Monday morning.

12. *January 16.* Nela Farley learned about necklace stolen from Blythe Webster and realized the necklace was in Marian Grant's purse.

13. *January 16.* Nela Farley entered Haklo after hours and placed necklace on Blythe Webster's desk.

14. *January 16.* Unidentified caller to *Clarion* claimed Marian Grant was murdered, her fall caused by a skateboard placed deliberately on the second step.

15. *January 17.* Detective Dugan informed Haklo staff of the anonymous message. Theft (or claimed theft) of skateboard from the porch of Abby's cabin revealed.

16. *January 17.* Necklace once again missing.

Steve didn't need a reminder of the incidents. He'd written too many stories to forget a single one. Instead, he focused on dates. The car was set afire in September. After a lapse of two months, several acts of vandalism occurred. Was the car fire an anomaly, independent of the other incidents? Maybe the car fire gave someone an idea.

The fire caused no harm to the foundation. The later vandalism was clearly intended to cause problems for Haklo.

The fire could have been set by anyone. The destruction of the Indian baskets, water damage in Robbie's office, theft of Blythe's necklace, and use of Blair's letterhead could have been done only by someone familiar with the foundation.

The vandalism could have had any of several objectives: To harass either Haklo or its trustee, Blythe Webster, to mar the stewardship of the new director, to make the theft of the necklace appear simply to be another in a series of unlawful acts, or as an act of revenge by a disgruntled current or former employee.

Katie Dugan settled on the fact that no vandals had ever struck at Haklo until this fall. Katie believed newcomer Chloe Farley committed the vandalism but that her goal was to take the necklace. The lapse of time between the car fire and the destruction of the Indian baskets supported Katie's theory. Chloe likely would not have known until she'd worked at Haklo for several weeks that Blythe Webster kept a quarter-million-dollar necklace lying in a desk drawer in her unlocked office.

However, Chloe was not the only new employee at Haklo since summer. He thumbed through notes. Hollis Blair arrived August first. Abby Andrews was hired August fifteenth.

Steve stared at the list. Why was there a two-month lag between the car fire and the hacked baskets? Maybe when he knew the answer to that, he'd know the truth behind vandalism, theft, and murder.

He clicked several times on his computer. The burned car had been front-page news. Who had handled that investigation?

Nela turned into the main Haklo drive. She was alert as she passed the main building and turned left to drive to the employee lot, but she didn't see any police cars. Nela parked again between the Thunderbird and the Dodge. Louise's car was also in the lot. Nela looked in every direction as she walked to the staff entrance. When she stepped inside and the door sighed shut behind her, she scanned the hallway. No trace of police. It seemed strange to be wary of the police. Her uncle Bob had been a sergeant in the LAPD, a big, ebullient, loud man. Her aunt always worried. A cop never knew when a stopped car might harbor danger, yet every day cops walked toward cars, some with tinted windows. They carried a gun in a holster, but they approached empty-handed, keeping streets safe for ordinary people.

Lights spilled from Louise's open door. In Chloe's office, Nela dropped her purse into a desk drawer. Despite the lack of a police presence, she continued to feel apprehensive. What was Detective Dugan doing now? Driving to Haklo to interrogate Nela again? But the detective had no reason to inquire into Nela's activities Monday night. Surely she was focused on a search for the missing skateboard.

Nela hung Chloe's large jacket on the coatrack, checked the clock. She stepped to the open door between the offices.

Louise's office was brightly lit. She looked up. "Good morning, Nela." Although her face was wan, she made an effort to smile. "That's a pretty skirt."

"Thank you, Louise." Nela's wardrobe was limited by what she'd managed to put in one suitcase. The long swirling skirt was silk with a pattern of blue and black circles. She added a crisp white blouse and black pumps. It was one of her best outfits, one she'd often worn when working as a reporter. If she saw Steve . . . But she wouldn't see him. She'd turned him away, listened to the fading sound of his footsteps. The thought brought a quick stab of unhappiness. She wanted to see him. She didn't want to see him.

". . . put some more application folders on your desk. After you finish the summaries and deliver the morning mail, please pick up the proofs of a new scholarship

brochure from Peter." She looked a little defiant. "He sent
me the brochure online but I still like to look at paper." She
gave a decided nod and turned back toward her computer.

Nela settled at Chloe's computer. It was important for
her to act as if Haklo's troubles didn't affect her personally.
As she read and typed, willing herself not to think of Steve,
she listened, alert and wary, for the brisk sound of official
steps in the hallway. She felt like a fish in a barrel, easy
prey. As soon as possible, she had to figure a way to discover
the truth behind the tangled relationships at Haklo, what
mattered and what didn't matter, who had stolen a necklace
and committed murder to prevent exposure.

She'd started her investigation with Erik Judd. He'd been
willing to talk to her, but would any of the rest of the staff
be willing to respond?

Her fingers hung in the air above the keyboard.

Maybe there was a way to take advantage of her reporter
background. She glanced up at the clock. In a few minutes,
she was scheduled to deliver the mail to Haklo staff, starting, of course, with Blythe Webster. Monday morning, as
soon as Blythe heard from members of the grants committee about the obscene letters with the Haklo director's letterhead, she had set in motion a thorough search. She hadn't
been passive, hadn't waited for anyone else to take charge.
Tuesday the police dropped the bombshell of the anonymous
call claiming Marian Grant's death was instead murder.
Blythe made it clear at that meeting that all staff members
were to cooperate with the authorities. Yes, the police were
investigating, but Blythe might see a role for Haklo itself to
seek truth. And maybe Nela could help.

S teve dropped into the straight chair next to Mokie Morrison's desk. "Glad I caught you." Most of the other desks
in the detectives' room were unoccupied.

Mokie was cheerful. "Katie believes in old-fashioned shoe leather. At least she didn't send me out to check with the sanitation guys to see if anybody noticed a skateboard disappearing into the jaws of death last week. In case you're wondering, the jaws of death are those big choppers that grind up garbage when the guys throw stuff in. The choppers can turn metal pylons into mincemeat, damn near. The garbage guys need to watch their elbows and hands. That's just one hazard. Do you know anybody who works harder than garbage guys? Hang on and freeze their butts in winter. Hang on and bake in summer. And, man, the smell. And they're supposed to check out the trash before it splinters? I don't think so. Anyway, Katie's frustrated. Plus too many places in this case—the apartment behind the Webster mansion and the assistant curator's cottage on the Haklo grounds—don't have any convenient nosy parker neighbors. So I got no complaints about my assignment, but Marian Grant's banker and lawyer aren't ready to chummy up with the cops. Lots of mutters about court orders, sanctity of client information. Me, I think the whole idea that Marian Grant was murdered is just another poke by the Haklo Vandal, one more way to make things awkward for the T. It's kind of a blot on Haklo's shiny bright rep if somebody bumped off the COO. The hell of it is, nobody can prove murder or accident, but once the story's out there, some people will believe in murder and think there's a big cover-up."

Steve was casual. "Maybe, but it's funny that the tip was specific, a skateboard on the second step, and then it turns out one of the Haklo people is missing a skateboard. That gives the story some legs."

Mokie leaned back in his chair. "Nah. The Haklo Vandal used a skateboard in that call you got because the Vandal spotted a skateboard on the cabin porch and then, to muddy things up even more, filched the skateboard."

"The skateboard disappeared before the call was made."

"So? Can't say the Haklo Vandal doesn't plan ahead. Anyway, what can I do for you." Mokie smothered a yawn. "Got to be more interesting than listening to lawyers and bankers talk in great big circles."

Steve pulled some folded copy paper out of his pocket. "You covered the Camaro fire out at Haklo. I know it's been a while, but I'd like to run through what you remember."

"Oh, man." Mokie's eyes gleamed and he sat up straight. "Hot stuff."

"The fire?" Weren't fires always hot?

Mokie's eyes squinted in remembrance. "Nah. The babe. Stacked." He moved his hands in a modified figure eight. "Boobs with a life of their own. Hips . . ." He sighed. "Inquiring officer couldn't touch but he could dream. At least I got to sit in the back of the patrol car with her. Inches away." He wriggled his nose. "Gardenia perfume. Like a summer night in the bushes with a babe."

Steve shook his head. "If you can get past primal appeal, tell me about the fire."

Mokie grinned. "Man, you got to remember, first things first. Wow. Drop-dead gorgeous. As for the fire"—his tone was suddenly matter-of-fact—"let me take a look." He swung around to his computer, clicked a couple of times. "Yeah. Here it is. Call came in at three fifteen, car on fire in Haklo staff lot. Arrived at three twenty-two. Bystanders wringing hands. Fire truck arrived at three twenty-four. Flames shooting from Camaro windows. Fire out by three thirty-eight." Mokie's nose wrinkled. "Pretty bad stink. Plastic seats melted by heat, interior destroyed, car turned out to be totaled. A gardener called in the alarm, tried to douse the blaze with a watering hose. The sirens brought people outside and somebody alerted the Camaro owner, who came running outside. One Anne Nesbitt." A deep breath. "Man, I wish I'd been there to see her run. Daffodil yellow cotton top, molded, tight cream skirt. Very short."

"The fire," Steve reminded gently.

"Somebody splashed the interior with gasoline, stood back, and lobbed a wad of burning rags." He raised a crooked black brow. "That was pretty clever. The arsonist was smart enough to know there could be a flash explosion so the perp used a kid's bow and arrow. The bow was in a plastic trash barrel at the edge of the parking lot. No finger-prints. A piece of a plastic shaft, all that didn't melt, was found inside the car. Arson investigators can figure out a lot from residue. Anyway, that's the theory." He raised a crooked black brow. "I always figured it was some dame who was jealous of the victim. A bow and arrow sounds girlie."

"Did you trace it?"

Mokie raised both eyebrows. "Like we can trace the sale of a Walmart toy. You know how many Walmarts there are in a fifty-mile radius? You can bet the perp didn't get the bow and arrow in Craddock. No luck there. Actually, no luck any-where. I dug hard and didn't find a whiff of anybody who had a grudge against the babe."

"How about hard feelings on the staff?"

"Why? Because she's gorgeous?" A slight frown tugged at his brows. "Have to admit there didn't seem to be any loi-terers out there that afternoon. The gardeners didn't see any-body walking around. One guy claimed nobody came in by the service road. The other access was to park in front and either come through the main door or walk down the east road. The east road was closed off for some repair work that afternoon. The crew didn't see anybody. I asked her every which way I knew and she couldn't tell me anybody that was mad at her. I checked out which staff members were there that afternoon. You want the list?"

Steve nodded.

Mokie clicked twice. "Easier to say who wasn't there. Hollis Blair was in Kansas City at a meeting. Everybody else was on site. You can't say I didn't give it my all." His mouth slid into a suggestive smile. "I talked to her a half-dozen times. Finally"—a regretful sigh—"I had to give up. There was no rhyme, no reason." He pulled his cell phone from his pocket, slid his thumb several times over the small screen. "Take a gander."

Steve looked at the image. Mokie hadn't exaggerated. Anne Nesbitt was a babe, shining thick golden hair, delicate intriguing classic features, and, not to be missed by any male between ten and ninety, a voluptuous body.

Nela was midway through the stack of folders when Chloe's phone buzzed. "Nela Far—"

"Come to my office at once." Blythe Webster's voice was sharp with a tense undertone. The connection ended.

Nela took a steadying breath as she replaced the receiver. Obviously, Detective Dugan had shared her suspicions of Chloe and Nela with Blythe. Was Blythe going to fire Chloe and her substitute on the spot? Nela walked up the hallway with her shoulders squared.

She stepped through the open door to Blythe's office. Each time she'd been in this elegant office, there had been a background of tension. The first time she'd overheard the worried exchange between Blythe and Hollis occasioned by the arrival of obscene letters on Haklo stationery. The second time she had slipped inside with the stolen necklace, eager to leave the jewelry behind and escape. The third time Steve Flynn marched her inside, but the glitter of gold and diamonds had persuaded him that Nela—and Chloe—were innocent of wrongdoing.

Now the office was once again a backdrop to drama.

Blythe Webster stood rigid next to her desk. She wore her luxuriant dark mink coat and held a sheet of paper in one hand. On the desktop lay a white envelope that had been opened. "Shut the door. Where did this letter come from?"

Nela stared at the trustee's haggard face and realized in a welling of relief that Blythe had not called Nela into the office to accuse her or to fire her.

"The letter, where did it come from?" Blythe's voice wobbled. "Answer me."

"I didn't bring the letter. I haven't made deliveries yet this morning. I was summarizing—" She broke off. Blythe didn't care about Nela's work. She cared only about how the envelope had reached her desk.

In a jerky movement, Blythe reached toward the envelope, stopped inches away. She stared for a moment, pulled open the center drawer, picked up a pen, used the end to tip the envelope address side up. "There's no stamp. If the letter didn't come through the mail"—Blythe's words were reluctant—"someone must have put it on my desk." Her lips compressed, she turned and picked up the telephone receiver. "Rosalind, have there been any visitors in the building this morning?" She listened. "No visitors?" Her expression was grim when she replaced the receiver.

She looked at Nela. "Go to your office. Remain there. Do not discuss the letter with anyone."

S teve Flynn set a full mug of coffee on his desk. Arson of the Haklo employee's car seemed more and more like an outlier to the subsequent vandalism. His mouth twisted in an almost-smile. Mokie might be an old dog, but he hadn't forgotten the hunt. Maybe his instinct was right, some woman had set sexy Anne Nesbitt's car on fire in a jealous rage.

Steve laid out his notes on his desk, scanned them. Mokie had been thorough.

*. . . boyfriend in Norman, doctoral student. No hanky-
panky there. Known each other since college, never
dated anyone else. Nesbitt had no known enemies . . .
Acquaintances insist Nesbitt was on good terms with
everyone. . . . Gardeners working on west side of
grounds claim no strange cars in or out within half an
hour either side of fire . . . East-entrance road under
repair that day, closed, no cars entered from that direction . . . Perp could have parked somewhere else,
walked on foot, but no strangers noted . . .*

Maybe no stranger did arrive that afternoon. Maybe the
perp was already present, a member of the Haklo staff, the
crime carefully planned, the bow and arrow, gas tin, and wad
of cloth hidden near the employee lot. Yeah, there was an odd
lag in time between the fire and the destruction of the Indian
baskets, but he'd try to reconcile that puzzle later. For now . . .
He pulled out a fresh legal pad, picked up his pen.

KNOWN TO HAVE KEY TO HAKLO

Blythe Webster, Haklo trustee; Grace Webster, honorary
trustee; Hollis Blair, director; Louise Spear, executive
secretary; Cole Hamilton, advisory vice president; Francis Garth, business development research fellow; Robbie
Powell, director of public relations; Peter Owens, director of publications; Abby Andrews, assistant curator;
Chloe Farley (and thereby Nela Farley), administrative
assistant; Rosalind McNeill, receptionist; Kay Hoover,
chef; Erik Judd, former director.

He'd known Rosalind since kindergarten. Some people
could be badasses. Some couldn't. Rosalind couldn't. He
drew a line through her name. Kay Hoover was the grandmother of his best buddy in high school. She made pralines

to die for. Mama Kay thought about food. And family. And food. And family. He marked out her name. Two more quick strokes went through Chloe and Nela's names. He couldn't vouch for Chloe, but he believed Nela. If she was innocent, Chloe was innocent.

Now for a closer look at those with easy access to Haklo.

I n the chair behind Chloe's desk, Nela had a good view of the portion of hall revealed by the open door. She waited and watched. The sound she had expected was not long in coming. Not more than ten minutes later, brisk steps clipped in the hallway.

Nela had only a brief glimpse, but the glimpse was telling. Detective Dugan strode purposefully past, accompanied by a somber Blythe Webster. Dugan was in all black today, turtleneck, skirt, and boots. The cheerful color of Blythe's crimson suit looked at odds with her resolute expression, a woman engaged in an unwanted task. Two uniformed officers followed, balding, moonfaced Sergeant Fisher with his ever-ready electronic tablet and a chunky woman officer in her late twenties.

Nela eased from the chair and moved to the open door. She didn't step into the hall. Instead, unseen, she listened.

"The light is on, but the office is empty." Dugan had a clear, carrying voice.

The squeak of a chair pushed back. Rapid steps sounded. Louise Spear hurried past Chloe's doorway, didn't even glance toward Nela. "What's wrong?" Her voice was anxious, held definite foreboding.

"Where is Miss Andrews?" Dugan sounded pleasant, but firm.

"Usually at this time she's upstairs in the artifact room." Louise sounded puzzled.

"Sergeant, ask Miss Andrews to join us."

"Blythe, what's going on? Why are the police here?"

Blythe sounded remote, as if she were trying to remain calm. "The police have to make an investigation. I don't have anything to say right now. Let's see what happens."

Nela slid closer to the door. No one spoke until the officer returned with Abby.

Abby's face was fearful and pinched. She stared with wide, frightened eyes at the cluster of people outside her office. "What's wrong? Why do you want to talk to me?"

Blythe Webster spoke in a tight, contained voice. "Abby, it's necessary for the police to search your office. I have granted them permission to do so."

"Why?" Abby's breathing was uneven. "What are they looking for?"

Hurrying steps came down the hall. Hollis Blair strode forward, brows drawn in a tight frown. He looked from Blythe to Dugan to Abby. "I saw police cars. What's happening?"

Abby's voice shook. "They want to search my office."

Nela stepped into the hallway. She might be sent away, but surely it was only natural to respond to the arrival of the police.

Abby's delicate face twisted in fear. "I don't think they have any right. I haven't done anything." She lifted a trembling hand to push back a tangle of blond hair.

Hollis appeared both shocked and angry. "I'll take care of everything." He swung toward the police detective, who stood in the doorway. "Detective, I want an explanation."

Dugan was brief. "Information received necessitates a search of the office. The search will proceed."

"On whose authority?" The director bit off the words.

"Mine." Blythe Webster spoke quietly.

Abby turned toward Blythe. "I haven't done anything. Why are you—"

Dugan interrupted, "The search of the office is not

directed at you personally, Miss Andrews." But Dugan's brown eyes never moved from Abby's lovely, anxious face. "Please step into the doorway and see if you notice any disarray in your office."

Arms folded, a gold link bracelet glittering on one wrist, Blythe listened, eyes narrowed, lips compressed.

Two more uniformed police came from the main hallway along with Detective Morrison.

"Disarray?" Abby repeated uncertainly.

"Anything out of place? A drawer open that you left shut? Any suggestion that an unauthorized person had been in your office?" Dugan's questions came quick and fast.

"Oh my God." Abby hurried to the doorway. In a moment, she faced her tormentors. "I don't know. I don't think so. I don't know." Her voice rose in distress. "Why? What are you looking for?"

Dugan nodded toward Detective Morrison and the two newly arrived uniformed officers, a lean, wiry man with bushy eyebrows in a pasty face and the redheaded police-woman who had come to the garage apartment when Nela called for help.

Hollis Blair glared at Blythe, his handsome features strained, his jaw rigid. "Why wasn't I notified? There better be a damn good reason for this." He jerked a thumb toward Dugan.

The trustee's shoulders stiffened. She gave him a level stare, her brown eyes cool. Her expression was not hostile, but the distance seemed to increase between them.

By now, the hallway around Nela was crowded. Louise Spear stood a little to one side, eyes huge, staring at Abby's office, her face puckered in a worried frown. Other staff members hurried toward the clump of people, likely drawn by the arrival of the police and the hubbub in the west hall-way. Rosalind McNeill tried to appear grave but she almost bounced in excitement. Cole Hamilton moved back and forth uneasily, darting quick looks past Dugan. Occasionally one eyelid jerked in a nervous tic. Peter Owens, his gaze intent, looked from Blythe to Abby to Hollis. Francis Garth stood with folded arms, heavy head jutting forward, thick black brows lowered, massive legs planted solidly. Robbie Powell muttered, "Police again. This can't be good for Haklo."

Heels clicked on marble as Grace Webster arrived. She clapped her hands. "Never a dull moment."

Hollis moved nearer Blythe. "I'm the director. I should know if the police are called. And why."

"I'm the trustee." That was all Blythe said.

Hollis Blair stiffened. His angular face flushed. After a tense pause, he took two steps to stand beside Abby.

"Whoop-de-do, Blythe's in her dowager queen mode. Sis, I hate to break it to you"—Grace Webster's tone was saccharine—"but what are sisters for? That frozen face makes you look fifty, not a happy number for somebody who's barreling up on the big Four-O."

"I didn't know you were coming in today." Blythe's voice was cold.

"Can't stay away. Haklo used to be bo-ring. Not any-more." Grace yanked a thumb over her shoulder. "What's the cavalry here for?"

Blythe ignored the question, her face smooth, her eyes focused on the doorway.

Grace's look of amusement faded, replaced with anger.

The public relations director took a few steps toward Blythe. "The *Clarion* will pick up the call. We need to be prepared—"

Sergeant Fisher came to the doorway. "Detective."

The silence among the onlookers was sudden and absolute. Abby Andrews clutched Hollis Blair's arm.

Detective Dugan stepped into Abby's office. A muttered murmur, no words intelligible to those in the hall. The office door closed.

Blythe stood with a hand at her throat. Louise shivered. Abby wavered on her feet. Hollis slid a strengthening arm around her shoulders. Cole Hamilton's face drew down in disapproval. Francis Garth gazed at the assistant curator speculatively. Robbie Powell was impassive, but his eyes locked on the office door. Grace's look of defiant amusement fled.

— 14 —

Steve Flynn picked up a folder. He'd gathered up odds and ends of information about those with Haklo keys. Nothing had jumped out at him. No bright red arrow pointed to a vandal, thief, and murderer. Somewhere there had to be a fact that mattered. He settled down to reread the dossiers.

Blythe Webster, 39. BA in English, OU. After graduation returned to Craddock and lived at home. Younger sister still in middle school. Served as a hostess for her father. Unmarried. Craddock gossip in 2005 linked her to a handsome young landman who worked for Webster Exploration. Rumor had it that Harris Webster offered the landman a hundred thousand dollars to relocate—by himself—to Argentina. Harris told Blythe he knew a skunk when he saw one and he was saving her from an unhappy marriage. Blythe spent a year in Italy. She returned to Craddock when her father's health

worsened. At his death, she became the sole trustee of
Haklo Foundation. She traveled extensively and left the
running of Haklo to Marian Grant, COO. However, as
trustee, she always attended the annual conference of
small charitable foundations. Following the conference
this past summer in St. Louis, she took a renewed interest in the foundation. In short order, she instituted a
number of changes. From corporate luncheons to the bar
at the country club, the locals delighted in totting up the
casualties both inside and outside the foundation. Erik
Judd was fired. A grant to a local art gallery wasn't
renewed. Haklo ended support of a scholarship program
for Native Americans at Craddock College.

Steve glanced at a photograph. Shining black hair framed
an olive-skinned face. Her eyes, large and expressive, were
her most compelling feature. Her lips were perhaps a little
too reminiscent of her father's thin mouth. Her composed
expression suggested a woman with power. He'd often dealt
with Blythe Webster. She expected to be treated with deference. She could be abrupt and was reputedly wary in personal
relationships. That he could understand. How did you get
over knowing a man preferred cash on hand to your company? He knew odds and ends about her. She collected
Roman coins and had a take-no-prisoner mentality in her
dealings. She once drove a coin dealer into bankruptcy when
he sold a coin she wanted to a rival collector. She played
scratch golf. She was generous in her praise for employees
and gave substantial bonuses at Christmas.

Grace Webster, honorary trustee, 27. A strawberry
blonde who liked to have fun. Usually ebullient, though
she was often caustic with her sister. Her contemporaries
dubbed her the wild one. Five colleges. Never graduated.

Backpacked across Europe. A succession of boyfriends. Harris Webster was amused by her escapades. He told a friend that he never worried about Grace and men, saying she always had the upper hand, enchanting men but never enchanted. When her father died, she was angry that Blythe became the sole trustee. Everyone thought that Harris saw Grace as too young and carefree for the responsibility. Perhaps out of spite, she comes to Haklo daily when she is in Craddock and keeps up a running critique of Blythe's decisions. Their relationship is frosty. Her latest lover was a local artist, Maurice Crown, who delighted in satiric paintings. A recent painting juxtaposed the Haklo Foundation crest with gallons of crude oil gushing from a Gulf platform. Blythe promptly cancelled a grant to the gallery that featured Crown's paintings. Grace was furious, insisting foundation bylaws prohibited cancellation of grants except on the basis of criminal malfeasance. However, the trustee had all the power. Grace is markedly different from her sister, adventurous, enthusiastic, always ready to take a dare, impulsive, careless, optimistic. Perhaps the trait they hold in common is bedrock stubbornness. Each is always determined to do exactly as she chooses.

Steve had clear memories of summers at the lake and Grace's daredevil boat races. She appeared supremely pleased in her photograph, strawberry blond hair cascading to her shoulders, an exuberant smile, seductive off-the-shoulder white blouse. Her chin had the same decided firmness as her sister's.

Hollis Blair, director, 32. BBS in business, OSU. MA in art history with an emphasis on the American West, SMU. PhD in education, University of Texas. At 28, he joined the staff of a medium-size charitable foundation in Kansas City. Blythe Webster heard Blair speak at a foundation workshop in St. Louis last summer. After the session, she invited him to join her for dinner. She met with him several times during the weeklong workshop. Within three days after her return to Craddock, Erik Judd had been fired and Hollis Blair hired. He arrived August 1. He is affable, charming, outgoing, eager to please.

The photo had accompanied the press release put out by Haklo when Hollis became director. Chestnut hair, deep-set blue eyes, a bony nose, high cheekbones, full lips spread in a friendly smile. Steve had played golf with Hollis several times and found him good-humored and intelligent with perceptive questions about Craddock. The last time they'd met had been at a reception in early December for the new director of the chamber of commerce. Steve recalled a man who looked tired and worried. Hollis had brightened when he was joined by the Haklo assistant curator, Abby Andrews. At the time, Steve had thought it generous of Hollis to bring an assistant curator to a function. Apparently, he was interested in more than Abby Andrews's work advancement.

Louise Spear, executive secretary, 58. Widow. A grown daughter in Corpus Christi, three grandchildren. Louise started as a secretary at Webster Exploration in 1974, moved to the foundation when it was created. Louise is precise, careful, responsible, and follows instructions. She considered Harris Webster a great man. Haklo was second only to her family in her affections. She has taught Sunday School at the Craddock Methodist Church for 34 years. Kind, gentle, thoughtful, always ready to help.

Steve didn't bother to look at Louise's photo. He knew Louise. Casting her as a vandal, much less a murderer, was ludicrous.

Cole Hamilton, advisory vice president, 64. BBA 1969, OU. Widower. No children. Longtime crony of Harris Webster. When Haklo was formed, he left Webster Exploration to serve as senior vice president. Active in local charities, he served as a sounding board for Harris. A former member of the grants committee once said caustically, "Cole always loses at poker to Harris. That seems to be his primary qualification for his title. But he's sure he's indispensable, second only in importance to Harris." His advice always began, "Harris agrees that Haklo should . . ." A man who took great pride in being a part of Haklo. But Harris was dead and Blythe was now the trustee.

Steve turned to the screen, brought up several photos of Cole Hamilton. One had been taken with Harris Webster on the deck of a cruiser. Each man held up a string of fish. Harris's string was longer. The oilman's predatory face was relaxed. Cole beamed, basking in the moment. In a more recent picture at a November open house at Haklo, Cole's round face was morose as he stood by himself at the edge of a group.

Cole was no longer at the side of Harris Webster, the center of Haklo. After Harris's death, Marian Grant ran the foundation. Very likely Marian treated Cole kindly. Marian had been part of that close-knit group, Harris, Cole, herself, and Louise. But this summer Blythe Webster took over and soon there was a new director and Cole's title changed from vice president to advisory vice president.

Steve reached for the phone. "Louise? Steve Flynn."

"Yes." Her tone was tense.

He spoke easily. "I hear Cole Hamilton is being pushed out of his job."

"Steve, don't print that." A tiny sigh traveled over the connection. "I don't know what's going to happen about Cole. Just between you and me, Blythe has asked him to step down, but he won't turn in a resignation. I don't think Blythe wants to terminate him. In any event, he is the current advisory vice president. Let's leave it at that."

"Right. I'll wait until there's an announcement. Thanks, Louise."

The call ended. Steve looked again at Cole's pictures, such an affable, comfortable man, especially in the early photos. How much did his job, not just the work, but the prestige of being a part of Haklo, matter to a man who had no family and who had spent his life working for Harris Webster? Wasn't vandalism the kind of revenge a somewhat effete, deeply angry, and hurt man might take? Stealing the necklace was part of that pattern, striking out at the woman who was treating him badly. Cole Hamilton, soft-spoken and genial, scarcely seemed likely to kill. But murder might have been the only way to prevent exposure.

Steve looked at the next name on his list.

Francis Garth, business development research fellow, 47. BA, MA, University of Tulsa. PhD in economics, University of Chicago. Native of Pawhuska. Active as a member of the Osage Tribe. Prominent family, longtime civic supporters. Divorced some years ago, no children. Long-distance runner. Mountain climber. Taught in Chicago, a think tank in Austin, joined Haklo in 1994. A proponent of encouraging Oklahoma exports to foreign countries, especially Costa Rica. Knowledgeable about beef industry and exportable non-food crops. Instrumental in arranging grants for factory expansion. Passionate in his support of the Tallgrass Prairie.

Steve scanned the index in the annual report of the Haklo Foundation issued shortly after the end of the fiscal year in October. He flipped to the business development section. A figure jumped out at him. The business development budget last year had been two hundred and eighty thousand dollars. The current budget had been cut to one hundred and fifty thousand. Just as in Washington, money meant power. Francis Garth was an impressive man at the peak of his career, whose priorities weren't those of a new director.

Steve turned back to the computer. Burly, muscular Francis stared into the camera with a heavy, determined face. Not a man to welcome a downgrade. Would a bull of a man be likely to resort to vandalism? It didn't seem in character. But Francis Garth was highly intelligent, able to think and plan a campaign. A series of unfortunate incidents would damage Hollis Blair's résumé. As for murder, Francis had the air of a man who would, without a qualm, do what he had to do.

A very different man from Robbie Powell. And Erik Judd. Steve didn't hesitate to combine their résumés.

Robbie Powell, director of public relations, 44. BA in public relations, University of Missouri. Worked at PR agencies in Kansas City and later Dallas. Joined staff at a medium-size Dallas charitable foundation, became the protégé of the foundation director, Erik Judd. Judd, 55, was a University of Cincinnati graduate in social work. Worked in social service agency in Ohio, earned his PhD in finance, joined the Dallas foundation, within ten years named director. When Judd was hired by Harris Webster as director, he brought Robbie with him. They shared a home in the older part of Craddock, a rambling ranch-style house. When an anti-gay city councilman berated Harris for their lifestyle, the philanthropist's response was forcible and pungent. "I hired Erik to run my foundation and he's doing a damn fine job. Robbie's

dandy at PR. When I need a stud for breeding, I buy the
best bull out there. For the foundation, I bought the best
PR man available. I know the difference between the
foundation and my ranch." The Webster clout made it
clear that no hostility to its staff would be tolerated. That
power and changing mores assured acceptance by Craddock society. Erik was highly respected for his accomplishments as was Robbie. But past success didn't matter
to Blythe when she decided she wanted new ideas and
younger leadership.

There were plenty of file photos taken over the years, individually and together, of Robbie Powell and Erik Judd: Robbie making a presentation at a Rotary luncheon, Erik shaking
hands with a visiting congressman, Robbie handing out prizes
at a livestock show, Erik in earnest conversation with Harris
Webster. Robbie's young blond good looks had aged into
well-preserved smoothness, hair always perfectly cut, face
tanned, expensive clothes well fitted. Erik's dramatic personality might amuse some, but he always got the job done and
he was known for kindness and thoughtfulness. He was also
a scholar and in his free time wrote highly acclaimed essays
on early Oklahoma history. Under his direction, Haklo had
maintained a reputation as a conservative, well-run foundation, nothing flashy but year after year of steady growth.

Steve was thoughtful. Robbie and Erik were highly
respected for their abilities. On a personal level, they were
committed to each other. Until this past summer, they had
very likely never imagined a cataclysmic change in their
lives. Steve had seen too many men who had lost jobs in the
last few years to dismiss the effect of that loss. He'd heard
that Erik had withdrawn from many activities, presumably
to concentrate on writing a history of Haklo. Was he
depressed or was he genuinely enjoying time to be a scholar?

How angry was Robbie at the injury to Erik? Erik was polished, civilized, erudite, and now diminished. Robbie was
quick to react to slights and never missed an opportunity for
a dig at the new director. Did the acts of vandalism cause
more injury to Hollis or to Blythe?

Steve picked up the next dossier.

Peter Owens, director of publications, 38. BA, MA in
media relations, University of Maryland. Wife, Denise.
Owens and wife met in college, married shortly after
graduation. He worked at publications in various cities,
moving to accompany his wife, Denise, from one teach-
ing post to another. She was named an assistant professor of English at Craddock College six years ago. He
worked for a local horse publication and met Marian
Grant when he wrote a series of articles about breeding
seminars hosted by Haklo. He became director of Haklo
publications three years ago. Owens and his wife have
twin nine-year-old daughters who are stellar swimmers.

Steve had met both Owens and his wife. Peter was casual,
understated. Denise was intense, vocal, and self-assured.
There were two photos, the official photo online at the Haklo
website and a picture at the college last spring with his wife
and a visiting poet. The official photo was bland and unrevealing. At the university event, he stood with his hands in
his trouser pockets, smiling pleasantly. He was perhaps six-
two, shaggy dark hair, horn-rimmed glasses, relaxed
demeanor. He stood a pace behind his petite, dark-haired
wife, who was engaged in intense conversation with a heavy-
set, white-haired woman.

Abby Andrews was the last entry, but definitely not least,
thanks to a file in her computer and a missing skateboard.
However, this dossier contained very little information.

Abby Andrews, assistant curator, 23. BA in anthropology, University of Kansas. 3.7 grade point average. Active in her sorority and several campus activities, including yearbook staff and student council. Met Hollis Blair when he spoke to the anthropology club. Blair hired Abby to be his assistant in Kansas City one month later. He arrived in Craddock August 1. Abby came to Haklo August 15.

In Abby's Haklo staff photo, she stared gravely into the camera, her lovely features composed. She wore a string of pearls with a pale blue cashmere sweater. The *Clarion* always carried photos of new Haklo staff. Abby appeared very young with a smooth, unlined face.

Steve tapped impatient fingers on his desk. There was nothing odd or peculiar in her background. A nice recent college grad. Yet, an obscene letter was found in her computer and a skateboard went missing from the front porch of her cabin.

Steve's face crinkled. Why was she living in a Haklo cabin?

He speed-dialed Louise. "Just rounding up a few points. Tell me about the Haklo cabins. Their history and function."

Louise's tone was bland. "Harris thought it would be appropriate for visiting scholars and scientists to be able to stay on the foundation grounds. Eventually, it was decided the cabins would be ideal for summer interns." Full stop.

"And?" Steve prodded.

"The cabins have always been useful for guests."

"Abby Andrews isn't a guest."

"I think Hollis offered her a cabin since she is paying off student loans."

"Right. Thanks, Louise." He wasn't sure that the knowledge mattered, but it was one more out-of-the-ordinary fact about Abby Andrews. Except it wasn't out of the ordinary once her relationship with Hollis Blair was evident.

He felt great uncertainty about the importance of Abby Andrews. Surely the idea that she engineered the vandalism, which hurt Hollis, didn't make sense. But on another level, it made all kinds of sense in Katie Dugan's initial premise that the point of the vandalism was to make the theft of the necklace possible. Student debt was a crippling factor for a lot of college graduates, and a quarter-million-dollar necklace could pay off loans and then some.

As for the missing skateboard, it became important because of his whispered message. He'd based that message on Nela's insistence that there had been a skateboard on Marian's steps. How and when had Nela learned—or guessed—that Marian Grant stepped down on a skateboard and fell to her death? Nela said she could not tell him how she knew. He felt a ripple of uneasiness.

"Hey, buddy." He spoke aloud. "Don't get spooked." But his Irish grandmother would have looked at him and said softly, " 'There are more things in heaven and earth, Horatio, Than are dreamt of in your philosophy.' "

Maybe so, but he wanted to know the basis for Nela's claim. He didn't think Nela was protecting Chloe. Chloe might have known that Abby's skateboard was missing. However, it seemed unlikely that Chloe would link a missing skateboard to Marian's fall. Why would she? Was it possible that Chloe was suspicious about Marian's fall and for some reason saw Abby as a threat to Marian? It seemed very unlikely. But, as he had also learned long ago, if you want to know, ask.

He picked up his phone.

* * *

The office door opened. Her face impassive, Detective Dugan looked at Blythe. "Miss Webster, we can use your assistance."

The trustee's eyes widened. She gave a tiny sigh. Her demeanor was that of a woman whose fears have been confirmed. She pressed her lips together and moved purposefully into the office.

As Blythe stepped inside Abby's office, Dugan firmly closed the door after them.

Grace turned toward Abby. "What have you got in there?"

"I don't have anything—"

The door opened. Dugan walked out. "Miss Andrews, come this way."

Tears brimmed in Abby's violet eyes. She clung to Hollis's arm. "Why? I haven't done anything wrong."

"I have a few questions."

Hollis Blair stepped forward. He was combative. "Abby doesn't have to answer your questions."

Dugan nodded. Her voice was mild. "In the search of Miss Andrews's office, a diamond-and-gold necklace was discovered in a filing cabinet. Miss Webster has identified the necklace as the one taken from her desk. If Miss Andrews prefers, we can take her into custody for questioning in regard to grand theft." She turned to Blythe. "Now my officers need to search the cabin where Miss Andrews resides. Do we have your permission to do so?"

"Yes." Blythe's voice was thin. She didn't look toward Abby. She turned to Louise. "Get a key. Take them there." Her words were clipped, brooked no disagreement. She didn't wait for an answer, but swung away, headed for her office.

Louise Spear stared after Blythe. Louise's face was pale

and apprehensive. She was obviously upset. But she had her orders and she had taken orders for many years.

Dugan nodded at Sergeant Fisher and the plump woman officer. "You know what to look for. Call me if anything is found."

The police officers followed Louise into her office.

Abby took a step toward Dugan. "I didn't steal that awful necklace. Someone put it in the cabinet." She looked at Hollis in appeal. "I didn't take it."

Hollis Blair was grim. "Of course you didn't take it. I'll get a lawyer for you."

"I shouldn't need a lawyer." Abby's thin face, twisted in despair, was no longer pretty, but desperate and frightened. "It's all a lie."

Dugan was brisk. "We will take your statement at the station. If you wish to have counsel present, that is your prerogative. We'll go out the front entrance. This way." She gestured toward the main hallway.

Abby shot a panicked look at Hollis.

He gave her a reassuring nod.

Dugan and Abby walked together toward the main hall, Hollis a step behind. Dugan was purposeful, striding fast. Abby's shoulders hunched as she hurried to keep pace.

Grace looked puzzled. Her expression was distant, as if her thoughts were far away and not pleasant. She moved swiftly toward the main hall. Peter Owens glanced toward Louise's office. "I guess the show's over for now." He moved toward the rear stairs.

Cole Hamilton spoke in a soft aside to Robbie. "All these new people were a mistake. I told Marian it didn't look right for a man to bring a pretty girl in as soon as he gets a new job. It wasn't like there wasn't a pretty young thing in the office. Why, Anne Nesbitt was pretty enough to please anyone. He noticed her. What man wouldn't? But a nice girl.

Now I wonder if Abby set her car on fire so there wouldn't be another young girl around."

He intended his comment for Robbie, but Nela was near enough to overhear.

Robbie's eyes gleamed in his old-young, pleased face. "A lust for diamonds. They say some women can't resist them. But vandalism to serve as a smoke screen was clever. I wouldn't have thought Abby was that clever."

Francis Garth's heavy voice was stolid. "She's nice. Pleasant. Pretty if you like them young and callow. But not clever. She doesn't have the nerve to be a vandal—or a murderer."

Francis's words thrummed in Nela's mind as she returned to Chloe's office, sank into the chair behind the desk. She agreed with Francis. And that put the question squarely to her. What was she going to do now?

From down the hall, Grace's strident voice carried clearly. "What's the deal? You gave the cops carte blanche to search. First Abby's office, now the cabin. How'd you know—" A faraway door slam cut off Grace's voice in midsentence. Nela wondered how forthcoming Blythe would be with her sister.

Nela knew the answer to Grace's question. Someone had placed a letter on Blythe's desk. Obviously, the message suggested a search of Abby's office for the missing necklace.

But Nela knew more than Blythe or any of the others. Nela had put the necklace on Blythe's desk Monday night. Some time after Nela's foray into the building Monday night, the necklace was removed. Today an anonymous letter on Blythe's desk indicated the necklace could be found in Abby's office.

The sound of voices and footsteps faded in the hallway. Finally, there was silence. Abby Andrews was in a police cruiser, on her way to the police station.

Nela retrieved her purse. She slipped the strap over one shoulder. She walked down the hall to the staff exit, car keys in one hand, cell phone in the other.

—15—

The connection was surprisingly clear. ". . . don't know if you remember me, Chloe. This is Steve Flynn for the *Clarion.*"

Chloe's husky voice burbled with delight. "How sweet! I love the *Clarion.* You know that feature you do every Sunday, the Craddock Connection? That's the nicest thing, stories about everyday people like firemen and teachers and bricklayers. I loved the one about the lady at the nursing home who was turning a hundred and nobody knew she'd been a nurse on Corregidor during WWII. It just makes you think," Chloe Farley said solemnly. A pause and she rushed ahead, "I'm from LA and you can live in an apartment house and never know anybody. Nela always told me everybody has a story. Instead, most newspapers just write about politics. Of course, Craddock has a few drawbacks. I get tired of roosters crowing. I never heard a rooster 'til I came to Craddock but there's one in the field next to Leland's trailer. I'll bet you want to do a story about Leland and me and our trip. Oh, you can't believe the water here in Tahiti. It's like looking through blue glass and the shells—"

Steve tried to divert the flood. "When you get back, we'll do a big story. Right now I want to ask about Marian Grant's fall down her apartment steps."

"Marian's fall?" There was no hint of uneasiness or wariness in Chloe's froggy tone. "That came as such a surprise. Why, she was so graceful—"

Nela turned the heater up full blast, but the VW was icy cold. Yet there was a deeper chill in her thoughts as she called the *Clarion*, gave Steve's extension number. Once she spoke, there was no turning back. She wasn't surprised when the message came on: *I am either away from my desk or engaged in another call . . .*

She waited until the ping. "Steve, it's Nela." She was brisk. "Blythe got an anonymous letter this morning, saying the necklace was hidden in Abby's office. Blythe called the police and they found the necklace in a filing cabinet. Dugan's taken Abby to the police station. I'm on my way there now. I'll tell Dugan how I found the necklace in Marian's purse and that I brought the necklace to Haklo Monday night and left it on Blythe's desk. I won't mention you." She clicked off the phone, put the VW in gear.

Steve ignored the call-waiting beep.

". . . hard to imagine Marian falling. She had an air, you know. Why, it would be easier to imagine Tallulah Bankhead in a pinafore." A throaty gurgle. "My gram thought Tallulah Bankhead was hilarious. Gram loved to quote her and Bette Davis. People would be surprised if they knew how women told it how they saw it even then." It was as if she spoke of a time far distant. "Of course, Marian never talked like that. Marian was serious." Chloe drawled the word. "But that's all right." Her husky voice was generous. "Marian was *somebody*. You knew that the minute you met her. I even had that feeling staying in her apartment. And Jugs is a sweetheart, which shows she had a soft side. If you need a quote, I'd call Louise Spear or Cole Hamilton. They'd known her forever. Anyway, got to go, the catamaran's ready . . ."

Steve replaced the phone. If there was any guile involved in Chloe Farley's discursiveness, he'd find a pinafore to wear. So how and where did Nela come up with a skateboard on Marian's steps? He didn't want to ask her again. Her refusal to explain had been definite. Why?

He tussled with the question as he punched listen to retrieve the message from the call he'd missed.

"Y ou can sit there." The policeman—or maybe he was a detective because he didn't wear a uniform— slouched to a seat on the other side of a utilitarian metal desk. There were nine or ten similar desks across the room, some with occupants, most empty.

Nela remained standing. "I'm sorry." She was polite but firm. "I have to talk to Detective Dugan."

"She's busy. I'll take down the information. I'm Detective Morrison." He gave her a swift, admiring glance, then his narrow face smoothed into polite expectation. "Whatever it is, I can handle it."

A door rattled open behind her. Quick steps thudded on the wooden floor.

Morrison looked past her. "Yo, Steve. Haven't seen you move this fast since they handed out free gumdrops at the county extension office."

"Mokie." But Steve's voice was abstracted and he was looking at Nela.

She half turned to see the now familiar freckled face and bright blue eyes.

He stopped beside her. "I came as soon as I got your message."

She was glad and sad. Glad to know he would be with her. Sad to know she was going to cause him trouble. "You don't have to stay. You don't have anything to do with any of it." The words were quick.

He gave her a swift, lopsided grin. "I signed on Monday night. I did what I did—and I'm damn glad I did. But you're right. Katie has to know."

Mokie Morrison was looking from one to the other, his brown eyes curious and intent. "Sounds like an episode in a soap. Not that I watch soaps." The disclaimer was hasty. "My ex loved *As the World Turns*, still in mourning for it."

"I can't get in to see her." Nela's voice was anxious.

Steve turned to Mokie. "Tell Katie we've got stuff she needs to know now."

T he office was small. Thin winter sunlight slanted through open blinds. Katie Dugan's sturdy frame was replicated by the shadow that fell across the legal pad and folders open on her desk. The office was impersonal, no mementos on the desktop, a map of Craddock on one wall, a map of Oklahoma and a bulletin board with wanted circulars, notes, and department directives on the other. Two metal filing cases. The detective's face was impassive as she listened and took notes.

There was tight silence when they finished.

Nela was intensely aware of Steve's nearness. They sat side by side, separated by only a few inches, on worn wooden chairs that faced Dugan's desk.

Dugan's cool gaze settled on Steve. "Why should I believe you"—a flicker toward Nela—"or her?"

Steve was affable. "How does it help either one of us to lie?" He retrieved his cell phone, touched, pushed it across Dugan's desk. "Note the date and time. Ditto the next pic. Maybe enhanced details will prove one was taken at the Haklo staff entrance, the other in Blythe Webster's office. Nela was your main suspect until the necklace was found in Abby's office. If Nela had kept quiet, she and her sister would be off your radar. Right?"

There was a touch of frost in Dugan's voice. "I'm not smart enough to see the possibility Abby Andrews was picked to be a fall guy?"

Nela felt a sickening swoop of disappointment even though she'd expected Dugan to be hostile.

Steve's face looked suddenly tough. "You know me better than that. I know you look at everything. Always. We're trying to help, Katie. Give us a chance."

"Maybe it would have been a help if you people had told me the truth from the start." Dugan's broad face was equally tough. "I got news for you, and not the kind to put in the *Clarion*. Everybody's on my radar. Including your girlfriend." Her cold gaze moved to Nela. "Maybe you found the necklace in the purse. Or maybe your sister asked you to take care of it, but you got cold feet. Maybe—"

Her phone rang. She glanced at caller ID, picked up the receiver. "Dugan . . . So anybody who took a close look would find it?" She raised a dark eyebrow, looked sardonic. "Yeah. Check for prints. Want to bet nothing doing except for the owner's? Test for a match on the stair rail. Right. Thanks." She replaced the receiver. She turned to Nela, went back to her attack. "Or maybe you decided the necklace was too damn hot to keep. I learned a long time ago that a pretty face doesn't mean squat. You could be lying your head off. Or you could be telling the truth down the line. If you are, then something strange is going on out at Haklo and that necklace is at the heart of it. If you left the necklace on Blythe Webster's desk, the water gets muddy. We found the necklace in a filing cabinet in Abby Andrews's office. The tip came in an anonymous note left on Blythe Webster's desk. Traffic has been pretty busy in and out of her office, apparently. The upshot? Anybody could be the perp." She looked steadily at Nela. "Including you."

But Nela was thinking. Paint flecks . . . "They found the skateboard, didn't they? You told Louise to take the officers to Abby's cabin and they found the skateboard there."

Dugan stiffened, like a hunter on point. "Lady, you seem to know everything. You know too much."

"You said to check for a match on the stair rail. What else could it be but the skateboard?" Nela tried to speak naturally, as if she didn't see Jugs's glowing eyes. "I read in the *Clarion* that there was a call claiming there was a skateboard on Marian Grant's stairs. Abby claimed someone took her skateboard. Now it's back. Doesn't it figure after the necklace was planted in Abby's office that the skateboard would be back?"

"Next thing I know"—Dugan's voice was sardonic—"you'll be filling out an application to be a cop. Thanks, but I can figure out what may or may not have happened. If you're telling the truth, I appreciate the fact that you came forward. If you're lying to me, I won't be fooled. Now"—and she looked from Nela to Steve and back again—"nothing said in this room is to be repeated, revealed, discussed—or printed. Go out the back way. I don't want anybody seeing you two leaving here. If either one of you gets loose lips, you'll be my guest at the county jail." She stared hard at Nela. "Ask Steve about the county jail. It makes the city jail seem like a resort."

They stood in an alleyway behind city hall, a few feet from a row of trash cans.

Nela hugged Chloe's coat tight, warding off not only the

cold but the chill of fear. "Somebody put that necklace in Abby's office and the skateboard at her cabin. It has to be the killer. How else could the skateboard show up again? It's diabolical. Abby said the skateboard was missing and now they've found it in her cabin. You heard what Dugan said. It was some place where it wasn't hard to find."

Steve looked thoughtful. "Maybe the murderer got a little too cute. Katie will give a fish eye at how nice and easy the evidence is falling in her lap. But she won't cross Abby off her list. There's been a lot at this point, the obscene letter file in her computer, the necklace, the skateboard." He hunched his shoulders against a cold gust.

The wind was frosty on Nela's face, tugged at Chloe's big coat. "Your ears are red from the cold. You need a coat."

He grinned. "Last I heard they didn't have an ear coat in my size."

Nela laughed and felt a surge of gratitude. Steve had made her laugh when she was half scared, half mad. But the laugh died away. She reached out, gripped his arm. "I'm sorry about everything, Steve. Katie Dugan was your friend. Now she doesn't trust you."

"Katie's got a big bark. She'll figure things out. But we have to play it her way. You'd better get back to Haklo. I'll drop by the station later in the day, see what the official line is. I'll be over to see you tonight." It was a statement. He paused. "Okay?" The tone was light, but his eyes were serious.

"If you were smart"—her voice caught in her throat—"you'd stay away from me."

"Not," he said quietly, "in this lifetime." He reached out, gently framed her shoulders with big strong hands, turned her around. "Walk straight and you come out on Alcott. You can take it to Main."

She walked away without looking back, still feeling the strength of his grip on her shoulders, and knew he stood, red hair stirred by the wind, ears red with cold, hands jammed in his pockets, and watched until she reached the end of the alley.

Nela put the McDonald's sack with a cheeseburger and fries on Chloe's desk. She glanced at the clock. It was a few minutes after one. She stepped to the connecting door to Louise's office, ready to apologize for her lateness.

Louise sat at her desk, but she wasn't working. She stared out the window, her pale face lined and unhappy, unaware of Nela's presence. Indeed, she seemed to be very far away, sunk in a somber reverie. One hand fingered the collar of her pink blouse. The pink added a note of cheer to her gray jacket and skirt.

Nela said quietly, "Excuse me, Louise. I'm sorry I'm late getting back from lunch." She could eat while she worked if Louise had some tasks for her.

"It doesn't matter. I won't need you now. I'm"—she appeared to make an effort to be matter-of-fact—"going to look over some materials this afternoon. I'll need to concentrate. Please shut the door."

Nela was dismissed. She nodded and closed the door. She settled at Chloe's desk, ate without tasting the food.

Her phone buzzed. "Nela Farley."

Rosalind McNeill's words tumbled. "Everything's off schedule." Her voice dropped to a conspiratorial whisper. "After somebody dropped that anonymous letter on the T's desk, she quizzed me like she was a private eye. But she didn't waste any time calling the cops. First thing I know, they're trooping in the front door and the T's waiting for them like she's a commissar. When they found the necklace in Abby's office, I thought I was in a Brad Pitt movie. You know how the cops whisked Abby off in a cruiser? I thought they'd lock her up and throw away the key. Not so. Abby and Hollis just got back. They came in the front door, which is crazy, too, but everything's jigsaw today. Maybe if the cops take you away, the cops bring you back. I'll bet the director was right behind them in his snazzy Cadillac sports car. The T bought the Caddy for him, said it was more appropriate than the old Ford he used to drive. Anyway, they came in the front, Hollis looking like Sir Galahad and Abby clinging to his arm, pretty much in a Victorian swoon. She hung back, kept saying she couldn't bear to be here, and he was all manly and stiff upper lip that she was innocent and the innocent don't have anything to fear. So she sucked it up and they went down the hall and she turned to go to her office—"

Nela heard steps in the hall and looked up in time to see Abby Andrews walk past. Abby stared straight ahead. Porcelain-perfect face pale, shoulders tight, she looked young, vulnerable, and scared.

"—and Hollis marched into the T's office and closed the door. A closed door at Haklo means something pretty stiff. Anyway, I guess we have to keep on keepin' on. Neither hail nor sleet nor cops nor damsel in distress can stay the appointed rounds, so if you've got a minute you might drop around and get the mail. I've got everything sorted."

Nela hadn't given the morning mail delivery a thought after Blythe summoned her. "I'm sorry. I'll be right there."

The long blue plastic tray, almost three-fourths full of envelopes, rested on top of the horseshoe-shaped reception counter. Rosalind looked up with a smile and bounced to her feet, her brown eyes excited. The soft splash of water in the tiled fountain between the reception desk and the French windows to the courtyard was cheerful, a restful counterpoint to Rosalind's vitality. Before Nela could pick up the tray, Rosalind leaned on the counter, looking eager. "Did Louise fill you in on the cabin?"

"The cabin?" Everyone standing in the hallway outside Abby's office this morning heard Dugan ask for permission to search Abby's cabin, but Nela maintained a look of polite inquiry. "She didn't say anything about it."

"Well"—Rosalind looked around to be sure no one was near—"when the officers came through here, one of them—the tall, skinny one—was carrying something in a big billowy plastic sleeve and I'll bet I know what it was." She looked triumphant. She didn't wait for Nela's response. "Abby's skateboard was supposed to be missing. Well, they found it—I guess in her cabin—and I'd like to know the story behind that."

"Someone could have taken the skateboard and put it back."

Rosalind squeezed her face in thought. "Someone else here at Haklo?"

"Who wrote the anonymous letter? You can bet it wasn't Abby."

Rosalind's eyes were huge. She looked uneasy. "I guess somebody doesn't like Abby very much."

As Nela walked down the hall, the plastic tray balanced on one hip, she wondered, was there bitter enmity toward Abby? There had certainly been an effort to focus blame on her, the file in her computer, the use of her brother's skateboard to commit murder, the discovery of the necklace in her office, the reappearance of the missing skateboard. Was Abby a target simply because she made a good scapegoat? Or was she a vandal, thief, and murderer? Did she really care for Hollis Blair or was she willing to see his career jeopardized so that she could steal a quarter-million-dollar necklace? However, there was the clear fact that Abby's latest problems had been caused by an anonymous letter. Did Abby have a gambler's instinct and the guts to do a double bluff, write a note that accused her, then use the fact of the note to assert innocence? Had she decided the necklace was too dangerous to keep and well worth sacrificing to escape an accusation of murder?

Nela pictured the strained face of the girl walking toward her office. Abby had been oblivious to Nela sitting at Chloe's desk so Abby's expression wasn't formed with the expectation of presenting an air of innocence. But she had good reason to be fearful, whether innocent or guilty.

Nela stopped at Blythe's closed door. She knocked, then turned the knob. She felt an instant of déjà vu. Monday morning she'd stepped inside with the mail, interrupting a tense conversation between the trustee and the director. This afternoon, she walked in on the two of them again.

There was a decided difference today. Blythe was nodding, her expression reassuring. Hollis had the air of a man unexpectedly encountering good fortune. His bony, appealing face was grateful. ". . . appreciate your understanding. Like I told Abby, we'll get to the bottom of everything."

"Excuse me, may I leave the mail?" Nela hesitated in the doorway.

Blythe nodded and waved at the in-box. A ruby ring flashed as red as her crimson suit.

Hollis unfolded from the chair. Despite his lanky height, he looked very young as he gazed down at Blythe. "I'll tell Abby. I told her to rest for a while, then go up to the lab. She'll feel better if she keeps busy, and there are a bunch of donations to catalog. Knowing you're behind her will be a huge relief."

"Hollis, I think you may be right that Abby is innocent." Blythe was thoughtful. "Things certainly look black against her but it's silly to think she'd hide the necklace, then put a note on my desk saying the necklace was hidden in her office. And if she did hide the necklace, who could possibly have known about it?"

Just for an instant, his jaw was rigid. "The whole idea that she'd do anything dishonest is outrageous. As for the police, I think even that hard-faced woman detective is having second thoughts. We were waiting for her. Then, when she came in, she hadn't really started when someone buzzed her and she left. When she came back, she didn't say a word about Abby being a person of interest or give a warning. If she had, I would have said nothing doing 'til we got a lawyer. I still think maybe I should see about a lawyer. Instead, she said she just had a few factual questions. I thought"—he was earnest—"that it was all right for Abby to answer those. Dugan asked a few questions, then said we could go." He was like a man who receives an unexpected bonus check in the mail and wonders if it's for real. "I know you expected the worst." His lopsided smile was rueful. "I wish you could have seen your face when I walked in and said we were back. You looked like you'd seen a ghost. So, now we have to hope the cops turn up the truth." He turned away from the desk and moved past Nela with a brief nod.

Blythe's smile faded as he stepped into the hall. She looked tired and grim.

Nela placed a half-dozen letters and several mailers in the upper box, but she didn't turn away. "Miss Webster, may I speak to you?"

Blythe looked at Nela in surprise. Until this moment, Nela knew her presence had scarcely registered with the trustee. Nela might have been a robot carrying out assigned duties. "Yes?" Her response was clipped. Clearly she was impatient, in no mood to waste time with Nela.

Nela knew she was taking a gamble, but as Gram always pointed out, "Sure, the answer can be no, but it will never be yes if you don't ask." Nela was glad she'd chosen her best blouse and the skirt that swirled as she walked. If nothing else, she felt more confident and professional. She placed the tray on the corner of Blythe's desk, noted the slight thinning of the trustee's lips. She also shed, just a little, the deference of a minimum wage employee. "Miss Webster, I was between assignments at home and I was glad to be able to come to Craddock and take Chloe's place while she's gone. I'm an investigative reporter—"

There was a flare of alarm in Blythe's eyes. Certainly Nela now had her full attention.

"—which makes me skilled at asking questions and discovering facts. I can help you protect the foundation."

Blythe frowned, her thin dark brows drawn down. Her brown eyes had a hard stare. "How?" The demand was sharp. "There have been too many stories already. I'm sick of stories about Haklo." There was a distinct chill in her tone.

Nela realized Blythe thought Nela was threatening to write an exposé revealing that only a member of the Haklo staff could have committed some, if not all, the acts of vandalism, including the destruction in Marian Grant's office.

"I'm not talking about writing a story. Here's what we"— she placed a slight emphasis on the noun—"can do."

As Blythe listened, her rigid body relaxed and she no longer looked wary.

S teve Flynn's freckled face was thoughtful. As far as Katie Dugan was concerned, he and Nela hadn't been in her office, certainly had not heard her conversation with the officers searching Abby's cabin. But she'd tipped her hand when she'd dryly commented that there likely wouldn't be any prints but to check with the paint flecks on the stair rail. Nela had instantly made the connection. Katie had neither confirmed nor denied Nela's guess that the missing skateboard had been found. To get the quotes he wanted from Katie for a story, he had to have some outside ammunition.

Steve punched his speakerphone.

"Hey, Steve. How's everything?" Robbie Powell's voice was smooth and bland.

"Doing a roundup on the latest at Haklo." Steve was equally smooth. "What's the statement about this morning?"

Robbie was too much of a pro to stammer and stutter. Instead, he was silent for an appreciable moment. Finally, he cleared his throat. "Haklo Trustee Blythe Webster this morning received an anonymous letter suggesting that her missing necklace was hidden in a staff office. Police were summoned. The necklace was found and is currently being held by police as evidence."

"Whose office?"

"That information has not been released."

"And the further search?" Robbie might assume Steve's information came from the police. But if the point ever arose, Steve certainly hadn't made that claim.

Robbie didn't question the fact that Steve knew about the second search. "I have not spoken with a police officer. Haklo Foundation remains confident that the police investigation will be successful." A pause. "If you have further questions, please contact Detective Dugan." The connection ended.

The delivery of mail afforded Nela quick glimpses of staff members, to whom, after a perfunctory nod, she became invisible, cloaked in the comfortable anonymity of a cog in the well-oiled Haklo machine.

Louise Spear, sunk in apathy, held a folder at which she gazed with empty eyes. The brightness of the Baranovs' print seemed almost shocking in contrast to the paleness of her face.

Abby Andrews hunched at a desk covered with a welter of papers in her small, spare, utilitarian office. Her young face was pale, her eyes red-rimmed.

In the east hallway, Hollis Blair's office was not as large as either Blythe Webster's or Marian Grant's, but still imposing, with red velvet drapes, oak-paneled walls, a broad oak desk, a sofa and several easy chairs grouped on either side of a shiny aluminum coffee table. Filled bookcases lined one wall. Seated at his desk, he spoke into the speakerphone, his face grim. "I don't want a criminal lawyer. That looks bad, like she might be guilty. You've represented the foundation for years—"

A woman's brisk voice interrupted. "As you've explained the circumstances, it wouldn't be appropriate for me to represent her. Of the names I suggested, Perry Womack is one of the best. And he's welcome"—the tone was wry—"in polite society. Now if you'll excuse me, I have another call waiting."

The remaining staff offices were on the second floor. Grace Webster occupied the corner front office to the west, directly above her sister's office. The difference in decor was interesting. Blond Danish modern furniture, jagged slaps of oil on unframed canvases, swirls of orange, black, crimson. A sculpture of partially crushed Coke cans, coils of rusted barbed wire, and withered sunflower stalks stood stark and—to Nela—ugly in the center of the room. A casually dressed Grace lounged on an oversize puffy pink sofa, eyes half closed as she held her cell to one ear. ". . . missed you too. Two weeks is too long. Way too long . . ."

The large second-floor east office, the same size as Marian Grant's on the first floor, had a shabby, lived-in, fusty, musty air with stacks of books, framed photographs tucked on curio stands. The desk held more pictures, but no computer monitor. There was an aura of yesterday, pictures of a young, vigorous Webster Harris and an eager Cole Hamilton with a bush of curly brown hair. There was no evidence of work in progress. He looked up from a worn book with a frayed cover, then his eyes dropped back to the page.

Robbie Powell's office was light and airy with calico plaid drapes that matched the sofa, splashes of color in photographs of outdoor scenes, and a sleek modern desk with three computers. He reclined in a blue leather swivel chair. His smooth voice was as schmoozy as a maître d' escorting high rollers to their usual table. ". . . hope you and Lorraine will mark the donor dinner on your calendars if you're not in Nice or Sydney. We'll definitely have lamb fries in honor of the Lazy Q. You know—"

The interruption over the speakerphone was brusque. "What's this I hear about somebody pushing Marian down some damned stairs?"

Robbie's face tightened, but his tone remained soft as butter. "Now, Buck, you know gossip runs wild sometimes. That's absolutely false. Now the dinner—"

"The dinner be damned. There's no getting around the fact that a bunch of strange things have been happening out at Haklo, and I don't give money if it's going to be wasted cleaning up after vandals. Or, for God's sake, killers."

Francis Garth barely glanced up from the keyboard as Nela deposited the incoming mail. His massive hands dwarfed the keys. His heavy face was somber beneath the thatch of thick brown hair. He looked like a man thinking hard and darkly. His office was bare bones, uncarpeted floor, obviously worn wooden desk, wooden filing cabinets. The only decoration was a representation of the Seal of the Osage Nation depicting a blue arrowhead against a brilliant circle of yellow. A peace pipe crossed an eagle feather in the center of the arrowhead.

Pride of place in Peter Owens's office was a low broad wooden coffee table covered with brochures, flyers, and pamphlets. Deeply absorbed with a sketch pad and a stack of photographs, he scarcely noticed the arrival of the mail. Working, he had an air of contentment, a man enjoying thinking and planning.

As Nela hurried down the stairs to the rotunda, carrying the empty tray, she hoped that she would be smart and lucky. At some time between the disappearance of the necklace and Marian Grant's fall, Marian had gained knowledge of the whereabouts of the necklace and the identity of the thief. When had she found the necklace? Surely there had been some act, some word by Marian that revealed how or when she came into possession of the stolen necklace.

Thanks to Blythe Webster, Nela could now ask questions as she wished. Nela accepted the fact that no matter how carefully she phrased her questions, she might alert a murderer. One of the persons with a key to Haklo hid ruthlessness and danger beneath a facade of civility. Nela understood the risk, but she had a chance to make a difference and she was going to take it.

She hurried across the rotunda to the reception desk. There was no better place to start than with Rosalind McNeill, who saw staff members come and go as they moved about the foundation.

At the slap of the tray on the counter, Rosalind whirled around on her desk chair. Her eyes lighted and she popped to her feet. "I saw you go in the T's office and Hollis come out. He looked like a man who just got sprung from death row. Is Abby in the clear? I figure since she and Hollis came back, the cops must have learned something to clear her. What's going on?"

"The investigation is continuing, but the detective is looking at everyone at Haklo, not just Abby." Nela thought it might cheer Abby if that word trickled back to her. "I talked to Blythe Webster and offered to help since I have a background in investigative reporting. She agreed that it would be a good thing for me to gather information from staff members." Speaking with Rosalind was the next best thing to putting up a public placard. How better to establish herself as the new eyes and ears of Haklo?

Rosalind's eyes widened. "That's cool. Gee, I wish I could perch on your shoulder." Her gaze was admiring.

"Miss Webster authorized me to speak to everyone on her behalf. Rosalind, I want you to think back to Marian Grant's last week here. Start with Thursday . . ." The day the theft of the necklace was discovered.

— 16 —

Mokie Morrison brushed back his one strand of black hair, slanted his eyes toward Dugan's closed door. "I've seen feral hogs in a better mood."

Steve grinned. "When was the last time you were in the woods?"

"Boy Scouts. I went on a campout. Once and done. We met up with two copperheads, a cave with bats, and a feral hog. I haven't been outside the city limits since. But today"— and he was almost not kidding—"I'd pick the snakes, bats, and hog over Katie."

"Yeah. Well, I got a deadline." He gave Mokie a mock salute. His smile slid away as he knocked lightly on Katie's door, turned the knob.

She looked up from the papers spread on the desktop. "Yeah?" Her broad face was as inviting as a slab of granite.

"*Clarion,*" he said gently, making his visit official. He stepped inside, closed the door, pulled folded paper from his pocket, turned it lengthwise. He already had a soft-leaded pencil in his other hand. Without an invitation, he dropped into the wooden chair. "I talked to Robbie Powell out at Haklo. He said Blythe Webster received an anonymous letter saying the stolen necklace was hidden in a staff member's office. Robbie said to check with you about the necklace and the second search."

Katie briefly compressed her lips, obviously not pleased by Steve's questions. "The necklace was found." Full stop.

"Where?"

The reply was grudging. "In a filing cabinet. Miss Webster identified the necklace, which is now in police custody."

Steve's glance was chiding. "Where was the filing cabinet located?"

"The discovery was prompted by an anonymous letter. At present, there is no proof that the occupant of the office knew of the presence of the stolen property. Therefore, the identity of the office occupant is not necessarily relevant."

"What prompted a search elsewhere on the grounds?"

"Information received in the anonymous letter."

"Where did the search take place?"

"No comment."

"Was anything found that appears to be linked to Marian Grant's fall?"

Her eyes narrowed. She knew he knew about the skateboard. "No comment."

"Is there a person of interest?"

Katie shook her head. "Not at this time."

Steve felt like high-fiving Katie. She hadn't succumbed to the lure of evidence against Abby that had been so nicely and neatly wrapped up and delivered to her. "How did the anonymous letter arrive?"

"That has not been determined."

"Did the letter come through the mail?"

"No."

"Did the contents or envelope contain fingerprints?"

"The only fingerprints belonged to Miss Webster, who opened the envelope and read the letter. She immediately notified police."

"Was the letter handwritten?"

"No."

"Was the message printed?" Should there be another search of files in Haklo computers?

"No."

Steve figured that out in a flash. Words, maybe even pictures, pasted on a blank sheet. That took time. Last night or this morning, someone from Haklo had worn gloves, patiently clipped needed words from newspapers or magazines.

"Did you send somebody through the wastebaskets out at Haklo?"

"You're quick." That's all she said.

"Katie"—Steve's voice was quiet—"you want to figure out what happened out there and whether somebody killed Marian Grant. I do, too. I want to clear up the mess. I don't want Nela Farley hurt."

Katie's eyes narrowed. "But you just met the woman. What's with the white knight to the rescue?"

Steve looked at Katie. They'd known each other for a long time. They had a careful relationship because he was a reporter and she was a cop. But they were—deep down, where it counted—friends. "You know how it works, Katie. You look at someone. Your eyes meet and there's more there than you can ever explain or describe. You and Mark. Me and Nela. Maybe everything will be good for us. Maybe not. But for now, it's me and Nela. I think she's honest. I want to help her. The best way to help is to figure out what the hell happened at Haklo. Can you and I talk it out for a minute?" He put down the sheet with notes on her desk, placed the pencil beside the paper. "Off the record."

* * *

Marian had an air. Everybody always kept on their toes around her. She was her usual self that week except"— a little frown creased Rosalind's round face—"she was really mad about the necklace. The necklace disappearing upset her even more than the vandalism. That was Thursday. Friday morning she looked distracted, as if she was thinking hard. But she looked really upset again Friday afternoon."

"Friday afternoon?" Nela prompted.

Rosalind gestured toward the French windows to the courtyard. "It's been cold since you came to town, but that week—Marian's last week—we had a couple of beautiful days. It was in the sixties that Friday. Marian loved the courtyard. Sometimes she'd take a cup of coffee and go out and sit in the sun with a book of poetry. She said poetry helped her think better. Oh, golly." Rosalind's eyes widened. "She was reading *Spoon River Anthology*. She didn't know she was going to have her own epitaph the next week." Rosalind's voice was a little shaky. She paused for an instant, then continued, talking fast, "I was on the phone with a teacher calling about a school tour group. I looked up as Marian came inside. She looked odd. I worried maybe she didn't feel well. Of course, it may just have been being out in the courtyard and seeing the fountain still messed up. Like I said, the vandalism really made her mad. But she had a weird look when she came in. She walked past me and turned to her right. She was heading for the west wing. I didn't see her again."

Hollis Blair's face crinkled in thought. He looked bemused, interested, finally eager. "Blythe's got a good idea. And she's smart to send you around to ask. You know, she's a nice person but even people who have known her for years find her a little daunting. She's been swell to me. And like she said to me, just because the necklace was in Abby's office, it doesn't mean Abby had anything to do with any of it. I know that Blythe had to call the police when she got that letter."

He gave Nela an appealing smile and his eyes were warm and appreciative. His lopsided grin had aw-shucks charm. He was a big, handsome, rawboned guy. Consciously or unconsciously, he made any woman aware that she was a woman. Nela suspected he had been charming women since the day he went to kindergarten and he had probably discovered that intense looks and an air of total focus paid huge dividends.

"At least Blythe hasn't blamed me for everything that's happened." His relief was obvious, then he looked discouraged. "Everything started so well here at Haklo, then things began to fall apart. But let me think about that last Friday." His brows drew down. He shook his head. "I talked to Marian that morning. She was quite pleasant. I didn't see her that afternoon. But I can tell you one thing." He was forceful. "The idea that Abby would hurt anyone is crazy. Absolutely crazy. As for that damned necklace, somebody put it in her desk."

"Why?"

Hollis stared at her. "How would I know? To get rid of it? Abby spends a lot of time up in the artifact room. Her office is often empty. Just like those letters. It was easy to use her computer."

"You don't think someone chose Abby's desk for a particular reason?"

"I don't know why anyone would be ugly to Abby." But there was an uneasy look in his eyes.

Louise Spear's eyes widened in surprise. "Blythe said you could ask questions?"

Nela stood a few feet from Louise's desk. "When I

explained my background, she agreed that I might be able
to find out something useful about Marian's last week. The
police now know that Marian had possession of the necklace when she died. The police believe she threatened the
thief and that's why she was killed." As she spoke, she
sensed the same change in perception that she'd felt in
Blythe's office. To Louise, Nela was no longer simply a
pleasant replacement for a flighty young assistant. It was a
reminder of how easily people made assumptions about
worth based on a level of employment. Nela hoped that she'd
never simply relegate people to the guy who parks the car
or the girl who does nails or the frail inhabitant of a nursing home. It didn't matter what people did or where they
came from or their accent. Either everyone was important
or no one was important. Steve would agree. The quick
thought surprised her, pleased her.

"That's the week the necklace disappeared." Louise looked
sick. "And then Marian died. That awful necklace."

"Do you have any idea when she might have discovered
the thief?"

Louise slowly shook her head. "She was upset when the
necklace was stolen. But Friday morning, she seemed more
her usual self. She was busy making plans for the donor
dinner. That was very special to her. She was looking
ahead . . ." Louise shivered. Her face drooped with
sadness.

Nela knew every word was painful for Louise. She hated
to make her remember, but Marian was dead and beyond
help, Abby was alive and needed help, and she and Chloe
were still on the cold-eyed detective's list. "Did you see her
Friday afternoon?"

Louise sighed. "The last time I saw Marian was Friday
morning. She was cheerful, making lists, thinking of a
speaker. She loved planning the dinner. Tables are set up in

the rotunda. She always had the portrait of Webster that hangs in her office placed on an easel between the twin stairways. She never said so, but I think to her it was as if he were there. She always opened the evening with a recording from one of his last speeches. It's a very big event. It won't be the same without Marian."

Louise's description of Marian's last week tallied with Rosalind's. Nela felt convinced that she was on the right track. Marian had been upset by the theft of the necklace, but the next day she was her usual, competent, businesslike self until that afternoon. Nela knew without question that Marian had been in possession of the stolen necklace when she died. Had she found the necklace Friday afternoon?

Louise fingered the ruffled collar of her pink blouse. "What did Blythe say about Abby?"

"We didn't talk about her. I think Blythe agreed that it was important to try and discover how Marian knew who took the necklace."

"The necklace . . . I've tried and tried to understand." Louise's expression was drawn and weary. "Sometimes things aren't what they seem and it's easy"—her voice dragged—"to think you know something. But we can't get around the fact that the necklace was found in Abby's office. Abby either hid it there or someone put it there to get her in trouble." She looked away from Nela, her face tight. "She shouldn't have been there. But I saw her . . ." She sat up straighter, looked at Nela with a suddenly focused gaze. "It's good that Blythe asked you to help. That makes me feel much better. Maybe things will get sorted out after all."

Nela looked at her sharply. "Who did you see? Who shouldn't have been where?"

Louise looked uncomfortable. "That doesn't matter. It's easy to be wrong about things, isn't it? Besides, having you talk to everyone makes everything better. I'm not as worried now." She reached for the phone. "I must make some calls about the dinner."

Nela had been dismissed. She stood in the hall for a moment, heard Louise's voice. "Father Edmonds, I was wondering if you would do the invocation . . ."

As Nela walked away, she puzzled over Louise's disjointed comments. They'd been talking about Abby. Had Louise seen Abby somewhere that surprised her? Why was Louise relieved that Nela was asking questions? That fact had lifted Louise's spirits, which seemed odd and inexplicable.

A bby's office was empty. Nela took the back stairs to the second-floor west wing. As she'd expected, she found Abby in the long room with trestle tables where donations and artifacts were sorted and examined and exhibits prepared to be sent to schools around the state.

At the sound of Nela's steps, Abby looked up from a back table that held an assortment of Indian war clubs. Abby held a club with an elongated stone head. Some of the clubs were topped with ball-shaped polished stones, others with sharp metal blades, one with sharp-tipped buffalo horns. Propped against the wall behind Abby was a long board upon which she was mounting the clubs along with short printed annotations denoting the origin and tribe.

Abby watched, eyes wide, body stiff, as Nela crossed the room. As soon as Nela mentioned that Friday afternoon, Abby relaxed.

"I was working up here that day." She sounded relieved. "I don't think I ever saw Marian on Friday. Why does that matter?"

"She was upset Friday afternoon. I think she discovered the identity of the thief. She came to the west wing."

Abby spoke sharply. "She didn't come up here. I don't know what she did."

* * *

"Friday afternoon?" There was a curious tone in Grace Webster's throaty voice. Even in a plaid wool shirt and jeans and boots, she reflected high gloss, Western casual at an exorbitant price. "You're here at Blythe's direction? That's interesting." She looked past Nela, seemed to focus her gaze on the jarring sculpture with its strange components. Grace's face had the hooded look of a woman studying her cards and not liking the hand she held.

The silence between them seemed to stretch and expand.

Nela said quietly, "If you saw Marian—"

"I didn't." Her gaze moved from the sculpture to Nela. "I don't think we will ever know what happened with the necklace. In any event, it's now back. Sometimes"—and Nela wasn't sure whether there was warning or threat in Grace's eyes—"it's safer not to know."

Pink stained Cole Hamilton's cheeks. "Things have come to a sad state when Blythe sends an outsider to ask questions. I don't believe any of this is true about Marian. Whoever took that necklace was just trying to make trouble for the foundation. It's been one thing after another ever since that girl's car was set on fire. I know what's behind that." His tone was sage. "She was too pretty." He was emphatic. "Too many pretty girls always causes trouble. I knew when Louise hired that girl that there would be trouble. Not that she didn't behave herself. But every man here, except those of us who know how to be gentlemen, couldn't take their eyes off of her. And before we turn around, there's another pretty girl and this one's obviously an old friend"—there was more than a hint of innuendo in his tone—"of Hollis's. Erik knew better than to hire pretty girls. But nothing's been the same, not since that bumptious young man took over.

Why, he's barely thirty. As for that necklace, no one took it to sell or it wouldn't still be around. And that pretty young woman may have the brains of a feather but even she wouldn't be foolish enough to keep the thing in her office. It was just more troublemaking. How would Marian know anything about that? The whole idea's nonsense. Mark my words, someone took the necklace and put it in Abby's office to stir up more trouble. And it has, hasn't it?" He didn't wait for a reply. "Marian's fall was an accident and that's all there is to it."

R obbie's young-old face congealed into a hard, tight mask. "If anyone's asking questions, it should be me."

"Miss Webster said she was sure everyone would cooperate." Nela stared at him. "Do you object to telling me if you saw Marian that Friday afternoon?"

His green eyes shifted away, fastened on the penholder on his desk, a red ceramic frog with bulging eyes. "I caught a glimpse of her in the main rotunda that afternoon." He frowned. "I'd been down in the library. Erik was doing some research. He often comes in the afternoons. I was on my way to the stairs. Back upstairs. Marian came in from the courtyard. She didn't look as though her thoughts were pleasant. So I walked faster. I didn't want to talk to her when she was in that kind of mood."

"Mood?"

"I'd seen Marian in her destroyer mode before when something threatened her precious Haklo. I didn't know what had raised her hackles, but I knew it was a good time to keep my distance."

Nela thought he was telling the truth. But was he describing Marian's demeanor because he was well aware that Rosalind, too, would have seen Marian's obvious displeasure? Maybe he was telling the truth because he felt he had no choice.

* * *

Nela walked swiftly from Robbie's office to the stairway. She still needed to speak with Francis Garth and Peter Owens, but she wanted to see the library first. In the library, Nela stopped in the doorway.

Erik Judd sat at one of the writing tables, papers spread out around him. He had the look of a man whose mind is deeply engaged.

She glanced from him to a French window opposite the doorway that opened into the courtyard. If he lifted his head, he would have a view of the central portion of the courtyard.

"Excuse me."

He looked up at her, blinked, nodded in recognition. "Miss Farley. How can I help you?"

"I'm sorry to interrupt you, but may I ask you a question?" Since he no longer worked for the foundation, he was under no compulsion to answer simply because Blythe had authorized Nela to speak to staff. "I'm trying to find out more about Marian's last afternoon here. I will report what I learn to Blythe Webster."

He squinted from beneath his thick silver brows. "I see. Blythe is hoping someone might have information that will be useful to the police. Certainly, I will help if I can."

Erik didn't sound worried. But the mind behind the darkness at Haklo would always keep emotion in check.

"Mr. Judd, did you see Marian in the courtyard?"

There was a thoughtful pause. Finally, he spoke. "I had a brief glimpse. I'd been shelving books. When I turned to go back to the table, I saw her."

Nela knew one question had been answered. The library door had been open and Erik had glanced outside.

"She was hurrying up the center path toward the main hall. That's all I saw. I'm sorry I can't be of more help."

"Hurrying?"

"Moving with a purpose, I'd say." He frowned. "I thought something had happened to upset her."

Francis Garth's size made everything in his office seem smaller, the desk, the chairs, even the framed replica of the Seal of the Osage Nation on the wall to his right. Now he stared at Nela, elbows on the bare desktop, heavy chin resting on massive interlaced fingers. He was silent after she finished, his gaze thoughtful. He slowly eased back and the chair squeaked as he shifted his weight. "I don't think it is wise"—his voice was as heavy as his body—"to draw too many conclusions from a single glimpse of Marian on that Friday."

Nela persisted. "Marian Grant came inside the rotunda from the courtyard Friday afternoon and she was visibly upset."

Francis stared from beneath thick black brows. "Why?"

Nela shook her head. "I don't know. But everyone who saw her after that moment describes her as grim or upset."

Francis bent his big head forward. Finally, he lifted his chin. "I don't lie. But remember that truth can be misleading. I was checking on a matter with Louise, I think it was shortly after three o'clock. When I stepped out into the hall, Marian was coming out of Abby Andrews's office. She was"—he chose his words carefully—"deeply in thought. She moved past me without speaking." A pause. "I don't think she saw me."

Peter pushed his horn-rimmed glasses higher on his nose. As Nela finished, he shook his head. "I didn't see Marian Friday afternoon." He spoke absently, his thoughts clearly elsewhere.

Nela had done enough interviews to know when some nugget of information was almost within reach. Peter might not know about Friday afternoon. He knew something and was debating whether to speak.

"If you know anything that could help, please tell me."

He took off his glasses. He dangled the frames from one bony hand. "Ever since we found out that somebody killed Marian, I've been thinking about everything that's happened. I don't know anything about Marian that last Friday, but this fall she did something out of character."

Nela scarcely breathed as she listened.

"It was about a week after the car fire. She knew I was a good friend of a curator at Sam Noble." He glanced at Nela, almost smiled. "That's the natural history museum at the University of Oklahoma. You'll have to drive up and take a look at it one day. Anyway, Marian came in my office and closed the door. She stood in front of my desk and"—he squinted in remembrance—"as clearly as I can remember, she said, 'Peter, I need a favor.' I said sure. She said, 'See if you can get Anne Nesbitt a job offer from Sam Noble. Do it. Don't ask me why. Don't ever tell anyone.' She turned and walked out." His smile was half wry, half sad. "When Marian said salute"—he slipped on the horn rims, lifted his right hand to his forehead—"I saluted."

K atie Dugan looked at Steve Flynn quizzically. "If the circumstances were different, I'd say Nela Farley's a nice woman. She has a nice face. Of course, nice faces don't mean much when it comes to protecting family."

Steve grinned, almost felt carefree. "Katie, that dog won't hunt. I talked to Nela's sister. I've interviewed everybody from narcissistic, guilt-ridden, emaciated movie stars to nuns who tend to lepers. I won't say I can't be fooled, but Chloe Farley is about as likely to be involved in a jewel heist

as a kid running a Kool-Aid stand. Ditzy, happy, doesn't
give a damn about appearances or money or status. If you
knock out protecting her sister, Nela doesn't have a ghost
of a motive. Right?"

A small smile touched Dugan's broad face. "Yeah. And
she's got a cloud of soft black curls and a sensitive face.
Man, she's pulled your string. Quite a change from that
elegant blonde you married."

"Yeah." Steve had a funny squeeze in his chest. He
couldn't even picture Gail's face. All he saw was a finely
sculpted face that reflected intelligence and character and
a shadow of sadness. He met her two days ago and he'd
known her forever.

Katie reached for the thermos next to her in-box, rustled
in a drawer for foam cups. When they each held a cup of
strong black coffee, she raised hers in a semitoast. "Okay.
Just for the sake of supposing, let's say your girl's home free
along with ditzy sis. Where do you go from there?"

"Haklo. What the hell's wrong out there, Katie? I think
there's been a lot of misdirection." He spoke slowly, thought-
fully. He had the ability to recall printed material as if he
were looking at it, and this morning he'd outlined the start
of trouble at the foundation. "Let's look at what happened
in order: the girl's car set on fire, Indian baskets destroyed,
office sprinklers activated, frozen pipes from water running
in the courtyard fountain, stolen necklace—"

Katie interrupted. "Everything besides the necklace is
window dressing."

Steve spoke carefully. "Just for now, let's keep it in the
line of events, not make it the centerpiece."

Katie shrugged. "I get your point. I don't think I agree,
but finish your list."

"The necklace is stolen. Then Marian Grant dies in a
fall apparently caused by a skateboard, Nela Farley disrupts
a search of Marian's apartment, Nela finds the necklace in

Marian's purse, Marian's office is trashed, obscene letters on a Haklo letterhead are traced to Abby Andrews's computer, Nela leaves the necklace on Blythe Webster's desk, the necklace is missing Tuesday morning, an anonymous call"—he refused to worry now about Nela's source and his complicity—"links Grant's fall to a skateboard, Abby Andrews is missing a skateboard, another anonymous letter leads to the necklace hidden in Abby's office, skateboard used on Marian's stairs found in Abby's cabin." He paused to give Katie time to object but she remained silent, which he took as a tacit admission that the skateboard found in the second search at Haklo had matched the scrape on the rail of Marian's steps.

Katie sipped her coffee. "Hate to say been there, done that. I know all of this."

"What's the constant?"

She raised an inquiring eyebrow.

"Trouble at Haklo." At her impatient look, he barreled ahead. "All along, Katie, you've pitched on the necklace as the only thing that matters and, yeah, a quarter million dollars barks pretty loud. But think about the scenario. A lot of things happened before the necklace disappeared. You pitched on the idea that Chloe Farley set the girl's car on fire to scare her away and, after she got the job and had been there long enough to know about Blythe's carelessness with the necklace, Chloe decided to steal it and committed vandalism to make it appear that the necklace wasn't the objective. But if we wash out Chloe—"

Katie moved restively. "I've been a cop in this town for a long time. Haklo never had any problems 'til these new people came to town. Maybe Chloe Farley's not the perp. Maybe Abby Andrews planned everything. Sure, she's supposed to be sappy about the new director, but maybe she's sappier about a quarter million dollars. Plus every time we look, we find a link to her. But maybe she's not a dumb

blonde. Maybe she figured she might be suspected so she
set it up to look like she might be behind everything but
there's always an out, somebody else could have used her
computer, somebody took her skateboard, somebody sent
an anonymous letter tagging her with the necklace. A double
game."

"And she's lucky enough to go in Blythe's office and find
the necklace lying on top of the desk?"

Katie wasn't fazed. "Somebody found it. Somebody
moved it. Top of the list, Nela Farley and Blythe Webster.
Probably Louise Spear. I'll bet she's in and out of the trustee's office a dozen times a day. As for Abby Andrews, if
she's behind everything that's happened at Haklo, she'd be
nervous about anybody showing up there after hours, like
your girlfriend coming in the back way Monday night. Abby
lives in a Haklo cabin. Maybe she saw headlights. Maybe
she came out to take a look. Maybe she saw you waiting by
the staff entrance and stayed to watch. She would have overheard every word. When you and Nela went inside, she followed. If she stayed out of the way, you two would never
have seen her. But if she wasn't there, didn't take the necklace, it could have been anybody the next morning. People
pop in and out of offices all the time. Somebody came to
ask a question, do a tap dance, announce the end of the
world. Hell, I don't know. But it all comes back to the fact
that nothing like this ever happened until these new people
came to town."

A quicksilver thought threaded through Steve's mind, was
there for an instant, then gone . . . Not until the new people
came to town . . .

Nela wished she'd taken time to pluck Chloe's coat from
the rack in her office, but once outside in the courtyard,
she shivered and kept going, looking from side to side. In

spring, the courtyard would be magnificent. Flower beds bordered the walks. Benches surrounded a fountain. Even in winter it might have had an austere charm except for the back hoe and stacked copper pipe near the damaged fountain.

Nela reached the center of the courtyard, made a slow survey. Windows in the west and east halls overlooked the yard. Marian Grant could have chosen a place anywhere here for her moment of peace and poetry. However, when she came back into the rotunda, she had turned, her face set, and moved decisively toward the west wing.

Nela walked past the west wing windows, noting Louise's office, then Chloe's. Francis Garth saw Marian leaving Abby's office. She continued another ten steps. Bare yellow fronds of a weeping willow wavered in the wind that swirled around Nela, scudded withered leaves across the paved walk. Nela reached out to touch the back of a wrought iron bench, yanked back her fingers from the cold metal. The bench was turned at a bit of an angle. Someone sitting there had a clear view into the west hallway and, through the open door, into the interior of a small office. Abby's office. The desk faced the doorway.

Nela shivered again, both from cold and from a touch of horror. She knew as surely as if she'd sat beside Marian Grant that she'd lifted her eyes from her book and watched as someone stepped inside Abby's office.

Nela took a half-dozen quick steps, peered inside the window. Her gaze fastened on Abby's desk.

She looked and knew what had happened. Someone known to Marian had walked into Abby's office. Perhaps Marian had been surprised enough by the identity of the visitor to continue to watch. It seemed obvious that the visitor pulled the necklace from a pocket and placed it either in the desk or a filing cabinet. Wherever the necklace was put, Nela didn't doubt that a shaken Marian understood what was happening. She knew the theft was intended to implicate Abby and she knew the identity of the thief. She now had it in her power to protect her beloved Haklo.

K atie Dugan raised an eyebrow at caller ID. She lifted the receiver. "Dugan . . . Yeah? . . . Hold on." She covered the mouthpiece. "Blythe Webster's on speakerphone with Nela Farley. Apparently your girlfriend's been busy. Blythe wants me to hear what she found out. Since Nela will give you the lowdown anyway, I'm going to turn on my speakerphone. But you aren't here." With that, she punched. "Okay, Miss Farley, what have you got?"

Steve heard more than the sound of Nela's voice. It was as if she were in Katie's impersonal, businesslike office, looking at him with those bright, dark eyes that held depths of feeling that he wanted to understand and share. As she recounted her passage through Haklo, he gave a mental fist pump. Good going, good reporting. He made quick, cogent notes:

Rosalind McNeil pinpointed a change in Marian Grant's demeanor to her sojourn in the courtyard Friday afternoon. When Marian came back inside, she walked toward the west wing.

Louise Spear, worried and upset, focused on the necklace's discovery in Abby's filing cabinet.

Abby Andrews claimed she was upstairs in the laboratory and didn't see Marian.

Grace Webster said it might be safer not to pursue the truth about the necklace.

Cole Hamilton dismissed the idea of murder and linked the car fire and incidents around Abby to the presence of pretty young women. He said too many pretty girls always causes trouble.

Robbie Powell confirmed Marian's distraught demeanor as she walked toward the west hall.

Erik Judd claimed he caught only a glimpse of Marian.

Francis Garth saw Marian coming out of Abby Andrews's office.

Peter Owens claimed he didn't see Marian Friday. He revealed that, after the car fire, Marian asked him to arrange a job offer for Anne Nesbitt in Norman.

He and Katie listened intently as Nela continued, "I went into the courtyard. It was a pretty day that Friday and Marian went outside with her book of poetry. Not like today."

Steve knew the bricked area must have been cold and deserted this afternoon. There was a memory of that cold in Nela's voice.

"A bench on the west side has a good view of Abby's office. I think Marian saw someone walk into the office and hide the necklace. And then"—Nela's voice was thin—"I think Marian came inside and went to the office and got the necklace."

Blythe's words were fast and clipped. "Marian should have called the police." A short silence. "But she didn't. Instead, she obviously decided to handle everything herself. She should have come to me." Anger rippled in Blythe's voice. "I"—a decided emphasis—"am the trustee. I should have been informed. Oh." There was a sudden catch in her voice. "It's terrible. If she'd come to me, I would have insisted we contact the police. If we had, she would be alive now. Why didn't she realize that Haklo didn't matter that much, that Haklo wasn't worth her life? But she was Marian and so damnably sure of herself." There was an undertone of old rancor. "I suppose she accused the thief but promised she'd keep quiet if the thief left Haklo. I can see why Marian thought that was the best solution. Everyone would forget in time about the vandalism if it stopped. Instead . . ." Blythe trailed off.

Steve knew all of them pictured a dark figure edging up Marian's stairs and placing a skateboard on the second step, returning unseen in the early-morning darkness to watch a woman fall to her death, then pick up a skateboard with gloved hands and slip silently away.

"Anyway"—Blythe sounded weary—"perhaps this information will be helpful to you. Do you have any questions?"

Katie's face quirked in a sardonic smile. "That all seems clear, Miss Webster. Thank you for your call. And thank you, Miss Farley, for your report. I'll be in touch." As she clicked off the speakerphone, she raised an eyebrow at Steve. "Notice anything?"

"Yeah. Kind of interesting about the necklace. First, it's put in Abby's office. Second, Marian retrieves it. Third, the necklace is in Marian's purse. Fourth, the necklace is on Blythe's desk. Fifth, the necklace is found in Abby's office."

Katie flicked him an approving glance. "You got it. Starts with Abby, ends with Abby. What are the odds, Steve?"

S teve sat at his desk and tried to ignore the undercurrent of worry that had tugged at him ever since he'd heard Nela's report over Katie's speakerphone. Yes, she'd done good work. But there could be no doubt that she was now on the murderer's watch list. He forced himself to concentrate and maintain the coldly analytical, unemotional attitude that made him a good reporter. Figuring out what to accept and what to discard came down to more than the five *w*s and an *h*. There had to be innate skepticism that questioned motives and discounted conventional wisdom.

In the case of Haklo, there were facts. New staff members had been added, including the director. Six incidents of vandalism and a theft occurred between mid-September and this week, beginning with a car fire. Marian Grant died in a fall. There were suppositions. The vandalism was committed to detract attention from the theft of a quarter-million-dollar necklace. Marian Grant threatened the thief. Marian Grant was murdered.

Steve accepted the facts, but there were two pieces of information, one that came to him, the other picked up by Nela in her talks today with staff, that entirely recast his ideas about what happened at Haklo and why.

He glanced at the clock. Just after seven. He reached for his cell, shook his head. He'd told her he was coming. As he slammed out of the office, a couple of folders and a legal pad under one arm, the worry he'd fought to contain made his throat feel tight. He had lots to say to Nela. He hoped she would listen.

—17—

Jugs's ears tilted forward. He stared toward the front door, luminous green eyes unwavering.

Nela's heart lifted. He'd said he would come. She shouldn't feel this way. She hadn't felt this way in a long time. Not since . . . Her gaze shifted to Bill's photograph. But it was only a picture and there was, always, the desolate feeling of nothing there, nothing, nothing.

She was on her feet before the sound of a rapid knock. She'd left the porch light on. When she pulled the door back, Steve looked down at her. In the bright glare, his wiry red hair looked like a patch of flame and his blue eyes were commanding and insistent. His broad freckled face again surprised her because he wasn't now a mirror image of a smooth, always-young celluloid figure. His face was not only the face of a man who could be kind and pleasant and thoughtful, but the face of a man with a hardened worldview and a memory of loss and betrayal. He was a man who had to be reckoned with and who'd taken up space in her life in a brief span of hours. But that was how life happened. Things changed, not just in hours but in minutes. Bill had walked up a dusty road in a distant land and the world turned gray and cold for her.

Cold . . . Steve's ragged diamond-patterned sweater was familiar now. Before she thought, she blurted, "Don't you ever wear a coat?"

"Too much bother. You okay?"

The query surprised her. There was worry in his eyes, worry and concern. She felt a flicker of happiness. She'd been so alone and now she didn't feel alone anymore, not as long as he was here.

He looked into her eyes, saw her response. His smile was as warm as an embrace.

With a quick breath, Nela stepped back, knew she talked too fast. "I'm fine. Come in. Let me get you some coffee."

She felt steadied as she served fresh hot coffee in thick white pottery mugs. They sat on the sofa, Nela taking care to provide space between them, disconcertingly but gloriously aware of his nearness.

Jugs jumped to the coffee table, sliding a little on Steve's papers.

Steve grinned. "Hey, boy, you're in the way."

Jugs gazed at him for a moment, then flowed to the couch, settled between Steve and Nela.

As Nela reached down to stroke the black-and-tan striped back, Steve moved to smooth Jugs's bristly ticked coat. Her hand brushed Steve's. There was an instant's pause, the two of them still, then Steve reached for the mug, spoke rapidly.

Nela listened, trying to corral her thoughts and her feelings. Steve was so near, so big, the remembered warmth of his touch, Bill, emptiness, Chloe, Haklo . . .

". . . and here's some stuff I put together about the people who have keys, plus I was in Katie's office when you called this afternoon." He handed her several sheets of paper.

Nela read swiftly. Steve's bios added substance to her personal encounters with the staff members. She stopped reading when she turned to the sheet with the italicized head: *Nela Farley's Report to Katie Dugan*. She started to hand back the sheets.

He gently massaged behind Jugs's prominent ears, prompting a throaty purr. "Read all of it."

Everything was as expected except for one surprising twist. In Nela's report on Cole Hamilton, Steve had marked *too many pretty girls always causes trouble* with a canary yellow highlighter.

Nela repeated the sentence, looked at him inquiringly.

"That could have been an outlier. Nobody else has talked about pretty girls. But I picked up a vibe from Mokie Morrison this morning. He's the cop who tried to deflect you from Katie. Mokie is a man with an eye for good-looking women. When he talked about Anne Nesbitt"—Steve's grin was wry—"if he'd melted in a puddle right there in the squad room, I wouldn't have been surprised. Apparently she was hot." Another wry smile. "Presumably she still is. But here's what I wonder." He leaned back against the cushion. "Maybe we've been off on the wrong track, right from the start. The conventional wisdom dismissed the car fire in September, like it wasn't a part of the stuff that started happening in November. What if the car fire was part of everything? What if somebody was angry about pretty girls?"

Nela stared. "Why?"

His gaze was serious when he answered. "Short answer, sex. Long answer, people can get twisted up in knots about love or lust or whatever you want to call it. Now"—his eyes narrowed—"I'm thinking something off the wall. Not the usual triangle stuff. But how about this. Anne Nesbitt apparently packed a potent punch. There are women"—there was an undertone of grimness in his voice—"who are like pots of honey to bears. Bears can't help themselves. They have to nose around. Cole Hamilton may be old but he isn't dead and he all but said in his gentlemanly way that testosterone bubbled. Maybe one of the bears thought he had a chance with her and then Hollis Blair arrives."

"He really cares about Abby." Nela shook her head. "He wouldn't go after someone else."

"Maybe not. But he has an aura around women. Right?"

Nela understood what Steve meant. "Yes." She didn't have to say more.

"In fact . . ." He broke off, pulled out his cell, found a number. "Hey, Robbie. I got a question. You're a canny guy about people. You notice things. Think back to late last summer. I understand Anne Nesbitt was a pretty gal. Did Hollis Blair notice?" Steve listened, looked satisfied. "Pretty blatant, huh? . . . No, nothing to do with much of anything. Just a bet with a friend. We got to talking about Anne Nesbitt and I swore she was a magnet for males. Right . . . Thanks."

"Robbie doesn't like Hollis."

Steve laughed. "Despises him, actually." He was abruptly serious. "But Robbie notices things. He said every man up there but him found one reason or another for a nice chat with Anne every day. That included the director. With Hollis, I think it's pretty much automatic pilot. Hollis learned a long time ago that ladies like him and he's ready to soak up a little sun when he can. But maybe somebody thought the handsome young director had cut him out."

Nela felt a wash of horror. "And he set her car on fire? That's unbalanced."

Steve's gaze was somber. "Someone is desperately unbalanced. Step back and look at the vandalism. There's a fury in everything that's happened."

Nela wasn't convinced. "Anne Nesbitt left. Why the other things?"

"Hollis Blair is still there."

Nela slowly shook her head. "I can't imagine anyone at Haklo being that"—she looked at Steve, used his word—"twisted." If Steve was right, someone she'd met, spoken with, perhaps shared a smile with, had a monstrous ego willing to destroy, steal, and ultimately kill because of jealousy. Or was the viciousness not even prompted by jealousy? Perhaps the motive was uglier, darker. Perhaps a perceived affront would not, could not be tolerated.

"There's something bad out at Haklo." He looked uneasy. "Like a nest of rattlesnakes. That's why"—he reached out, took her hand—"I want you to back off. I've already told Katie what I think. She listened. She'll be looking at them."

Them . . .

Nela knew the list was short. If Steve was right, the vandal, thief, and killer was either Cole Hamilton, Francis Garth, or Peter Owens.

"Nela, stay in your office. Stay out of it. Leave everything to Katie."

A fter Steve left, Nela poured another cup of coffee, carried it to the sofa, settled by Jugs.

The cat turned his wedge-shaped face toward her.

She stared into Jugs's brilliant green eyes.

". . . *You wanted him to stay . . . He likes me . . . I like him . . .*" Slowly, Jugs's eyelids closed.

Nela petted his winter-thick coat. "Sure he likes you. Who wouldn't? Cats rule, right?" She would be very alone now if it weren't for Jugs. He was alive and warm, his presence comforting. Maybe some evening somewhere, she and Steve would sit with Jugs between them and they could talk of books and people and places, not of death and murder and anger.

Did everything hinge on the theft of the necklace? If not, the entire picture changed. If Steve was right, if the car fire was central, the first act in an unfolding drama of passion, then it mattered very much why the fire was set.

Had one of the men felt scorned by Anne Nesbitt and been determined to punish her? Perhaps there had been momentary pleasure after Anne left. Nothing else happened until the attraction between Hollis and Abby became obvious. The next vandalism destroyed the Indian baskets precious to Abby. The rest of the incidents caused difficulties for Hollis, his first directorship marred by the unsolved crimes, for Blythe as the foundation trustee, and for Abby.

As for the necklace, the intent might never have been money but a hope of implicating Abby. Marian Grant found the necklace in Abby's office. Marian knew who had taken it. That knowledge cost Marian her life. But when the stolen jewelry—thanks to Nela—appeared on Blythe's desk, the necklace ended up in Abby's office. It had never mattered that the necklace was worth a quarter million dollars. Moreover, once again placing the necklace in Abby's office indicated a depth of obsession. The thief should have been worried about the return of the necklace, wondering if someone was going to be a danger. Instead, the vendetta against Abby continued.

Nela shivered.

Jugs stirred, looked up. "*. . . Afraid . . .*"

Nela felt a catch in her throat. Yes, she was afraid. She saw faces, Cole Hamilton almost cherubic with his fringe of white curls, heavy, bull-like, massive Francis Garth with a dark commanding stare, lanky, professorial Peter Owens with his genial smile.

Which one?

* * *

J ugs gave an irritated chirp as Nela moved restlessly deep in the night. She was aware of him but only dimly. Distorted dreamlike images jostled in her sleep-drugged mind. But once, with sharp clarity, came the lucid thought: Grace warned me. Or were her words a threat? *Sometimes it's safer not to know.*

N ela carried with her a sense of danger Thursday morning. The hallway seemed cold and remote with no hint of life or movement. She walked faster, but the quick clip of her shoes emphasized the silence. She pushed open Chloe's door, turned on the light. The connecting door between Chloe's office and Louise's was open as usual, and a cheerful shaft of light spilled across the floor.

Nela crossed to the doorway.

"Good morning—" She spoke to emptiness. Louise's coat hung from the coat tree. There were papers on her desk, but Louise wasn't there.

Nela turned away. She checked her in-box. It was empty. Nela had completed the stack of applications Louise had given her yesterday. She glanced at the clock. A quarter after eight. Nela would have been glad to have tasks to do. It would be nice to be absorbed, pushing away worries about Haklo and the investigation. But surely Katie Dugan had realized that Nela wasn't covering up for Chloe, that the necklace was only a part of a whole, and that none of the peculiar events at Haklo had anything to do with Nela or with Chloe.

Nela settled at the desk, waited. Time seemed to crawl. The minute hand moved with stately slowness. Another quarter hour passed. It was too early to make the morning round of mail deliveries. Finally, restless, Nela opened a side drawer, fished out a legal pad. She wrote a half-dozen statements in no particular order, fast. She liked, when writing a story, to pluck out the most interesting facts. Then with a quick scan, she'd rank them in order of importance and that's how she'd structure the story.

In the adjoining office, Louise's phone rang. And rang. Finally, it clicked off. Nela almost rose to go answer but she'd not been instructed to take Louise's calls and she might well prefer to later pick up messages.

Nela returned to her fast-draw observations:

Blythe Webster's active role as trustee began this summer.

Grace Webster resented her sister's appointment as sole trustee yet she made it a habit to be present at Haklo when she was in Craddock.

The vandalism began after Erik Judd was fired.

Hollis Blair seemed to effortlessly charm women.

Francis Garth was a huge man with a strong personality. Whatever course he followed, he would be formidable, either as friend or adversary.

Nela tapped the pad with her pen. Did any of these observations point to the figure behind the events at Haklo?

Chloe's phone rang.

Nela looked at caller ID: Craddock Police Department. Nela lifted the receiver. "Nela Farley."

"Miss Farley, Detective Dugan. Do you have time to talk?"

"Yes." She felt a twist of amusement. Nice of Dugan to ask. If she had questions, she could insist they be answered.

"I have a question I can't ask Steve Flynn. Wrong gender." Katie Dugan was brisk. "I know a bit more about you now. You're a reporter, used to sizing people up. I want you to consider three men: Francis Garth, Cole Hamilton, Peter Owens. You're an outsider at Haklo. Your impressions will be fresh."

Nela realized that she was being treated as an equal although she should always remember that Katie Dugan was a woman who could play many roles. "How can I help?"

"Francis Garth. Cole Hamilton. Peter Owens. Think sex."

Nela got it at once. There is office decorum and there is the rest of life, from an encounter on a beach to a glance across a crowded room. Men are men and women are women and there are glances and smiles and eye contact that say more than words ever could. Not that the lines often didn't blur. Hollis Blair could no more be around a woman without sending out a primal signal than he could forego using his diffident charm in any setting.

Katie nudged. "You're sitting in a bar and Francis Garth's on the next stool."

Removing the men from Haklo, placing them in a dusky, crowded bar with music and movement and the splash of whisky over ice cubes, she saw them without the veneer of work. "Francis Garth." Nela's tone reflected her shift in perception. "Magnetic. Powerful. Definitely a man who notices women." She felt a flicker of surprise as she continued. "Cole Hamilton may have the aura of a kindly older man, but he's very aware of women." As Steve had observed, Cole Hamilton was old, but he wasn't dead. "Peter Owens has that tweedy, professorial aura, but he's very masculine. Any one of them could be sexually on the prowl."

M im looked up from the page layout on her monitor, gray eyes inquiring. She was to Steve unchanged and unchanging, a rock in his life, her short-cut white hair making her thin, intelligent face look young and vibrant. She had the air of a sprinter ready for the gun, poised, ready to go. She never wasted words, suffered fools impatiently, incompetence never.

Steve propped against the edge of her desk. "You know everybody in town." He grinned. "If I were a cub, you'd snap, 'Don't tell me something I already know.'"

She raised an eyebrow, waited.

"I want the backstairs gossip on Francis Garth, Cole Hamilton, Peter Owens. Bed playmates. If any." There was no playfulness in his voice. The request was serious.

Mim was always self-possessed. The only indication of surprise was a brief flicker in her eyes. Then, she gave an abrupt nod. She didn't take the time to say *not for publication*, to warn that she couldn't vouch for gossip, that of course she picked up scurrilous comments about Craddock movers and shakers that she never shared. She wasn't going to tell Steve something he already knew. "Francis reportedly has been sleeping with the mayor's wife, but lost out this summer to Mack Harris." Mack Harris was a tall, rangy rodeo champion who'd bought a ranch near Craddock. "Cole Hamilton spends a lot of time at the Cowboy Club and he likes 'em young." The Cowboy Club was a gentlemen's retreat with gambling, music, and dancing women dressed as briefly as Dallas Cowboys cheerleaders. "Denise Owens and the twins spent the summer at her parents' lake home in Minnesota. My granddaughter's on the same swim team as the Owens girls and there was a lot of surprise that they stayed away all summer. Press of 'work' kept Peter in Craddock."

W ith one ear cocked for the sound of Louise's brisk steps in the hall, Nela tidied and straightened the office, finally began to rearrange the contents of the center drawer in Chloe's desk. As she worked, she ignored the ringing of Louise's telephone. Trinkets and odds and ends brought her sister near, as if Chloe were smiling at her with laughing eyes: two ticket stubs from the Oklahoma City Civic Center production of *Peter Pan*, keepsake menus from a half-dozen Oklahoma City and Norman restaurants (on the menu from Legend's in Norman, Chloe had written in huge letters with a half-dozen exclamation points: *Better Than the Best!!!!!!*), a map of Turner Falls, a dog-eared copy of *Far Side* cartoons, jacks and a rubber ball in a plastic bag, a Rubik's cube, a deck of cards. The motley collection was typical of her quirky sister.

Finally, Nela picked up a much creased and folded sheet of ruled paper. She sensed something that was not meant for other eyes, not even those of a loving sister. She gently laid the folded strip in the back center of the drawer, returned each item. She had just closed the drawer when the staccato tap of heels sounded, coming fast, coming near. They stopped just short of Chloe's office. "Louise?" Blythe Webster's tone was sharp, just this side of angry. "Louise . . ." There was an exasperated sigh.

Nela knew that Blythe had realized Louise's office was empty. A flurry of steps and Blythe stood in Chloe's doorway. Blythe was trim in a soft gray cashmere sweater and black slacks. Impatience was evident in every line of her tense body. Her face was tight with irritation. "Where's Louise? I keep calling and I get her answering machine."

"I haven't seen her this morning." Nela glanced at the clock. Almost ten. She'd been at work for two hours. "She wasn't in her office when I arrived."

"Not here?" Blythe's voice was odd. "She's always here. She would have told me if she were going out."

"Her coat's in her office." Nela meant to be reassuring but realized that her voice held a question.

"Well." Blythe seemed at a loss, uncertain what to do. Then she looked relieved. She pulled a cell phone from a pocket, touched a number.

In only an instant, there was a faint musical ring, a

ghostly faraway repetition of the first few bars of "Oklahoma."

Nela pushed up from her desk. Blythe was right behind her. The musical ring continued twice again, louder now as they reached Louise's desk. Nela pulled out the bottom-right drawer. The last ring was ending. A black leather shoulder bag nestled in the drawer.

"Well, she's here if her purse is here." Blythe sounded relieved. "She's somewhere in the building. Find her for me." She swung on her heel and surged out of the office.

Nela was glad to have a task. The directive hadn't been delivered with grace or charm, but if you ran the ship, you could navigate any damn way you pleased. Anyway, she had her orders, she'd carry them out.

S teve wasn't a lazy reporter. He had one more call to make. In fact, it took five calls to track down Anne Nesbitt. The connection crackled.

". . . almost time for the next presentation. I'm at an elementary school in Bartlesville. It's such fun. I have a slide show of our dinosaur exhibits. Kids love it." She sounded sunny and happy. "How can I help you?"

"This is Steve Flynn, *The Craddock Clarion*. The police haven't given up on the arson of your car."

A pause. "Oh"—a small sigh—"I appreciate the police continuing to try but I think it had to be some kind of nut. Not anybody I knew. Like"—she paused—"how do they put it when the criminal is a stranger? A casual crime. That's what happened."

Steve picked his words. "There have been other problems since you left Haklo. It's important, in fact it may be a matter of life and death, to know if the destruction of your car is linked to later vandalism. I want to ask a serious question.

Was a male staffer at Haklo hitting on you? If so, did you rebuff him?"

She didn't rush to answer. "Men are"—now it was she who spoke with care—"often very nice to me. Some men always see women in a certain way. Hollis Blair was very friendly, but he was never over the line. Hollis"—there was good humor in her tone—"is a guy who automatically sends out signals to women. The other men were interested, but I made it clear that I'm in a committed relationship. I've been fortunate in both school and jobs that I've dealt with nice men who recognize boundaries. No one bothered me at Haklo."

Steve ended the call with a feeling of bewilderment. He'd been so certain . . .

Rosalind waggled a hand in greeting. She was speaking brightly into the phone. ". . . some unexpected repairs have to be made and the foundation won't be available for tours this Saturday. If you would like to reschedule, please call." She gave the number. "We're very sorry for the cancellation. Again, this is Rosalind McNeill at Haklo Foundation." She hung up and heaved a sigh. "The T is definitely out of sorts. But I kind of get her point. She cancelled the Saturday tours. She said there's not a good feeling here." Rosalind's round face suddenly looked half scared, half uneasy. "She's got that right. Anyway"—she managed a smile almost as bright as her usual—"I have the mail tray ready." She nodded at the blue plastic tray on the counter.

Nela started to explain she was looking for Louise, then realized she would be visiting each office with the mail and she could combine the tasks. She would, however, change her route and end up at Blythe's office. Hopefully, she would be able to report Louise's whereabouts when she delivered

Blythe's mail. And, in fact, her answer might be right here at hand. Rosalind knew who came and who went.

"Is Louise in Hollis's office?" Louise handled correspondence and projects for both the director and the trustee.

"The director isn't here this morning. He called in and said he would be in around noon." Rosalind's face took on a conspiratorial glow. "Abby called in, too. She said she had an appointment and would come in around noon." Rosalind raised both eyebrows.

Nela had not paid particular attention, but remembered that Abby's office had been dark. Nela had assumed Abby was upstairs in the artifact room. She didn't care about the twin absences of Hollis and Abby. "I guess Louise is upstairs." She gestured toward the broad steps of the curving twin stairways to the second floor. "What time did she go up?"

Rosalind was too good-natured to be offended by Nela's lack of interest in the activities of the director and assistant curator. Her smile was cheerful. "I've been here since eight. I haven't seen Louise this morning. She must have taken the back stairs."

Nela received the same answer everywhere she delivered mail. No one had seen Louise. Nela deposited mail in the in-box on Grace Webster's desk. There was no jacket on her coat tree, no evidence she had been to Haklo this morning. Nela very much doubted that Grace had bothered to inform Rosalind of her presence or absence.

There was no one left to ask.

As she stepped out of Grace's office, the plastic tray held only the mail for Louise and for the trustee. Nela headed for the back stairs that led down to the first floor of the west wing. She would leave Louise's mail, and if Louise had since returned to her office, all would be well.

Light spilled into the hallway from the open door to the

artifact room. Abby had called in, said she wasn't coming until late morning. There was no reason for the light to be on if Abby wasn't working. Possibly Louise was there.

Nela walked faster. She reached the doorway and stopped. She glanced across the room. Her breath caught in her throat as she stared at death.

Louise's body lay facedown in a crumpled heap near the back table where Abby cataloged and mounted Indian war clubs. Yesterday Louise's pink blouse had been soft and pretty with the gray wool suit. Harsh light from overhead fluorescent panels threw splotched dark stains on the back of Louise's gray suit into stark relief.

—18—

Muttered voices and heavy footsteps sounded from the far end of the hallway near the staff entrance and the back stairway to the second floor. Nela assumed more police were arriving as well as the medical examiner and a forensic unit and all the various people involved in a homicide investigation. This time there was no question as to the cause of death. Homicide by person or persons unknown. Louise Spear had walked into the artifact room sometime late yesterday afternoon and someone, someone she knew, someone with a key to Haklo, struck her down, crushing the back of her head.

Nela sat numbly at Chloe's desk and waited. Dugan had taken only a moment to talk to Nela—how did she find the body?—then directed Nela and the other shaken and shocked Haklo staff members, who'd gathered in the upper-west hallway, to remain in their offices until further notice. Rosalind, eyes red-rimmed, brought lunch, ham sandwiches, chips, coffee. Nela forced herself to eat. The day was going to be long and hard. She needed energy to recall and tell Katie Dugan what she knew. Louise Spear had been worried and upset yesterday, but it had never occurred to Nela that Louise was in danger. Her distress had seemed natural, the care of a woman who had served Haklo for so many years. If only she had asked Louise what troubled her . . . *If only* . . .

Nela was painfully aware of the spread of light through the connecting doorway. This morning she'd assumed that any moment Louise would return to her office.

More steps, these coming from the other direction. "Yeah, yeah, yeah, I'm not going to talk to her. I'm on my way upstairs, but I want to see her, Mokie."

Nela came to her feet. Steve was coming down the hall.

"Katie'll have my head on a platter if any of the witnesses talk to anybody." Mokie's gravelly voice was steely.

Nela realized with a chill that there must be officers stationed in every hall to prevent conversation and ensure staff members stayed sequestered.

"That includes you, Steve." It was an order.

"Not to worry." Steve's voice was nearer, loud, determined. He came through the open door in a rush.

She moved to meet him.

He reached her, gripped her shoulders. His broad freckled face was grim, but his blue eyes looked deep into hers, saying, *It's bad, I'm here, I'll help.*

She drew strength from his reassuring gaze and from his touch, the warmth and certainty of his hands.

"I know it's rotten." His voice held a recognition of the grisly scene she'd found and taut anger at the death of a woman who had been good and kind and generous.

"I kept hunting for her." Nela hated thinking how long Louise's body had lain there. "And all the while—"

Mokie stood in the doorway. "Save it for Dugan." Mokie's voice was gruff.

Nela glanced at Mokie, nodded. "Right." She looked back at Steve.

He tightened his grip on her shoulders. "I've got to cover the story. I'll see you tonight. I'll bring dinner."

The afternoon dragged, one slow hour after another. Nothing to do. No one to talk to. Only the sounds of people coming and going. She tried not to remember what she had seen, tried to figure who might have committed murder, knew the list was long. All the staff members had been present late yesterday afternoon. Erik Judd had been in the library. Any of them could have killed Louise.

It was a quarter to five when footsteps came near, purposeful, quick steps. Detective Dugan came through the open door, followed by Mokie Morrison. He was much taller, but Dugan carried with her an air of command.

Dugan flicked a thumb at Mokie. He settled in a chair a little to one side, pulled out a small recorder, turned it on. "Office of Nela Farley, temporary assistant to murder victim. Time: four forty-six p.m. Investigating officers Detective Dugan, Detective Mokie Morrison. Investigation into homicide of Louise Spear."

Dugan didn't draw up a second chair. She stood in front of Chloe's desk, arms folded, and stared down at Nela. Although her white blouse, gray cardigan, and gray wool skirt would have been proper attire in any office, she looked every inch a cop, eyes sharp and questioning, face hard. "When did you last see Louise Spear?"

"Just before I left yesterday. A few minutes before five." When had Louise died? Why had she gone upstairs to the artifact room? That was where Abby worked. Once again, always, there was a link to Abby.

"Where did you see her?"

Nela gestured toward the connecting doorway. "In her office. I stood in the doorway, said good night."

"Did you talk to her?"

"Not then. I talked to her earlier in the day. She was very upset after the necklace was found in Abby's office. When I came back from lunch, she was sitting in her office and she looked dreadful. She wasn't doing any work. And later, I talked to everyone, asking about Marian Grant's last day—"

"We'll get to that in a minute." Dugan was impatient. "Tell me about Louise Spear."

Nela's eyes narrowed as she tried to remember Louise's words. "Louise said she didn't see Marian in the afternoon, that the last time she saw her, Marian seemed fine. Then Louise started talking about the necklace. Louise said that things sometimes weren't what they seemed to be, but we couldn't get away from the fact that the police found the necklace in Abby's office. It was all a little confused. She said either Abby put it in the cabinet or someone put it there to get Abby in trouble. And then she said"—Nela hesitated because the words seemed so damning now—"that 'she shouldn't have been there. But I saw her.'"

Dugan's expression was thoughtful. "'She shouldn't have been there. But I saw her.'"

When Nela opened the apartment door, Steve wished he could wipe away the pain and distress in her face. She carried too many burdens. He wanted to see her smile. He wanted her eyes to light up with happiness. He wanted her to know laughter and carefree days. And nights. Preferably with him. He held up a carryout bag. "Greek food. And"—he paused for emphasis, waggling a red can of coffee mixed with chicory—"I brought the Flynn special, coffee that will stiffen your spine."

Nela had already set the table.

He put the coffee on to brew while she emptied the sacks. "Dinner first, then I'll bring you up to date. But nothing about Haklo while we eat."

They feasted on chicken kabobs and Greek salad, finishing with baklava and steaming mugs of chicory coffee. "Can't end a meal at the Flynn house in the winter without coffee that barks." He looked toward Jugs, in his usual place at the end of the table. "Sorry for the language."

Resisting a second piece of baklava, Steve raised his mug in a salute to Jugs. "I don't usually like to share a girl with another guy, but I'll make an exception for you, buddy."

Jugs looked regal, front paws outstretched.

"Jugs is a gentleman." Nela smiled. "He has definite ideas on the proper place for a cat during meals, but he minds his manners."

Soon enough the dishes were done and they were in the living room.

Jugs settled between them on the sofa.

Nela smoothed Jugs's bristly coat, welcomed the warmth. "Tell me, Steve." The brightness from their cheerful interlude fled her eyes.

He didn't have to look at notes. He'd covered the investigation all through the afternoon, written the lead story with five minutes to spare on deadline. "You are the last person to admit seeing Louise, so she was alive at a few minutes before five. Her death occurred sometime between five and nine p.m. They can figure that from the state of rigor mortis. The autopsy will likely be more definitive. Katie thinks she was killed shortly after five p.m. For some reason, she went to the artifact room. There's no indication from the position of the body that she fought her attacker. Instead, she was apparently struck from behind, a blow that crushed the base of her skull. She fell and was hit at least three more times. Death from massive trauma. The weapon was a Plains Indian war club, a rounded polished ball of stone fastened by a strip of leather to a handle. The stone has a circumference of seven inches. The handle is eighteen inches long, partially wrapped in hide. On the length of the handle, there are several prints belonging to Abby Andrews along with some unidentified prints. Katie doubts the murderer was thoughtful enough to leave prints, and likely the unidentified prints belong to a previous collector or shop owner."

"Abby was cataloging the clubs. Of course her prints are on them." Nela had a quick picture of Abby yesterday as Nela crossed the room.

Steve shrugged. "Yeah. A point in her favor. Or a point against her. Everybody knew she was handling the war clubs. If she killed Louise, she didn't have to worry about gloves. Like you said, her prints are all over the clubs. Some of the prints are smudged either by Abby or by gloves worn by the murderer. If somebody else hefted the weapon, they must have worn gloves. But why not? If it was after five o'clock, maybe the murderer was already in a coat, ready to leave. Louise wouldn't be surprised at gloves in this weather."

"I don't see why Louise went to the artifact room."

"That's easy, whether the killer's Abby or someone else." Steve felt confident. "Abby could ask Louise to come up, say she needed to check out something with her. If it's someone else, it's even easier. Abby had the tail pinned on her a half-dozen times Wednesday. The murderer says, 'Louise, I may have found something in the artifact room that implicates Abby but I don't want to take it to the police unless you agree.'"

"Why did the murderer leave on the light?" Nela shivered. "That bothers me. I keep thinking about the light on all night and Louise lying there dead."

Steve didn't believe the light mattered one way or the

other. "Maybe the idea was that the light would attract attention and Louise would be found sooner rather than later."

"She would have been found early today by Abby, except Abby and Hollis were gone this morning. I don't think Grace ever came in today, although she wouldn't pay any attention if she had."

"Why do you say that?"

Nela gave him a quirked smile. He noticed for the first time that she had a hint of a dimple in her right cheek. "Grace wouldn't consider it necessary to personally check on anything. She and Blythe are accustomed to having others take care of details for them. When Blythe came here Friday night, she hadn't given a thought to who would take care of Jugs. She'd assumed it was taken care of. Minions can always be dispatched."

"You aren't a big fan of the Webster sisters?"

Nela considered the question. "Neither for nor against. As Fitzgerald said, 'the rich are different.' But"—and she looked a little shamefaced—"to be fair—"

Steve was touched by her rush to be generous. She had a kind heart. And that, he realized with an odd sense of sadness, was nothing he would ever have said about Gail.

"—Blythe is doing her best to find out what happened, even though I don't think either she or Grace were fond of Marian. Too much history there because of their father and mother. As for Grace"—and now she again felt the prickle of unease that she'd experienced when she spoke with Grace Webster about Marian's last day—"I don't know if she was warning me or threatening me when we talked about the necklace and she said that 'sometimes it's safer not to know.'"

"It could have been either?"

Once again Nela gave a question grave consideration. "It could have been either."

"We have to look at everything again." He hated the sense

of uncertainty that enveloped him, but they had to face facts. "I was positive the car fire meant a lot, that one of the men was hot for Anne Nesbitt, that she'd brushed him off. I talked to her. If one of them was interested, she didn't pick up on it. I think she was telling me the truth. She would have known, right?" He wondered if she knew how he felt, sitting so near her.

Nela looked at him. Her eyes widened, then her gaze slipped away. Her voice was soft when she answered. "She would know."

He felt a quickening of his breath and then her eyes moved to the photograph of the dark-haired man in the latticed frame with its carefully worked border of red, white, and blue ribbons. Steve willed his voice to be businesslike. "So, scratch the idea that one of the men was getting back at her. That means we still have to figure out whether the vandalism started with the car fire or whether the fire gave someone a clever way of setting up camouflage to steal a necklace or whether the necklace was just one more way of attacking Haklo and making life miserable for the director and the trustee." His lips compressed for a moment. "It's like trying to catch minnows with your bare hands, too many of them and too slippery and fast."

Nela smoothed Jugs's fur.

Steve gazed at her long fingers, a lovely hand, smooth, graceful, gentle.

She look at him with quick intelligence. "If the objective was to steal the necklace, would there have been so much destruction? The Indian baskets were slashed. A crystal statuette was thrown at a mirror in Marian's apartment. The mess in her office was more than just the aftermath of a search. I think"—she spoke slowly—"someone is frighteningly angry."

"And scared." He tried to sort out his confusion. "Scared

as hell, now. That's why Marian and Louise died. I don't think there was ever a plan to murder anyone. It was a campaign to cause trouble. Maybe Abby Andrews really did see a way to snatch a quarter million dollars worth of jewelry. If so, her heroine-tied-to-the-tracks posture is an act. But there are other reasons Haklo could be the target. Blythe decided to get really involved at Haklo this summer. Grace not only resents her sister's status as sole trustee, she's mad because Blythe squashed support for her lover's art exhibition. Erik Judd lost his job and Robbie Powell's been furious ever since. Cole's miserable about being pushed out as a vice president. Francis's budget has been whacked. Peter may be looking at the end of in-house publications if Blythe decides to use a local agency and that might ease him out of his job. Or maybe my first instinct was right and Anne Nesbitt's wrong. Maybe one of the overtures at the workplace wasn't gracefully deflected and somebody was infuriated by Hollis's usual approach to a good-looking woman."

Nela looked discouraged. "What troubles me is that when I think of everyone at Haklo, I see nice faces."

"I do, too. We have to hope Katie gets a break somewhere. She's smart. If anyone can ever figure out the truth, it will be Katie. She'll put on pressure. Somebody will crack. The murderer has to be in a panic now. Everything's spiraled out of control." He reached out, gently touched her shoulder. "Tomorrow will be better." He gathered up his papers. He wished he believed his words.

He stood and Nela came to her feet.

He looked down at her. She seemed small and vulnerable to him. He wished he could take her in his arms, reassure her, lift her face . . . "Yeah. Well. I better let you get some rest." He needed to leave before he said things he knew she didn't want to hear from him now. The best he could manage sounded lame and awkward. "We'll get through this."

Jugs twined around his ankles. He looked down, managed a grin. "Hey, Jugs, you'll look after the lady, right? Promise?"

"I'll count on Jugs." She managed a smile, said swiftly, "We'll talk tomorrow."

As the door closed behind him, he carried with him a memory of her smile.

As Nela picked up the coffee mugs, she heard a clatter behind her. She knew the sound now, Jugs pushing through the cat flap. She turned and glimpsed the end of a black tail as the flap dropped. It would be interesting to know what Jugs did when he was outside, what he saw, the thoughts in his mind. Was he watching Steve climb into his car and leave? Or was he immersed in stalking a mouse? Were mice frisking about on cold January nights? Surely a sensible mouse was ensconced behind a wall or nestled in a corner of the garage.

She knew Jugs's evening pattern now. He would return in a little while. She would be glad of his company tonight. They'd already established a routine, Jugs padding into the guest bedroom just before she shut and locked the door.

Nela rinsed out the mugs and the coffeepot. The apartment seemed empty without Steve. He brought strength and calmness and she wished that he were still here.

A knock sounded at the front door.

Nela dried her hands and stepped out into the living room. Had he left something behind? But the coffee table by the sofa was clear. As she walked toward the door, she felt eager. Perhaps he had something more to say. Perhaps they could talk for a while yet and she could feel safe and content. He hadn't left anything behind, except a vivid memory of his presence. She smiled. Not a coat certainly. She would have to encourage him to wear a coat.

She had left the porch light on for him to see his way to his car. She opened the door and felt an instant of déjà vu. Blythe Webster had worn her elegant mink coat over pajamas on Friday night. She again wore her mink, but tonight the coat was open to reveal a black sweater and slacks and ankle-high black leather boots, not pajamas and sneakers.

She appeared haggard, worried. "I couldn't relax and I decided to walk on the terrace. I saw Steve Flynn come down the stairs. I suppose he wanted more information about Louise since your office was next to hers. Anyway, I thought maybe he'd told you more about what's happened. I can wait and see what's in the paper in the morning, but I'm so upset about Louise. Do you mind telling me what he said?"

Nela understood. When something horrible happens, facts don't ease the pain, but there is a desperate hunger to know what there is to know.

Blythe's tone was almost beseeching. "If it isn't too late . . ."

Blythe's unexpected diffidence surprised Nela. Here was a woman who was accustomed always to having her way, accustomed to ordering, not asking.

"Of course." Nela held the door wide. "Please come in." She stood aside for Blythe to enter, then closed the door and led the way to the living room. Nela sank into the easy chair.

Blythe sat on the edge of the sofa, facing Nela. Behind her stretched a shining expanse of flooring. The bookcase next to the front door was bare tonight. Nela never saw it without remembering Marian's Coach bag and the secret it had held.

Light from a lamp beside the sofa emphasized Blythe's haggard appearance. One eyelid flickered. Lines were grooved deep beside her lips. Perched there, she looked small in the long luxurious coat.

Nela abhorred fur coats, sad that small living creatures

were killed when cloth would serve as well. But tonight she found the huddled figure on the sofa pitiable. Blythe looked as if she would never be warm.

"I'm afraid none of us know very much." Nela marshaled her thoughts, made an effort to repeat all that Steve had said.

Blythe hunched in the big coat, absorbing every word. Her features remained tight and stiff. She looked much older than her late thirties.

A clatter.

Blythe's eyes flared. She jerked to look behind her. "Oh, it's the cat."

Jugs stood just inside the front door, the pupils of his eyes huge from his foray into darkness. He sat down just past the bookcase.

Nela smiled. "It's too cold out tonight even for Jugs."

Blythe let out a sigh. Her tense posture relaxed as she once again faced Nela.

Nela knew nothing she could share would ease the core of Blythe's distress, but she laid out the possibilities, one by one. ". . . and everything may hinge on why Anne Nesbitt's car was set on fire." Nela leaned forward. "Perhaps you can help. You were there every day. You know these men. Did one of them make a play for Anne Nesbitt?"

Not a muscle moved in Blythe's face. "Anne Nesbitt." Blythe's tone was cold.

Jugs paced silently across the floor, stood a few feet behind the sofa. He looked at Nela with his huge green eyes. "*. . . angry . . . angry . . . danger . . .*"

Nela stared at Jugs.

Anger.

Abruptly, Nela felt the presence of anger, hot as flickering flame. When she mentioned Anne Nesbitt . . .

Bill once told her that you could never fool a cat. A cat always knew exactly what someone thought and felt. There might be a smile, a face ostensibly expressing sympathy or welcome, but a cat knew the truth. A cat knew if there was sadness or heartbreak or fear or horror or love or hatred.

Or anger.

Slowly Nela turned her gaze to Blythe.

The older woman's posture hadn't changed, but naked now, unmistakable in that hard tight face, were eyes that glittered with fury.

Nela's recoil was instinctive. She reached to push up from the chair.

"Don't move." Blythe's right hand darted into the capacious pocket of the fur coat. In an instant, she held a black pistol aimed at Nela.

Nela sat rigid in the pretty chintz-covered chair, her hand gripping the arm. Was the feel of chintz beneath her fingers the last sensation she would ever know? Nela's chest ached. The hole in the barrel of the big gun seemed to expand. The gun never wavered in the grip of the small hand with brightly painted, perfect nails.

Nela looked into the eyes of death. "You hated Anne Nesbitt. Because of Hollis."

Blythe went to Kansas City and met Hollis, a handsome, lanky man who made women feel admired, attractive, desirable. It was in his nature. The woman across from her responded, but she didn't see that the admiring glances, the soft touch of a hand were meaningless. She'd once lost love, her father buying off a man she thought cared for her. She was lonely, hungry for a man. Marian Grant and Louise Spear saw the danger. Hollis's easy charm was automatic, any woman, anytime. Blythe thought he was hers for the taking and Hollis turned interested eyes on Anne Nesbitt.

Blythe's lips quivered. "We danced at the hotel. I thought . . . Oh, it doesn't matter what I thought. He was a lie. He made a fool of me. I brought Hollis here. I made him the director, introduced him to everyone, bought him a car, and then he went after that sluttish girl, had the nerve to tell me how beautiful she was. I thought when she left . . . but that's when I realized he'd been involved all along with Abby. She's a simpering, stupid, irritating fool. A nobody. I could have fired her, but I knew a better way." There was a flicker of malicious delight across her face. "No one ever suspected me." She was pleased with herself.

Nela's thoughts whirled. She was cornered. There was no one to help her, no one to save her. But she would fight. At the end, she would lunge to her feet, slam the coffee table hard against Blythe's legs, jump to one side. That's when the gun would roar. Perhaps if she kept Blythe talking long enough, she could take her by surprise. She'd keep her talking . . . "You're very clever, Blythe. You planned everything well. You must have felt confident that Abby would be blamed for the vandalism, but Marian saw you put the necklace in her office."

"Marian threatened me." Blythe's voice trembled with outrage. "She said I had to 'find' the necklace, say it had never been stolen. She said I had to step away from Haklo, leave the running of it to Hollis, move to the house in La Jolla."

A clatter at the door.

Blythe heard the sound behind her. This time she didn't look around. "I always hated Marian. She stole Dad from Mother. I had to be nice to her, but I hated her. She thought I would do whatever she asked. She said she had hidden the necklace."

This time it was not Jugs entering through the cat flap. Jugs crouched a few feet behind the sofa, tail flicking. His head turned to watch the figure coming inside.

Nela forced herself to look at Blythe, not at the figure that stepped inside, face somber. But there might not be hope there for Nela, either. "You took Abby's skateboard and put it on Marian's steps. You knew when she jogged and you were there to get the skateboard after she fell."

Blythe looked satisfied for an instant, then anger again distorted her features. "Marian told me the necklace was in a safe place. I was wild all week. I was afraid to go in the apartment during the daytime. There's always someone around, the housekeeper or one of the maids. I couldn't take a chance someone would see me. They knew I didn't like Marian. I hadn't been to Marian's apartment in years. At night your stupid sister was here and then I thought I had my chance Friday night. I had to find the necklace. No one told me you were in Marian's apartment."

How ironic that Blythe had desperately searched the apartment and Marian's office only to find the necklace, courtesy of Nela, lying a few days later in the center of her desk.

Near the front door, Grace Webster listened, too, her rounded face drawn and sad.

"I found the necklace in Marian's purse." Nela nodded toward the bookcase by the door, felt a lurch inside, prayed that Blythe didn't turn around.

Blythe's gaze never wavered, nor the gun in her hand. Another spasm of anger twisted her face. "Her purse?" There was a sudden blinking of Blythe's eyes. "Oh. A safe place. I thought she meant she'd hidden it away. I should have taken her purse but I didn't know anyone was here and I couldn't afford to be seen. I thought about taking the purse as I ran across the room. If only I had."

Grace Webster, slim and athletic in a rose turtleneck and gray slacks, walked nearer on the thick soles of running shoes.

Nela continued with only a flicker of a glance at Grace. "I put the necklace on your desk Monday night. You found it there Tuesday morning and thought you had another chance to destroy Abby, but Louise saw you, didn't she?" Now Louise's troubled words were clear. *She shouldn't have been there. But I saw her . . .* Louise wouldn't have been surprised if Abby had come down to her office from upstairs, but the trustee didn't visit the offices of employees. Not usually. Not except the day Blythe came because she knew Louise lay dead upstairs and she wanted her found. Staff came to the trustee's office. Blythe shouldn't have been there . . . but she was.

Blythe sagged inside the big fur coat. Tears trickled down her cheeks. "Louise came to my office Wednesday and said she was glad I'd asked you to find out more about Marian's last day. Then she asked if I'd seen anything when I came to Abby's office. I couldn't have her tell anyone I'd gone to Abby's office. I told her I'd been worried and had dropped by to talk to Abby but she wasn't there. I told Louise I'd see if Abby would meet with us upstairs a few minutes after five. Just before five, I slipped upstairs and put one of the clubs just inside the door. I left the light on. I waited until I thought everyone had left. I put on my coat and gloves and stopped at Louise's office and said we could run upstairs and talk to Abby. We went inside and I said that Abby must have just stepped out and we'd wait for her. Louise walked over to look at the exhibit of clubs. I came up behind her . . ."

Grace Webster briefly closed her eyes, opened them. She looked at the woman huddled on the couch, the woman who was her sister. There were memories in Grace's haunted gaze, perhaps of an older sister pushing her on a swing, of family dinners, of sunny days and laughter, of a special link between an older and younger sister that quarrels might fray but never quite destroy.

Grace came around the end of the sofa. Her eyes dropped to the gun, rose to her sister's face. "You didn't know what you were doing, did you, Blythe?"

Nela looked into Grace's stricken blue eyes, saw a warning, a command.

"Gracie." Blythe still aimed the gun at Nela, but she looked up at her sister in dismay. "Gracie, why are you here? You have to go away. I can't let her tell the police."

"Everything's all right, Blythe. There won't be anything for her to tell."

Nela felt a rush of terror.

"You won't remember anything about your conversation with Nela. We'll go home now and call Dr. Wallis. You've simply been confused. Sometimes you get confused." Grace spoke with emphasis. She stared into her sister's eyes. Slowly she edged between Nela and the pistol in Blythe's hand.

Nela understood. Grace was telling her sister that she could pretend confusion, perhaps mental illness.

"Dr. Wallis will explain to the police that you are so upset you didn't know what you were saying." Grace was soothing, calm. "Everything will work out. Come home now."

Blythe shook her head. "Oh, no. I have to make sure she never tells anyone."

"Hush now. Don't talk anymore. I'll take care of everything."

Blythe bent to look beyond Grace at Nela. "She'll tell the police."

"That's all right. People can say anything, but there's no proof." Grace's voice was reassuring. "People don't know about your blackouts—"

Nela saw the surprise in Blythe's face and knew there were no blackouts.

"—and how sometimes you do things and don't even remember."

Nela watched the sisters. Blythe didn't have blackouts. But Grace was trying to save both Nela and her sister. The Webster money would probably protect Blythe from the death penalty, but no matter what happened, Blythe was burdened by guilt, would always be burdened.

Grace held out her hand. "I'll take the gun now."

"Why are you here?" Blythe was querulous.

"I saw you leave the house. When you didn't come back, I thought I'd better see. I couldn't find you anywhere, but your car was in the garage. I looked everywhere and finally I knew there was only one more place you could be. Now"—she was firm—"give me the gun. I'll put it back in the safe."

Slowly Blythe handed the gun to Grace.

"Thank you. The safe's a better place for it, don't you think?"

Grace held the gun in one hand, gripped Blythe's elbow with the other. It seemed to take forever for them to cross the space between the sofa and the door, Blythe talking faster and faster, words spewing, "Louise would have told someone . . . I had to keep her from talking . . . I didn't have any choice . . . Gracie, you see that I didn't have any—"

The front door closed.

Shaking, Nela came to her feet, struggling to breathe. She ran to the door, shoved the wedge into place, then raced across the room to the telephone. She yanked up the receiver, punched 911. "Help, please come. Blythe Webster has a gun. Her sister took the gun, but please come. One Willow Lane, behind the Webster mansion. Blythe Webster killed Marian Grant and Louise Spear. Please hurry. Get Detective Dugan. Grace Webster took the gun—"

Muffled by distance, Nela heard shouts. She strained to listen over the calming voice on the telephone. "Detective Dugan is off duty. Please explain . . ."

Jugs stopped a few feet from the door, shoulders hunched, ears flicked forward. His acute hearing picked up movement and sound long before anyone in the apartment would know someone was coming up the stairs.

Nela now heard thudding on the steps.

The doorknob rattled. "Open up." Blythe's shout was angry.

Nela gripped the phone. "Hurry, please hurry." Where was Grace? Why had Blythe returned?

"Ma'am, remain calm. A car is en route. The car will be there quickly. If you can—"

Nela broke in. "There's a murderer trying to get inside."

Blythe's voice was hoarse and desperate. "Let me in. I have to come in. This place belongs to me. Open the door." The pounding on the door was loud, sounded like the hard butt of a gun against wood. Had Blythe managed to wrest the gun away from Grace?

"Blythe, stop." Grace's voice rose above the banging on the door.

The pounding stopped. "Go away, Grace. I can't talk to you now. You mustn't interfere. I have to be safe. Don't you see? Go away."

A shot and a panel of the door splintered.

Nela ducked down behind the desk.

Sirens wailed.

Nela's head swung back and forth. She needed a weapon. Her only chance was to find something to use as a club. When Blythe shot away the doorknob, Nela would strike. Stumbling to her feet, she ran to the small table beside the sofa, grabbed the brass table lamp, yanking its cord from the socket.

She was midway to the door when a deep voice shouted, the sound magnified by a megaphone, "Police. Drop that weapon. Police."

Nela stopped and listened.

"Drop that gun."

A final shot exploded.

—19—

The wind ruffled Steve's hair, tugged at his old gray sweatshirt. The day was beautiful, the temperature nudging sixty. "We'll stop in Norman, have lunch. There's a great new Mexican restaurant downtown. We'll have plenty of time to meet Chloe and Leland's plane."

Nela liked the way Steve sounded, as if they were going to a fun place and there would be fun things to do. Each day that passed eased some of the horror of the night that Blythe held a gun and planned for Nela to die. Grace had done her best, but Blythe was wily. She'd grabbed the gun from Grace, struck her sister and stunned her, then whirled to run back to the garage apartment stairs.

When the police came, when voices shouted out of the night and lights flooded the stairway, Blythe had lifted the gun to her own head. When they gathered around her on the concrete patch below, her body lay quite near where Marian Grant had been found.

Nela pushed away the memories. She didn't have to think

about Blythe now or about Haklo and its future or whether
Chloe would want to return there to work. She did have to
make plans, for her and for Jugs. Ever since that dreadful
night when she'd called Steve, she and Jugs had stayed at
Mim Barlow's house. But Nela had to decide soon where to
go, what to do.

On the highway, Steve turned those bright blue eyes on
her. "You won't go back to California."

Was he asking? Or telling?

Or hoping?

NATIONAL BESTSELLING AUTHOR
CAROLYN HART

Dead, White, and Blue
A DEATH ON DEMAND MYSTERY

Summer is a hectic time of the year for Annie Darling,
bringing swarms of tourists to her mystery bookstore, Death
on Demand, for the latest beach reads. But Annie still finds
time to enjoy herself. The Broward's Rock Fourth of July
dance is just around the corner, and the island is buzzing
with excitement—Shell Hurst included . . .

Shell is the kind of woman wives hate—for good reason—
and most of them wish she would just disappear. But when
she does, and a teenage girl is the only one who seems to
notice, Annie can't help but feel like someone should be looking for her.

The residents of Broward's Rock grow uneasy when a second
islander mysteriously disappears. Annie and her husband,
Max, know something dangerous is brewing. They soon find
themselves following a twisted trail marked by blackmail,
betrayal, and adultery.

carolynhart.com
facebook.com/AuthorCarolynHart
facebook.com/TheCrimeSceneBooks
penguin.com

M1230T1212

FROM NATIONAL BESTSELLING AUTHOR

CAROLYN HART

DEATH ON DEMAND MYSTERIES

"Annie Darling is a great character...
[A] one-of-a-kind heroine in cozy fiction."
—*Cozy Library*

"Well-developed characters and a complex, fast-
moving plot make for a satisfying read."
—*Publishers Weekly*

carolynhart.com
facebook.com/AuthorCarolynHart
facebook.com/TheCrimeSceneBooks
penguin.com